A
GOOD
LIE

A

GOOD

LIE

A novel

Roberta Temes

LUMINARE PRESS

WWW.LUMINAREPRESS.COM

A Good Lie
Copyright © 2021 by Roberta Temes

Printed in the United States of America

Luminare Press
442 Charnelton St.
Eugene, OR 97401
www.luminarepress.com

LCCN: 2021914745
ISBN: 978-1-64388-701-2

To David, with love

*"Being a parent wasn't just about bearing a child.
It was about bearing witness to its life."*

— *Jodi Picoult*

CHAPTER ONE

Suzanne

THE YELLOW PILL MADE ME WORSE; MADE MY HEART RACE.
The little white pill made me too sleepy; I could barely
open my eyes. Then they sent me up here, to the ninth
floor, the loony bin.

Downstairs, the main hospital is bright and bustling.
Up here, windows are covered with thick iron bars and no
visitors are allowed.

Here they gave me a new drug, a small pink pill. The
pink pill was miraculous. For the first time, when I woke
up in this cold, sterile room, I never once thought about
cutting. Just naturally my thoughts went elsewhere. I
could think about the other patients—some were making
a racket; I could think about the volunteers who brought
my lunch to me—some dropped the tray in my lap and
dashed away in fear; I could think about the bright fluorescent lights and wonder why they buzzed and hummed and
yet my room seems dark; and I could think about nothing
when I needed a break from my brain.

It was a relief not to have to use so much will power and so much self-control. I was getting better on those four milligrams. I no longer needed to see my blood in order to relieve desperate darkness. But then one of the psychiatric residents said, "Oh, you're doing so well we can lower your dosage to two." Well, of course my thoughts went right back to cutting myself. It was an automatic urge. I didn't want to have it, but it appeared. I know you must be smart to get into medical school and to graduate from it, too, but even I know you don't tamper with dosages that are working.

So, I'm back to cutting. Cutting into my arm stops the agony. Sometimes I pierce the skin on my thighs—I can more easily hide those marks and then those scars. But mostly I try hard, very hard, to get cutting urges out of my mind. I don't want the hospital to think I'm worse than I really am. Yesterday I didn't cut myself, but then I couldn't stop from tearing apart my pillow and stabbing into my mattress. My sickness, my craziness—I guess I am crazy—is running my life. It's also ruining my life; I used to be normal. What's happened to me? Why am I here?

I've lived in this tiny town my whole life and never knew there was a hospital behind the new tract homes until it was time for me to be admitted. And I certainly didn't know they had a floor devoted to crazy people.

Occasionally one of the more colorful patients, or maybe they're called inmates up here, I don't know, escapes and pops into my room. She's a big gal, tall, like me, but unlike me she has a raucous attitude. She calls me 'curly girlie' and now the others, or at least those who can speak, stick their heads into my room whenever they pass by and shout, 'curly girlie' and then continue on their way to the patient lounge. I want to tell them that's no way to address a professional woman, but my voice doesn't seem to work.

My curly black hair has always been my trademark. Not that I didn't try to iron it flat with all kinds of devices, including a real iron, when I was in high school. That seems like a lifetime ago. I have to remind myself college graduation was just a few years back.

I'm sitting on my bed, although it's really a skinny cot, thinking about those school days, Iowa State, Class of '62, when my thoughts are interrupted. A young guy is walking into my room. He's tall, dark-haired, and dressed in jeans and a red shirt. No suit and tie for him, and yet he carries himself like a doctor. Looks at my chart, confidently looks at me. "How's it going? I'm Dr. Peters," he says with a friendly smile. He's staring at me for too long. He doesn't know I hate eye contact these days. He sits on the frumpy chair opposite me. Even though this is not my house I'm embarrassed that the stuffing is seeping out of his chair.

This doc does not want to analyze my dreams, nor does he want to dig around in my childhood. That's what the Freudian doc did. He told me he was following the lead of the famous Dr. Freud, and then he'd sit and say nothing. When the silence got unbearable for him he'd ask, " Do you ever think about harming your mother?"

This new doc has shown up without a checklist, nor does he have a brown leather briefcase nor black doctor satchel. He has a canvas backpack strapped to his back.

"I'm Suzanne," I mumble, staring at the scratched-up tile floor.

"I know. I saw your chart. I'm pleased to meet you. Would you prefer to be addressed as Suzanne or as Mrs. Franno?"

"Suzanne's fine," I say and lift my eyes as far as his beard. Beards were a new big thing for the boys I went to school with. Now it seems beards are part of the 1965 dress code for doctors, too.

Dr. Peters takes off his backpack and pulls a brown paper bag out of it. The bag is loaded with food—two apples, two bananas, two cans of ginger ale and some chips. He opens up the black folding table that's against the wall and centers it between us—me, on the bed, and he, on the chair—and unloads all the food.

"Let's talk and let's snack," he says as he reaches for an apple. "Please help yourself." My room has peeling paint and a sickening stench, but this is the first fresh fruit I've seen in months. I accept. Around here they don't believe in fresh food. Baloney on white bread, red Jell-O and plain macaroni are the foods we are offered almost every day for lunch. For supper we get a mystery meat along with potatoes, and either carrots or green peas straight from the can. Both meals end with a miniscule container of milk, but we don't get cups or glasses or straws. It's clumsy.

And so we begin—me and Dr. Peters.

"Suzanne, how did you get here? What happened?" He sticks out his chin and opens his eyes really wide. Why is he so eager for my answer? Doesn't my chart tell him?

I look down at my lap. My hands are playing with the little pieces of elastic sticking out of the hospital-issued pink cotton pajama pants I'm wearing. "I don't know, exactly. I do know I used to be normal. I think my mind was overtaken but I don't know by what."

"Try guessing. Your answer doesn't have to be exact. Try to figure out how you got up here."

Shrugging my shoulders I say, "I guess they moved me up here from the maternity floor. I was too mental for them down there."

"Too mental?"

"You know, crying and yelling. Not eating. Not getting out of bed." I shudder thinking of those days.

Dr. Peters doesn't recoil. He casually asks, "Do you remember anything from the maternity floor? Do you remember what you were yelling?"

I can remember some things. I remember the doctor who always wore a bow tie and had a trail of people following him around—I think they were students or interns and he was supposed to be teaching them. He would talk to them about me, but he never spoke *to* me.

I also remember the fancy doctor who dressed as if he were going to a party. He was the one who threatened me. I'd cower in bed when he approached. He'd stand over me shouting, "You'd better get well. Pull yourself together. Try harder or you'll be in big trouble."

"I do want to get better. I do, please believe me," I would quiver.

"Prove it," he'd yell and dash out to the next patient. He might have been in cahoots with the nurse who never smiled and told me, "I hate my job because of women like you. You are lazy and irresponsible." She said I didn't deserve to ever leave the hospital. There were a couple of other nurses who were nice and kind and understood me. They tried to protect me from the mean one. "Mrs. Franno needs to sleep now," they'd say, to chase her out of my room.

Dr. Peters doesn't rush me. I look up at him and explain, "Mostly, when I was yelling, I was asking them to tell me what to do to get better. To help me."

"It sounds like you were asking the right questions. Good for you."

I can't believe it. Dr. Peters thinks I was right. He's not labeling me and he's not trying to change my ideas. He thinks I was right. I almost smile.

He continues, "Did they help you? Did they explain what was happening to you?"

"Well, they helped me to eat by forcing food into my mouth. Disgusting dried-out oatmeal one time, smelly bread spotted with white stuff on it, another time."

I reach for one of the ginger ale cans. The forced-food memory needs to be cleansed out of my mouth. "No one ever explained what was happening to me. Can you?"

"Can you guess?" Dr. Peters asks. He's patient and waits for my response.

"I don't know. Maybe I had amnesia? Sleeping sickness? Something came over me, I know that. I'm not myself. I used to be regular." I do want to answer Dr. Peters. I try harder. I close my eyes to concentrate. "Um . . . did I have a nervous breakdown?"

Dr. Peters sits back in his torn chair and muses, "That's an interesting phrase, nervous breakdown. Not a medical term, though. In years past they said those symptoms you had—tiredness, extreme sadness, no appetite,—were indicative of diseases called neurasthenia and melancholia. Some people would just call it a crack-up." He sits upright, puts his face directly over the table, and asks, "What makes you think you were having a nervous breakdown?"

I don't want to tell him about my cutting. When they give me the right dosages of meds those urges disappear. I like Dr. Peters and I don't want him to think I'm crazy. I never cut before I was in the hospital. Those urges began only when the numbness took over my brain.

"My symptoms are pretty much gone now. I'm much better. No important symptoms left. What do you think?"

"I don't know your symptoms from months ago, but you do appear to me, today, to be healthy and alert. We don't need to talk about symptoms if you don't want to. In fact, we can continue our conversation tomorrow." He stands, grabs his pack, and says, " Enjoy this food and we'll talk again soon. Is it okay with you if I stop by tomorrow?"

A polite psychiatrist; will wonders never cease. "Yes, I would like that. Thanks."

"Bye, Suzanne," he says, making eye contact before smiling.

I smile back but I don't say anything. I gather the snacks, stash them in my teeny cubby and go to bed.

We make a schedule—I talk to Dr. Peters four times each week. Sometimes our talks last for one hour and sometimes longer. He listens carefully and asks lots of questions, most of which I can easily answer.

We talk in a small, crumbling office at the end of the hallway. There's a pail at the side of his desk that catches an occasional drip from a hole in the ceiling. The chair I sit on is a plastic porch or patio chair that I think used to be white. Now it's stained a filthy gray. Dr Peters' chair is a heavy dark wood that is bolted to the floor. At our first meeting he explained, "Some patients get into fights and look for weapons to haul at each other, hence my chair."

We talk about the work I had been doing at the pharmacy before I got sick. I think he's impressed that I know the different categories of drugs and that I understand, from working the retail counter, that often a trial and error approach is the only way to find the right medicine for a person. He consistently tweaks my meds and I don't complain. He knows what he's doing.

We talk about some of the TV shows I watch in the patient lounge. I don't enjoy the cartoons that my fellow-patients would like to watch all day. But then again, I don't enjoy the action-filled westerns, either. My taste is more family stories, comedies, and of course General Hospital. Sometimes I wish I lived near Port Charles General Hospital. I know it's a fictional hospital in a fictional town, but still.

It's not until we know each other very well that Dr. Peters starts talking about people. "Were you living by yourself before you moved here?" he asks.

I think about that. He makes it sound as if I packed up a moving van then checked myself in. Had I? No, I hadn't … I don't think so.

"I was living with my family," I respond. "Not my parents and my brother. My other family. My other parents."

"What about your parents and brother," he asks?

How do I explain that they are not a part of my life? "They have multiple problems; we are somewhat estranged. My husband's parents are the ones I consider mine."

Dr. Peters is not convinced. "Have your parents been here to visit you?"

"They don't know where I am." I'm ashamed to add that they don't care where I am. "My husband's parents are the caring parents."

And then I say his name. "Louie. Louie's parents," I blurt out. I pause. I'm confused. And now I'm starting to cry. I cry for a long time. Big, hot tears. This is the first time, since I've been up here, that I remember the name of my husband. I'm relieved that I could think of it. It's also the first time, I think, that I've cried. Until now my tears felt frozen inside my eyes.

During the next few sessions I cry a lot and that's a good thing. I was numb, or maybe it was total insanity, but for whatever reason until now I couldn't cry. That's one of the reasons I don't cut anymore. I don't need to induce pain just to prove to myself that I'm alive. I feel the pain. I am not numb; I'm alive.

These days, Dr. Peters and I talk about Louie and his family all the time. Bit by bit, I recall conversations we had, the meals we ate gathered at the little table always covered with a cheerful tablecloth, and I remember the way my life was just one year ago. They were a polite family and never brought up the fact that I was abandoned by my real parents. Louie's parents were hard-working; neither of them missed a day's work in all the years I knew them. They were kind, too. His mom treated me as a member of the household long before we were married, and she made a point of cooking my favorite meals. I can still taste those pork chops and her special blueberry pound cake. When the four of us sat at that square table in their flowery wall-papered kitchen, I felt like that chair and that place had been waiting for me for years. I belonged there, we were family.

I smile as I reminisce. "Louie loved me," I say. "He took care of me and regularly went out of his way to be kind to me. As soon as we started dating he took over the maintenance responsibility for my Chevy. He sensed I had no one to look after me and he knew I was uncomfortable going into Iowa Ike's Garage. When we planned our future, Louie's constant refrain was, "as long as you're happy, Suzanne, as long as you're happy."

"I've heard that your husband doesn't visit you," Peters says, at our next session. "Do you know why?"

I have no answer.

Eventually, he asks the big question: "You were on the maternity floor before you came to this unit. Why were you on the maternity floor?"

"Um…I guess I had a baby. Maybe. I did, yes, I did." I hesitate and then take a chance. I reveal the truth, even though so far every doctor I told this to didn't believe me. "While I was having the baby something happened to me. I mean actually the very minute the baby was born something really did come over me. I couldn't feel happy and then I couldn't feel anything and then I had that nervous breakdown or whatever it's called. In that minute I knew I could not take care of a baby. I couldn't even take care of myself. All I could do was wail. And then everything looked black."

Dr Peters doesn't contradict me. He wants to know more. "What looked black?"

"Everything. I was seeing the world through a black veil. At first, I thought it was something that happened to my eyes. Sometimes I still think that's what caused the blackness—a veil."

I remember how it was then. I felt nothing. I had no connection with myself or with anyone else. And everything hurt me. Every part of my body ached. And I couldn't cry even though I wanted to. I was too tired to let those frozen tears out; it would take too much effort.

Peters asks, "Is everything black now?"

"Lately, things are changing. I have days of no blackness, and some days of just little bits of blackness, here and there. But the big black veil is gone."

Dr. Peters says, "I've treated other women who've had similar experiences to yours. Sometimes something goes awry in your hormonal system during childbirth. It's only in the last year or two that scientists have learned how to take care of this and help new mothers return to their pre-pregnant state."

I am wide-eyed now. Other mothers have had this, too? I can get back to myself? I want to ask him if those other mothers have the same questions I do, but I don't know if I can make myself say these questions out loud. Can I admit to Dr. Peters that I'm not sure if I had a baby? And if I did, where would that baby be now? Could I have done something horrifying to that baby? Why can't I remember those minutes and hours in the delivery room? Why can't I remember what I did the next day?

I'm quiet. He's quiet. I guess he knows I'll be able to speak sooner or later. And I do. "Please, don't tell me that I did something terrible to the baby."

Now I beg him. "Did I? Tell me. Tell me, please. Did I hurt the baby? I didn't kill it, did I? Oh, God, what happened to my baby?"

Suddenly I'm exhausted. I can't move. Speaking is too difficult. I manage to whisper, "Maybe tomorrow you can tell me. I need to rest now."

Dr. Peters stands up and smiles. That's a good sign; he doesn't think I'm a monster. He says we'll talk more in a couple of days. He leaves and I slowly return to my room. I use all my strength to plunge under the covers. I'm crying again. My memories are right here with me in bed.

I'm remembering being pregnant and Louie talking to the baby through my stomach. I remember choosing the crib and the changing table and buying cute little infant outfits. We went shopping together. We did everything together as we prepared for our baby. We spent hours going through baby-name books, trying out silly names, sophisticated names, and now? Do we have a baby?

I wonder about that baby for many days and the next time I have a session with Dr. Peters I announce, "I'm ready to go downstairs and meet my baby."

He shakes his head. "Hospitals don't keep healthy babies more than a few days after childbirth. You gave birth quite some time ago. Your baby is at home."

I know I can trust Dr. Peters, so this must be true. I can breathe. I didn't harm my baby. "Well, then, maybe it's time for me to go home."

"There's a social worker, Mrs. Shepp, who will arrange your discharge when you and I think you are ready for home. I'll introduce you to her. That way, when you're truly

ready to re-enter real life, you'll have an established relationship with her. She's a mental-health professional, someone
you can continue working with after you're discharged."

Within a week, Shepp is at my bedside. Given how
slowly things happen here, that's a speedy response. I
wonder if it's because I need so much help or if it's because
they want to get rid of me.

Shepp is a white-haired, chubby, grandmother type
who I imagine bakes cookies and likes to hold babies on her
lap. She looks a lot like Mrs. Claus, if Mrs. Claus dressed
in colorful T-shirts, flouncy skirts, and Keds sneakers. She
and I decide to get together often. Very often. Before long
we're having what she calls *daily strategy meetings*. I'm still
talking to Dr. Peters a few times each week, so my days
are filled with good people who help me recover the old
Suzanne. I used to do everything a normal person would
do—go to work, go shopping, live in a family, feel capable
and competent. Some of that is coming back to me now.
Most days I can get out of bed without much effort; it
was overwhelming to wake up and face the day just a few
months ago. I had no feelings; I was numb.

We talk again about the fact that Louie has not come
to visit at all. I assume he's annoyed at me for staying so
long in the hospital, but I'm not sure about that. He's a
good-natured guy. He's never really been annoyed at me or
mad at me for any reason. Shepp suggests that we explore
the situation. That's how she approaches everything—"let's
explore the situation."

"With your permission," she says during one of our
meetings, "I'd like to invite Louis Franno to come here.
Do I have your permission?"

I say yes and think of what Louie will look like when he comes to pick me up. He'll have his ready smile and twinkling eyes lighting up his face. He'll be proud that I'm much better. We'll get back into the swing of things. I'll be happy.

Shepp calls him, but the phone says, "This is not a working number."

She writes to him, but the mail comes back marked "Return to Sender."

She phones the store, the family business, but the number is disconnected.

She attempts to visit Louie at the store, but the person up front says he is the new owner.

"Where," she asks, "is the former owner?"

The new owner answers, "I have no idea. I bought this from the bank. The bank bought the business and the house when the old owners moved out of town."

I no longer have the haze of illness to protect me. I'm able to understand what Shepp is saying. My shoulders slump, my tears flow. Over and over I sob, "Where is my husband? Where are my in-laws? What is happening to my life?"

This is unbelievable. Louie and his parents moved away? What about the business? That store is their life. What about the house? Is it empty? I wonder if this information is accurate.

Shepp comforts me the only way she knows how. She throws her plump arms around me, pulls me close to her bosom, and says, "We will make sense of this and you will become strong."

The next day Dr. Peters strides into the therapy room and announces, "It's time to talk about your baby. Let's begin those conversations."

"I did have a baby, right? A baby girl, right? Did I destroy her?" I croak, voice hoarse from crying. It's the only thing I can think of that would make Louie leave me. He was thrilled at the thought of becoming a dad. "Tell me the truth. Is that what made me crack up? Did I do something terrible?"

"No. Your daughter left this hospital with her father and her grandparents, swaddled in a pink blanket and perfectly healthy. The hospital has a closed circuit TV recording at all times."

"Please repeat that. What did you say?" And Dr. Peters says it again. It is true. My baby, my girl baby, is alive. I may have gone crazy, but not that crazy.

I continue my talks with Peters and with Shepp. They understand me. They're working with me to plan my life, to stay healthy, and to soon be discharged. They know I had bad luck after giving birth and now I believe them when they tell me that this happens to some mothers. Not many, but some. I'm not complaining, though, because I feel good now. Each day I have glimmers of my old self. I'm eating, I'm sleeping, I'm talking, and I don't want to cut myself and I don't want to stay in bed all day.

My sessions with Shepp and Dr. Peters are now devoted to solving the mystery of the disappearing family. They consult with security personnel in the hospital. We read the statement that Louie signed when he left with the baby, and we read the nurses' discharge reports.

There's an additional log: a record of what the hospital is calling 'an exit altercation' involving Louie. It happened quite a while after the baby went home with Louie. Apparently, hospital administrators called Louie many times insisting he come back to the hospital to claim the bag of clothing I wore the day I was admitted to the maternity floor. According to the log, Louie refused. He went to the hospital and said, "Please keep her bag of clothes here and also give this envelope to my wife if she ever gets to check out of the hospital."

"We can't do that, Mr. Franno. Take your bag, please."

"Please, I respectfully ask you, put this envelope in the bag and hold it for her. Please."

"We can't be responsible for personal items," they say.

"I promise not to hold you responsible for anything. Here, just put this envelope into that hospital bag and keep it all in the locker. Do what I tell you," Louie insists.

I smile at that. He was firm. He was loud. He was bossy. He was my Louie, just as I remember him—loving but domineering. Just like his mother.

"Mr. Franno, what are you doing?"

"I'm putting this envelope in my wife's bag and I'm attaching this label with her name on the outside so she's sure to get it…if she's released." The camera shows him shrugging. "She may never be released, anyway."

And with that, he attempts to quickly walk away. A security guard stops him but on the recording we hear him say, "I'm in a hurry. My mother is waiting in the car for me," and he brusquely pushes past the guard and races to the exit.

Shepp is on it and although it takes them a couple of weeks, the hospital does find that plastic bag. It shows up one day with a label on the outside in Louie's handwriting, just like he said. And in that bag is my plaid maternity dress. And I see my shoes. I am proud to see those pumps. I've always had the ability to comfortably walk in high heels, even when pregnant. And there is the envelope from Louie, too. The envelope contains no note, no letter, just a key and a piece of paper with an address. The key is on a key ring: a metal disc imprinted with the number 2.

That key and that mysterious address hasten my desire to leave the hospital. I want to know where Louie is sending me. Would the key open the door to my baby? I have a fleeting thought, a crazy thought. Maybe I really killed my baby and Louie saved the dead body for me in a special room.

I have an uneasy sleep that night. I dream I'm being led to a door that no one has been able to open and now it's my turn to try. I have a special key and I can open that door and enter the secret room. Just as I insert the key and the door budges I begin to awaken. A voice in my head says *Wake up, Suzanne, wake up*. In my dream I stop myself from doing something that might cause me too much pain. I protect myself. I am strong again.

I've been entitled to a day pass from the hospital for quite some time, and now I have a good reason to request it. Nathan is a graduate student in the School of Social Work and he's assigned to come with me and see to it that I stick to the plan Shepp and I have discussed. Maybe this is part of his internship—spending a few hours with a recovering crazy lady.

An obstacle to getting outdoors is finally shedding these hospital clothes and wearing real outfits. I can't wear anything from the found maternity bag because, well, it's maternity clothing. I explain my dilemma to the nurses and one of them says, "I bet we're both the same size. I'll bring you something tomorrow." And she does and she tells me to keep it and she surprises me with more clothes the next day, and the next. I tell her I don't want to deplete her wardrobe, but she says, "You're helping me. I've needed to get rid of clothing I've not worn since nursing school and you are making it easy for me to purge that closet. Thank you."

Although I've been out on the hospital grounds for a stroll now and then, the dazzling sunshine and noisy traffic startle me. Nathan walks to retrieve his car while I wait at the entrance. It's late autumn. Leaves swirl across the ground, the air is cool, and this is proof I've lost almost a full year of my life.

We drive to the address from Louie's envelope, me clutching the key ring the entire ride. It's a large building with a sign: Store-Your-Stuff. We show my key to a uniformed attendant. He's a serious-looking young man and I smile when I notice he has a beard. I'm tempted to ask him if he knows Louie but I say nothing and he points toward a line of steel doors and says, "Turn right at aisle 3; it's the second unit on your left."

My key fits in the lock. As we roll up the door, the first thing I see is my favorite chair—blue and white striped and straight-backed. It was a gift from my mother-in-law. She said every wife should have a special place to sit and think. I never did ask her what she wanted me to think about. Next, there's a cardboard box filled with books. The books are my pharmacy texts. I never did get around to buying books about babies and anyway my mother-in-law said she'd teach me whatever I needed to know. There's my old suitcase. It's the suitcase that I used on our honeymoon. We didn't go far. Louie's parents needed him in the store that week, so we got away for only a weekend. We went to Cedar Rapids, the nearest town with restaurants, hotels, and movie theaters. That one piece of luggage is crammed with clothes—my work clothes, my around-the-house clothes and my maternity clothes. Louie must have emptied my closet and shoved everything into it. This silly little storage space feels like home. I'd rather move in here than return to the hospital.

I see my big brown desk and there's a metal box labeled *Important Papers* on top of it. Also there's an old TV and a radio. I try out my chair. It's dusty but comfortable, just as I remember it. I decide to open the metal box when I get back to the hospital, away from Nathan's peering eyes.

Shepp is waiting for me when we return. She sees the box and suggests we take it into her office. She doesn't sit behind her desk, instead she pulls her chair around next to mine.

We begin. First, there's a pretty pink folder that contains my birth certificate, my pharmacy tech license, my college diploma, and a piece of paper I had never seen. It's titled Declaration of Nullity.

"You know what this is?" asks Shepp.

"No, I never saw it before."

"Well, I have seen these notices before. They indicate that your spouse is annulling your marriage. Did you know about this?"

"Know about it? I've been in the hospital for so many months I don't *know* anything except that my family is gone, and I don't know where they went." I'm afraid to think about this too much. I'm afraid it might drive me crazy again.

"Should we look into this further? Find a lawyer?" she asks, holding up that Declaration paper.

I sink into my seat. A lawyer? What would I want to fight for? I sigh and say, "The baby is almost one year old, and I don't know how to take care of it, so I don't want to fight this. I've cried for too many hours lately, there are no tears left. Whatever happened when I had my breakdown is done. Probably Louie found another wife, a more fit wife who knows how to be a mother. Maybe they went to another country to start over. Motherhood is supposed to be automatic. It wasn't for me. It knocked me over."

Shepp tells me to slow down, take my time, be kind to myself, but what she doesn't understand is that I am not as upset as she thinks. I know Louie still loves me, and I still love him. But I have my brain back. I can think again and I'm smart enough to know that love is not enough to hold a marriage together. I know that some things you just can't take back. The truth is, I can't say I was attached to that baby. Her new mother might be the true mother.

I look at Shepp and say, "I'm not ready to be a mother. I feel like I'm the baby. I feel like I was just born, and you and Dr. Peters are my parents. No, Shepp, no lawyers."

Shepp is about to say something but then closes her mouth. She probably doesn't want to agree to be my parent. Or, maybe she thinks that's a nifty idea. I'll never know. Instead, she digs into that metal box and hands me the next item.

It's a large envelope that embarrasses me when I open it. I wish Shepp wasn't here to see this. I want to hide it. Too late. It's stuffed with money. Rolls and rolls of fifty-dollar bills. And there is more. A note that says:

Suzanne, I will pray for you every night until the day I die. Louie.

CHAPTER TWO

Laurie

IT'S A FACT: I AM NOT GETTING MY DIPLOMA. ANOTHER stupid rule. All they have to do is pass me in History and I could graduate but no, they won't do that.

Sitting at our kitchen table, still savoring the taste of the chicken parm, I'm wondering what to tell Dad. He's having his usual ice cream and eating it in big spoonsful right from the carton. He doesn't yet know that when he comes to the graduation ceremony he'll see that Laurie Franklin is not on the list of graduates. Just a couple of reports that I didn't hand in and those stupid people ruin my life. They have no problem flaunting my name around whenever I win an art contest and no problem hanging my paintings in the principal's office. If it weren't for studio art I would have dropped out of school.

I do my best to never cause my dad any trouble. I know that he has a lot of responsibility ever since my grandparents moved. He cooks our meals—his version of cooking, that is—and helps me with my stupid homework. I want to be sure no teacher or principal would ever call him to complain about me because he's got more than enough to worry about now that he's opened his own store. He was proud to start his own business; many customers want him, and only him, to do their work. They know him from his old job at *House and Yard,* where he was manager of the floor coverings department. I try to help him. I designed a logo and picked out paint colors for the shop. I used to go there after school and work the phones and I did some billing. I had trouble handling the cash, though, because I'd often lose count. It was so boring.

While I begin clearing away the dishes I casually say, "Dad, I'm not sure exactly what I'm doing next year."

He puts his spoon down, which is how I know I have his attention. "What do you mean you're not sure? We sent a deposit to Jersey State, right?"

"Well, there's a special art college that might be better for me to go to."

"So, why don't you just go there? We'll get our deposit back and give it to art college, instead." Dad is always quick with answers. He resumes eating.

"It's not that simple, Dad. I need to show them a portfolio in order to be admitted. I don't have a portfolio, not yet, anyway. I think I should go to community college while I prepare one."

"Is community college what we used to call a junior college? And, honey, what's a portfolio?"

It's pathetic that my father, who knows so much about putting beautiful tiles and engineered hardwood on floors, knows nothing about what to put on walls. "A portfolio would be a collection of my artwork. Not necessarily the real canvas but a photo or slide of the real piece, for some of the art. And, yes, a community college is state-run and similar to a junior college and it's almost free. So, I've been thinking…"

He puts his spoon down again. "Uh, oh, here it comes."

Taking a deep breath, I ask if I could take the deposit money once we get it back from Jersey State.

"And what would you do with it?"

"I'll start building up my portfolio and also buy some new clothes, get into the city more often, and eventually when I can persuade the folks at the Motor Vehicle Office that I am Laurie *Franklin*, I'll get a car. Remember, I told you, when I went for my permit they didn't have the right paperwork for me. There was a mistake on my birth certificate. When I was born, some stupid clerk didn't know how to write Franklin and abbreviated it in a weird way."

I have to go back there. I have to fight it and prove who I am but it takes so much energy and time and gumption to go against the bureaucracy, even though I'm right and they're wrong. I'll probably never get my license. That's typical; nothing in my life ever goes the way it's supposed to.

Dad is silent and for a second he looks away from me and seems almost … guilty. I should be the one feeling guilty given how smoothly I'm avoiding mentioning my lack of graduation.

Dad says, "I'll give you some money now so you can start your own bank account. You do what needs to be done about college, honey, it's not my expertise. Then we'll take the next step when the right time comes."

He admits he doesn't know about colleges, is he aware that he also knows nothing about me and my life? He does not know that my teachers are stupid and that all my friends have dropped me, and he has no clue about graduation, or lack thereof. What he does know is that ice cream makes him happy, so he's back at it.

Grandpa and Dad used to eat ice cream together after supper while talking about their hardware store. I'd be watching TV and my grandma cleaning up and doing the dishes. When I would walk into the kitchen during a commercial, Grandpa would always give me a taste right from his dish; he wasn't worried about germs. Grandma would rush to give me my own serving; she did worry about germs. Now that it's just me and Dad we rarely sit and chat afterwards. I do homework in my room, and he returns business calls in the upstairs room that he calls his home office.

Don't get me wrong. I know it's hard for my father. He's had to be a mother and a father to me since the day I was born. I get it. But still…

Last night's talk with Dad was a downer. When he left for work this morning he did his usual—a smile, a pat on my back, and the same old words, "Have a good day, honey." I nod, as usual, as if a good day were possible.

On the mornings that I tell him I'm feeling too sick to go to school he gets that confused look on his face and asks, "Are you sure?" That's when he looks all around the kitchen, as if he's searching for someone to help me feel better or maybe tell him what to do next.

On the days that I do manage to get myself to school I'm usually ruined by second period because of one stupid kid in my math class. As soon as I walk through the door that kid always yells out, "Hey, Sad Sack."

My talent has saved me from being too, too, sad every day. Drawing and painting are the most important things in my life. I'm good at using a paintbrush to push away bad feelings. And if that doesn't work, I walk. On days like today, when it's almost summer and the weather is warm and daylight lasts for hours, I walk to downtown Truesdale, hoping I'll forget that Dad never understands me.

The action down here sometimes cheers me up for a few minutes. In fact, my sadness just lifted a little when I passed the bus depot. On the outside wall there's a showcase and the center picture in that case is mine. My art teacher chose four of my paintings to hang in public places around town. This one I made last summer. It depicts a little girl, smiling wistfully, as she looks up at her mother who is wearing a fancy dress and heading out the door.

Now, walking around downtown Truesdale, I'm giving myself a pity party. It's true; everything about my life is pitiful. Even my curly hair is pathetic—it resembles the springs under my mattress more than it does the hair I see on every other girl in Truesdale.

Walking in front of Angelo's pizza place would make a normal person feel happy. I love the aromas—the garlicy smell from the pizza dough, the strong scent of oregano—and I can almost taste the gooey, melted cheese and the hot simmered sauce, but then I remember—I'm not hungry. Still sad.

Next I pass Rhythms, the music shop. The sounds annoy me. I'm the only high school kid in the world who doesn't like music. It's true; I don't. Music makes me cry.

I don't know why, but I get teary and sometimes even sob out loud and I can't catch my breath—just from listening to music that everyone else loves.

Sole is the trendy shoe store. The shoes in their window look energetic. That really bothers me. Even shoes have more zest than I do. Town Books is around the corner, yet I can't muster the courage to go into this quirky shop that proudly proclaims that there's a book for everyone. I watch all the shoppers enjoying themselves, walking up and down Broad Street, chatting, laughing, wandering in and out of stores. Their happiness makes me feel sad and left out. Those seem to be the only feelings I'm capable of having these days—sad and left out. My happy feelings are dead. Why?

Sunny days make me unhappy, too. You're supposed to be cheerful on sunny days, I'm sure of that. Not me. The sun makes me warm, but miserable. I'm a freak, always lonely. Another freaky thing about me is I walk and cry at the same time.

I'm giving up on downtown as a mood changer, so my new goal is to reach Lyons Park. I'm almost there. Lyons is a place where I'm not too, too sad and when I settle down on the bench that faces the lake I'll be okay, especially if the ducks are out. It's peaceful here—most people don't come to this end of the park; I like having it all to myself.

After a couple of minutes I take out the sketchpad and pencils I always carry in my backpack. My sadness evaporates when I put pencil to paper. One thing I know about me is that I'm talented. Ever since I was a little girl I could draw, I could sketch, I could paint anything I saw in person or in my imagination. It's too bad that I

didn't go to a specialized art high school, which would
have been the right place for me, and I would have been
admitted, too, but Dad didn't know anything about the
application procedure.

I'm getting out my kneaded eraser and sharpener
when a nice couple walk by and smile. They look a little
older than me— maybe college kids, maybe recent college
grads—and they seem happy, so I'm surprised they notice
me. And not only do they notice me, they sit down on the
bench across the path and ask if they could "be of service."
I'm not kidding. Those are the words they use. They smile
too much for my taste.

"Hi, I'm Tom, and this is my friend Anna," says the
guy, pointing to the girl next to him. He is tall, dark, and
handsome, and she looks like she belongs on the cover of
Seventeen—perfect eyes, perfect nose, perfect hair, perfect everything. I feel gross next to her because I am so
ordinary—pale white skin with stupid freckles splattered
around my narrow face, blue eyes, curly black hair, not
skinny and not fat, not tall and elegant, just plain tall.
People don't usually notice me, no less choose to talk to
me, but these two want to chat. Eventually, I have to say
something, so I mumble, "I'm Laurie. Hi."

And then ... silence.

Tom asks, "Are you an artist? I see your supplies."

I don't really answer, just nod my head up and down
like a yo-yo and hope he knows it means yes.

"It's okay if you don't want to speak, Laurie. I just like
sitting here with you," says Anna.

Okay, well, that's creepy. Now I'm thinking maybe even
if I could talk, I wouldn't want to.

"It's fine to be quiet," she says. "No pressure to speak." And then they both continue their smiles. Big happy-face smiles. I stare at them, noticing their clothes are casual and sporty but not college-kid clothes. They are wearing expensive-store clothes.

After a couple of minutes that seem like hours, Tom says, "I'm running down the street to get some ice cream at Steve's. Do you want to come, Anna, or are you going to stay with Laurie?"

"I'll stay here. I'm hoping Laurie will let me watch her draw. Just get me something chocolate, okay?"

"Sure. And what do you want Laurie?"

What? Is he kidding me? I don't say anything. This might be a good time for me to leave. I begin to gather up my things when Anna says, "Come on, Laurie, be a sport. Tom, get Laurie that chocolate-strawberry mix that they put into those big cones," she says. "I know she'll go for that."

I stop collecting my supplies. Tom leaves, Anna just sits there, and I start picking at my nails. I don't know what else to do. Does she really want to watch me sketch? And what would I sketch with an audience scrutinizing my every stroke? Maybe if I sketch some scary stuff—mad faces, wild animals, Martians—they'll both realize I'm not a potential friend and they'll go away. I plan that drawing in my head but then I'm not sure if I really want them to go away.

When he returns, Tom hands me a huge cone over-flowing with chocolate on one side and strawberry on the other. I shake my head. "No, it's okay. I don't have any money on me."

"My treat. Please take it before it starts to melt and drips all over me," says Tom.

I take it, realizing all at once that I'm hungry and ice cream doesn't require any chewing so that's good. Chewing requires more effort than I can muster. The smooth, cold ice cream feels good going down my throat, and it brings me good memories of my family, too.

Anna interrupts my daydreaming. "It's really hot out here. We're in the hotel down the street. Do you want to come hang out in the lobby with us?"

"It's got great air conditioning," Tom chimes in.

He probably thought I'd want air conditioning because I'm wearing what my dad calls my "uniform"—heavy blue jeans and a thick gray sweatshirt. I wear them every day, even if it's hot. I like covering myself up as much as possible. Anna, on the other hand, is wearing a bodysuit tucked into trendy embroidered jeans. She looks cool in more ways than one. I never look cool in any way.

I am curious but too afraid to ask a question. I want to know why they were at a hotel. Are they from out-of-town? Were they in college? Where are their families? And why would they come to Truesdale?

"No thanks," I say, "I don't want to go to your hotel." I stand to leave, tossing the little that's left of my cone into the bin a few feet to my right and hope I'm not insulting Tom by throwing away some of what he bought me.

"We'll be back again tomorrow at about eight o'clock," says Anna, "look for us right here at this bench."

That's weird. Why would they come back? For me?

I walk away.

If we see each other again I wonder if it'll be like the times in school when I'd almost have a friend but then they'd try to change me. Once a girl who I thought could become a friend said, "Hey, the way you're sitting and looking at nothing reminds me of my grandma. Perk up, Laurie." Everybody notices; I have my moods.

I don't know why I'm returning to look for Anna and Tom this evening. I guess it's because I'm bored. I don't like to think about sad things and my school situation is sad. So, at eight o'clock I show up and there they are. They're friendly again and they look cool again.

Soon, we're getting together almost every evening, meeting at what we call "our bench." They talk to me about having patience and trying hard and not saying bad things about other people. Manners are important to them, and also smiling and greeting strangers.

They talk about things I never thought of. One evening Anna suggests we try to figure out the mood of people, and we go to the other end of the park where plenty of folks walk around. It sounds silly to me, but I go along with it, listening as she gives me tips about how to analyze strangers. Do they swing their arms? Do they take short steps? Are they in a hurry and walking rapidly? Do they stop to look around every couple of minutes? Where do they focus their eyes—ahead of them? Down at the ground?

Anna explains that she and Tom know what to say to people to change their mood, make them happier. "And if that happens after they spend a few minutes with us, we've done something to improve the world. It's also important for them to like us."

I ask, "Why do you care if strangers like you?"

"Once they like us, they will buy things from us. Selling is part of our Master Academy routine," answers Tom. "It's a privilege to introduce people to things they never knew they needed. Those things can improve their life."

"What?"

Anna looks at Tom and when he nods she says, "We belong to a group that helps people improve their lives and feel better about themselves every day. Master Academy is the name of our group." she says. "We've been trained in a particular way of speaking. We know how to calm ourselves and calm others, too, by using words. We don't smoke. We don't drink. We don't take drugs. We've become good copers because of our teacher, Master Shekett."

That's a strange name, and I say so,

"It won't seem strange if you're ever lucky enough to meet him. He is truly masterful."

"How could I meet him?" I ask.

"He's down the street at our hotel. He stays in his suite and doesn't come out. Pollution and noise disrupt his equilibrium. People come from all over to meet him. Each day with Master Shekett is a gift."

"And you guys? You live in that suite with him?"

"We're part of a select group chosen to work with him. We follow a study program that he designed for people who are under thirty years old and want to better themselves. We're almost finished and soon we move on to a different place. In Wisconsin."

Now they're getting weird again. I wonder what they are learning. Probably some bizarre subjects. I bravely ask, "What exactly do you study?"

"Oh," says Anna, "we learn about the inner workings of the mind. We learn how to influence people and how to avoid being influenced by the wrong people." She seems so sure of herself. Tom watches her with deep concentration and a smile on his face.

I have no clue what she's talking about. "Wrong people? What do you mean?"

"You know, people who think they know what we should do and how we should think. People who say they have our best interests at heart but really don't know who we truly are and what we need. Master says we must always be afraid of the kindness of strangers. They could be the enemy."

Maybe they're not so weird after all. I know plenty of people who think they're doing the right thing for me but have no idea who I really am and what I'm really all about. That's why I miss my grandma so much. She knew the real me. When my grandparents moved away to Florida, sadness came to live with me. The only times I wasn't sad were Christmas vacation, spring break, and the entire summer because that's when I went to visit them. Dad would take me down and then he would fly back to go to work.

In Florida, Grandma and I did everything together. We went to Disney and we did girl stuff—shoe shopping, manicures. She was a whiz on the first floor of every department store. When I packed up to go back to New Jersey I needed an extra carry-on bag just for all the samples she nabbed.

In Jersey the four of us lived together, ate our meals together, watched TV together. Thankfully, now that it's just me and Dad, we bought a new house so I don't have to face those memories every day.

Anna talks some more about the kindness of strangers. I say, "Those strangers to be wary of would be my teachers. I'm not graduating next week when I'm supposed to. My dad doesn't know yet. I might just forget to mention it and maybe he won't realize."

Anna asks, "What about your mom? Won't she know it's graduation time?"

"My mom died," I mutter, looking down. Whenever I tell people that I have no mom I avoid eye contact. If I look at them, they get too sad, and then I don't know how I'm supposed to react. I'm always making people feel bad for me and I don't even feel bad for myself. I'm the girl without a mother. That's who I am. After all these years it's not such a big deal.

"So sorry to hear that. My condolences," says Tom. He slyly glances at Anna who nods her head at him.

"I'm sorry, Laurie," Anna echoes. "My condolences, too."

I don't say anything more. What should I say—that I think it's okay not to have a mother? That they shouldn't feel sorry for me because I don't feel sorry for myself?

"We might be able to help you with your high school graduation problem," Tom says. "Master Shekett offers a program that ends with getting your high school equivalency diploma, the GED."

I shrug my shoulders. "It sounds good, but the thing is I have no money and I don't want to ask my father for help."

Oddly, Tom perks up at this. "Does he work? Is he in distress financially?"

"He owns his own business, and I know that he inherited money when my grandparents passed away. But we don't have enough money to live at a hotel every day like you guys do, and I don't want to ask. Not now. Not when he doesn't know about the trouble I'm having in school."

"Master supports us at the hotel," Tom says, then puts his arm around my shoulder. I hope he's not doing this to comfort me because he thinks I need sympathy, motherless child that I am.

Anna says, "Maybe you're supposed to be talking to us right now. Maybe it was not a coincidence that we met you. Think about it."

I'm beginning to get one of my headaches so I stand and once again start packing up my things.

"Don't go, Laurie," Anna says quickly. "Let's come up with a solution." She looks at Tom. "Do you think Master might allow Laurie to take the GED class in exchange for some work?"

I pause, my sketchbook halfway into my bag. "If I take the high school class would I then have a chance to take the Master Academy classes? They sound interesting." I'm not kidding around. My high school classes were bland. This stuff might be fascinating or at least not dull.

"That's rare. Those opportunities don't come up too often," Tom says. "Here's how those classes work. First you learn about the Master Academy community and you have private time with Master where he figures out the best way you can contribute to the community. After you make your contribution for many months, or sometimes years, you're permitted to attend Master's lectures. The lectures are about the ethics of work, how to set goals, how to achieve what you want in the world, and how to get along with people, even people you don't like."

This is too much conversation and too much to think about; it's making me nervous. I'm up and I'm out of here. "Good bye, it's time for me to go home."

While walking home I realize they are not encouraging me at all. Am I not smart enough for them? I know I could make a good contribution to their community with my artistic talent, but they didn't ask. Now I have a stomach ache in addition to my headache.

I skip a couple of evenings of meeting at the bench. But, this evening, after some quick and clever chatter with Dad, where I steer clear of school-talk and helpfully do all the clean -up, I walk toward Lyons Park. I miss my talks with Anna and Tom. Perhaps they gave up on me, but I'll take a chance because life hasn't been too bad the past few days. Is it because now I have two possible friends and some money in my pocket? I can treat them to ice cream this time. The weather is balmy and I pass open windows with softly swaying curtains. Maybe, just maybe, my life won't be pitiful anymore.

They're waiting for me, Tom, sporty in a beige short sleeve sweater and track pants, and Anna pure and lovely in a white dress. I wonder if they are a couple, a romantic couple, not just a Master Academy couple.

"Hi, guys!" I say, for once brave enough to speak first.

Tom stands up. "We've missed you. Is everything okay?"

"Yes. I've been thinking. I want to take my GED and then classes with Master Shekett," I say as I sit on my usual spot.

They give each other one of their glances.

"We discussed it with him," Tom says slowly, "but he's so much in demand that he must charge for his programs."

"I thought you said I might be able to do some work in exchange for a class."

"That's always a possibility, but to get the best from your relationship with Master Shekett you should try to work and pay for a class, too. We both did that."

"That not how I thought this works. Never mind." I'm disappointed. I was hoping for an adventure that could change my life. I stand up from the bench, smile at them, and say, "It was nice knowing you." I knew it. I am pitiful.

Anna says, "Don't go, Laurie. Let's try to work something out. Tom, do you think there's a way that Master Shekett might be able to make this happen for Laurie?"

I ask them both, "When you say I'd have to work, too, what kind of work would that be?"

"It's hard to say. Why don't you come along with us now and we'll see what we can do. It won't take long."

It takes me a couple of minutes to think this through. "Yes," I say and I do go along with them. I feel proud walking through town with two older, good-looking friends. When I see our reflection in the store windows on Broad Street, I hold my head up high and for a minute I feel like smiling—maybe I do smile; I don't know for sure.

I have new friends and I'm relieved I don't need to invite them to my house. It's awkward to bring a friend home because our house is not exactly a showplace. Dad doesn't pay attention to anything resembling interior decorating—in fact he prides himself on not paying money for furniture. Instead he brings home old junky furniture the people whose houses he's renovating are getting rid of. Ugly chairs, ugly tables, and one time even a black-and-white TV from the 1960's. He just piles it all up into his work van and proudly hauls it home.

One of the few times a friend visited, when her mother came to pick her up she said, "Oh, Laurie, I see your house is decorated in early utilitarian." I'm not exactly sure what that means, but I know it's not a compliment.

The three of us continue walking and finally we reach a tall red-brick building.

LIKE THEY SAID THAT FIRST NIGHT, THIS LOBBY IS TRULY air-conditioned. It's actually freezing. They lead the way. The hallway has walls covered with dark wood paneling, the carpeting is threadbare, there are a couple of hanging chandeliers, but only one of them is lit, and I might be smelling mold.

We reach room 130 and Tom knocks. After some scuffling sounds, the door opens to reveal a man who should have been a movie star if he is not one already. He's wearing a yellow shirt with the top buttons open, white slacks, and no shoes on his bare feet. His hair is white and poufy, as if it had been blow-dried, or maybe even teased. And he's wearing gold chains around his neck and a bracelet on his wrist. I think I may have spotted a bracelet on his ankle, too, but I don't want to look down again. It was startling enough to see his toes once.

My grandma would have called him spiffy, even with the bare feet.

"Well, well, Tom. And who is this lovely young lady?"

"Master, meet Laurie Franklin. Laurie, this is Master Shekett."

Master looks me up and down, kind of inspecting me, without saying anything. In that moment, I want to go home. Right now I don't care if my house is full of stupid furniture. I'm afraid I might throw up. I do not belong here, not at all.

Tom finally speaks, "Laurie would like to work toward her high school diploma. I told her you could help her reach that goal."

Master looks at me skeptically. "Is that so? Are you motivated to work hard?"

"Um…I think so."

He grins a phony grin and says, "Sorry, that's not good enough, sweetheart."

"I will work hard," I say. "Yes."

"That's the attitude. That's the attitude for success. You can have your first lesson now and we'll see how you do. Please enter. Sit in the red chair and we'll begin. Tom, are you sure she's ready?"

I barely have time to see Tom nod before he and Anna are out the door and I'm sitting on a huge overstuffed chair, and the barefoot Master smiles at me from across the room. There's a photo of him, Master Shekett, blown up and framed, on the wall. In real life and in the photo, Master is seated on a massive wrought-iron chair with high tufted pillows the color of sunshine. Behind him is a mahogany desk strewn with dollar bills and coins.

I'm starting to panic. My heart's beating too fast. I'm shaking. Am I doing a terrible thing? Should I be here with this man? Should I have trusted Tom and Anna? I'm trying to figure out how to make a run for it when my thoughts are disrupted by Master.

He is lecturing me. His voice is strong and...well... masterful.

"Laurie, you will do well in my program," Master says firmly. "You will reach your goal. And when you graduate you will be a finer person, a happier person, a person in control of her destiny.

"For your first lesson, you will repeat after me: 'I will stay on the path.' And then you will silently count to five and repeat that sentence. That sentence is your mantra. Soon you will say it in your sleep. And speaking of sleep, you may stay here, you may sleep here, you will live here. You meet our standards. I will get Anna to set up a comfortable room for you."

I am so shocked that I can barely blink, much less speak. Master stares at me. I am not quick enough to repeat the words. I don't know what to do. Can I just pick myself up and leave? What about Dad? This is not for me. Dad needs me at home. Meanwhile, Master is going on and on.

He's continuing to instruct me: "Now, you will begin: 'I will stay on the path.'"

I hear a voice say, "I will stay on the path. I will stay on the path." Only afterward do I realize I am that voice. It's me.

Even though Master says, "Good job. I'm going to notify Anna while you continue your chanting," this is all happening much too quickly for me.

I will explain everything to Anna, apologize for my mistake in coming here and then I'll just run out and run home. This is bizarre, and also a bit scary. But when Anna comes through the door she's so perky and smiley that my escape plan withers away.

"Hi, Laurie, I'm glad you got started on your program." she says. Then she notices my wary expression. "Laurie, please don't wimp out like some other newbies. You'll adjust. I know you're worried about your dad, but there's the phone. Tell him that you're having a sleepover. Just think, soon you'll be on your way to your diploma! And you'll make new friends. And you'll be making the world a better place—no arguing, no fights, everyone getting along because you will know how to calm people."

I pause to consider her words. I like the idea of being part of a group devoted to learning how to spread tranquility. What would be the harm in staying for a little while?

Anna says, "You will have friends here. I promise."

I don't leave.

When I call my dad, I convince myself that what I'm saying is partly the truth, or at least a good lie. "Dad, I'm with my friend Anna and spending the night," I say, watching Anna's smile grow as she stands there, blocking the doorway.

That night, Anna hands me a Bloomingdale's shopping bag with pink pajamas and a bunch of toiletries. The toothpaste is mint and the soap smells like roses. Before long I'm nestled in a cozy room with Anna on the next bed and somehow it seems okay. The crazy thing is that as I'm falling asleep, I hear myself murmur, "I will stay on the path, I will stay on the path."

CHAPTER THREE

Louie

I'M THE GUY WHO GETS THINGS DONE. I'M THE GUY WHO
takes charge. Not now. Now I'm the guy whose teenage
daughter has disappeared. A missing person, I would think,
but the authorities don't agree. "She called you. She told you
she'd be gone for a while. That's not a missing person," they say.

"Come on," I tell them. "Use your head. This is a girl
who has slept only in her own bed or in her grandparents'
house. This is not one of those runaway kids. This is serious."

Do the police come to our house? No. Do they open an
investigation? No. Is this phone call the only connection
I'll have with police? Yup; seems that way. "She's over 18,"
they tell me. "She told you she's leaving of her own volition.
There's nothing we can do."

They're ready to hang up, but I keep talking. "What
am I supposed to do? Twiddle my thumbs while my
daughter is missing?"

They give me some ideas. "Circulate her photo and
obsess over her last few weeks at home. Think of everything

she did and everything she said." They tell me to review her life; hints may be apparent from months or even years ago.

I think about Laurie's recent conversations. We talked about art school and about community college. That doesn't help. I go back and back and back. Finally, I'm at the beginning. Baby girl Laurie Sue, 7 pounds, 3 ounces, born December 1, 1964. I was so happy that my cheeks hurt from smiling. I looked at that newborn girl and could barely wait for my wife and daughter to come home from the hospital; we would be a real family.

On day two of baby Laurie's life my wife seemed strained and cranky. My mother said, "Baby blues. Suzanne will be better in a couple of days."

But she wasn't. Suzanne got sicker and sicker. She cried and she wailed. It hurts to remember all these details. Those days were tough. I haven't allowed those thoughts to come into my mind for years. I was in love with Suzanne and she was supposed to become the perfect mother to this perfect baby.

I remember the first time Suzanne walked into my dad's hardware store. She was tall, taller than me, and pretty. I was standing behind the counter and startled by her bright blue eyes and her great figure, and I thought her curly hair was adorable. She was asking for tape. "I don't know the name of it. It's not Scotch tape, I can tell you that much. My dad started using this type of tape since I've been away at school. I know what the tape looks like but not its name. And now he's run out and it's kind of important that we get more as soon as possible."

"Well, what will you be using it for?" I ask while trying to ignore my fluttering heart.

"We use tape to ... to... to... to wrap up things, you know, like a package." Suzanne turned red, she was flustered. I thought she was beautiful, even if she was a college girl.

"I'll bring a whole mess of tapes out to your house and your dad can choose the right one," I volunteered, hoping I wasn't blushing.

"No, no. That won't be necessary," Suzanne quickly said.

I sold her some duct tape and then courageously asked, "Maybe we could get together some evening?"

Suzanne immediately shouted, "no," and scooted out of the store as fast as her beautiful long legs could carry her.

How could she just hurry away? Didn't she feel those feelings that I was feeling? Wasn't her heart quivering, too? I knew I would see her again. I had to. I was in love.

She came into the store the next time she was on break from school. This time she needed two light bulbs. I was not happy; I didn't want to make a quick sale. I wanted to look at this gorgeous girl, this girl who had occupied my thoughts every day and every night since I first saw her.

Suzanne wasn't interested in lingering, but I had a plan. I said I'd place her family on our mailing list. The plan worked; Suzanne supplied her address. Two days later I set out to personally deliver my father's two pamphlets, "How to Save Time in your Kitchen" and "How to Save Money in your Workshop."

Parking my brown station wagon at the side of the road I took off my cap, placed the two booklets in a manila file folder, and headed for the weather-beaten, two-story, white house. I noticed the leader and gutter problem, the rusty mailbox, and the rotting window frames. I saw a couple of neglected bikes on the front porch, one missing a tire, the other missing a chain. The doorbell didn't ring, the knocker didn't knock. I used my fist to rap, then pound. Strange sounds came through the window. Wailing, shrieking, and then a woman's voice yelling, "Shut up, already. I'm coming to get you."

But she did not come. Nobody answered the door. I went around to the side of the house, and then the back, where through a window I could vaguely make out a skinny figure seated in a straight-backed chair. It was a man—a young man–and he was making weird noises—shouting and having some kind of a temper tantrum, thrashing his head back and forth.

I walked back to my car to check the address. As I did, Suzanne pulled up. I can see it now—her shocked face sticking out of the window of her shiny blue and white Chevy Bel-Air.

"What in the world are you doing here?" she shouted.

"Oh, I was just in the area and wanted to deliver these to you," I said, waving the booklets. "This is your house, right? Whoever's inside there's makin' a lot a noise. Everything okay?"

"Thank you," she said, ignoring my question, grabbing the folder, and rolling up her window. But she did not drive away, and I did not walk away. I continued to stand there, right in between her car and mine. I'm not the type to give up. She was looking down at her lap. I was looking straight at her. She knew that I knew that something was very wrong inside her house.

I still remember how, after a long minute of silence, she looked up, rolled down her window, and pleaded, "Please, don't come here anymore." At that moment I decided I would marry Suzanne and I would protect her with my love. These memories are killing me. I didn't protect her at all. And obviously I haven't properly protected our daughter.

The next time I saw Suzanne was when she came into the store for some batteries. We talked and I finally won her over. She agreed to a date and then to another.

Suzanne was secretive about her family and never wanted me to be near her house. She wouldn't speak about her home life and she arranged it so that I would have no reason to go there. She'd pick me up at my family's hardware store and we'd go from there to Virgil's Bowling Alley or the Winter Falls Theater, always in her Chevy. At the end of each evening she dropped me back to where my car was waiting.

My parents grew fond of her. My mom was impressed that Suzanne didn't look like the other college girls who came to the store. "Those girls wear bandanas on their head and sneakers instead of shoes," she said. "Suzanne dresses like a lady in a skirt and pumps."

When I told my parents about Suzanne's peculiar family my mom said, "We always have room for one more at our table. She can come here to eat any night she wants. And she can stay over in the guest room, too."

When Suzanne returned to school in the fall my family missed her. When she was back in town for winter break, they welcomed her. It was during those weeks that I finally learned the secret.

"We're not exactly a regular family," Suzanne confessed. "I wish we were. I wish we were like you and your mom and dad. Things are peculiar in my house because Joel, my brother, is a little *off.* He never learned to speak, and he doesn't really know how to control himself. My mother has to feed him, and dress him, too. He can't be by himself. When she has to go to the bathroom, she ties him to his chair and tapes down his hands. He's not smart enough to know what's dangerous and what's safe. Once, he ran out of the house and was sitting in the mud, down near the river. Another time, he darted in front of a car and the poor guy who was driving almost had a heart attack.

"My mother's whole life is Joel. She never complains about him, though. She criticizes me instead. Sometimes, my dad threatens to take me and move out. I'm not sure my mom would notice if I were gone."

Recalling this I can hear the tears in Suzanne's voice. I wanted to help her. I wanted to be her hero. "We do the maintenance work and carpentry for The Lane School for the Handicapped," I said. "Maybe Joel could be placed over there. That way he'd get professional help. What's wrong with him, anyway? Is he a mental case?"

Suzanne promptly cut me off. "He's never had an official diagnosis. And, if he did, it wouldn't be mental case. That's not a diagnosis, it's an insult." She explained that her mother wouldn't allow anyone from the county into their house, so Joel has never been formally tested.

When Suzanne stayed with my family her parents never did ask where she ate dinner and they never wondered where she slept. When she did go home, she'd return dejected and depleted. It would take a few days for her appetite to return and for her voice to sound strong again. As time went on, she went home less and less, and then she stopped going there altogether. Suzanne graduated and became a pharmacy technician at Bravo, the big drug store just outside of town, and soon enough we went with my parents to City Hall. My mom didn't want to invite Suzanne's family and neither did Suzanne.

When she was not herself after giving birth I thought it might be because she needed her family. A girl needs her mother at a time like that so I went to see her folks. They didn't care. Never asked if the new baby was a boy or a girl. I pleaded with her mother to come to the hospital to help Suzanne snap out of it. Her mother said she had to stay home.

The docs allowed Suzanne to stay in the maternity section a few extra days—back then people were compassionate and that was possible. No insurance companies complained about taking up a bed. We all thought Suzanne would soon get hold of herself. Baby Laurie came home and my mother took care of her. But after eight more days the hospital said Suzanne would have to leave the maternity floor, and they transferred her to Psychiatry, the mental floor with all the head cases. I couldn't believe this was happening. Suzanne was getting worse every day. She wouldn't eat, she couldn't sleep, and she stopped speaking. Her eyes had that glazed-over look that crazy people's eyes have. And this was my sweetheart, my Suzanne, the mother of my new baby, my daughter. And now where is that daughter? What has become of her?

When baby Laurie was one month old I brought her back to the hospital to see her mother, but Suzanne wouldn't come out to the visiting area to see her baby. Her own baby. She just shut her eyes. It was as if she didn't see me or hear me. She rolled herself up into a ball and stayed in the upper corner of her bed. I was shocked, and scared, too. We'd all thought she would want to see the baby, hold the baby, and that the adorable little baby girl would speed up her healing.

When I emerged alone from Suzanne's room, Mom passed Laurie Sue to me and marched right in to see her daughter-in-law. I'd heard her practicing her speech: *Stop being self-indulgent. You must come home and take care of Laurie. Louie is having a very hard time and so am I. We don't know what to tell the neighbors. We don't know what to tell the customers. Get your act together and get out of here. Now! Your baby needs her mother.*

But, when Mom came back she said, "I saw Suzanne's sunken eyes. I saw her mouth, turned down at the ends. I saw her pale skin, and when she looked up at me she said nothing. I wonder if she even knew who I was."

Baby Laurie cooed on the car ride home, but we were silent. This was more serious than we had initially thought. Next morning, Mom requested an appointment with Dr. Shonda, the Chief of Psychiatry.

"I am not optimistic," he said to us, standing erect, in his sharp suit and stiff lacquered hair. He didn't look like a doctor but he did look like he knew what he was talking about. We listened carefully as he said, "Some people get overwhelmed with new responsibilities. There are new dads who pick up and leave. There are new moms who take to bed and never get up."

"Never?" I couldn't believe it. But my mother did. Authoritative bearing and tailored clothes always impressed her.

"Sadly, yes. I've been here for thirty-eight years and every couple of years we have one or two who carry on and weep and shriek. Nothing helps them. They just weren't supposed to have a kid, I suppose."

We were living in Winter Falls, Iowa, far from a big city hospital. The old docs at our hospital were way behind the times. They were ignorant. Now I know that there was plenty of research going on about postpartum depression, but it was still months away from reaching our small town.

Dr. Shonda said that this was one of the hospitals where they used to do lobotomies on depressed patients. Lobotomies! That's where they drill holes in your skull and stick an icepick in there to move around the brain. Dr. Walter Freeman was the doctor who did more of these operations than any other doctor in the world. I looked him up and found out that many of the patients who lived through the lobotomies became like vegetables. Rosemary Kennedy, the president's sister was one of his patients. Freeman operated on her, he was so famous everybody believed in him. After the operation Rosemary Kennedy could barely function so she had to live in a nursing home the rest of her life. Operation Icepick is what they called these mass scale lobotomies and some doc got a Nobel Prize for it. I could hardly believe this.

When we came home from that hospital meeting we didn't know where to turn, and then my mother said she had an idea.

CHAPTER FOUR

Dot

ONE SUNDAY MORNING, ABOUT A YEAR AGO, I LOOKED UP from the counter where I was solving the *Sunday Times* crossword—in ink, mind you—and there he was, sitting in a booth at the back. He had seated himself, this chubby guy with a smiling face and a good head of wavy black hair. Middle-aged, adorable, a nice surprise.

My regular customers were still in church, and the condo and high-rise boom of the 1980's was just starting here in Huntington, so I knew most everyone in town. Who was this cutie?

"What brings you to these parts, stranger?" I asked, walking over with a menu.

"Just driving through. I live one town over, in Truesdale," he answered. "How's about some coffee to start, miss?"

He ordered. He was particular. He wanted ice cream on his waffles—cherry vanilla ice cream. I cooked. He ate. He paid. And on the way out he hesitated and then reached into his shirt pocket. "You haven't by any chance seen this kid, have you?" he asked, flashing a snapshot of a curly-haired teenage girl.

I'm not shy, so I asked, "Are you a cop or is she your daughter?"

He was hopeful, but evasive. "Have you seen her?"

"Sorry, no, and I'd remember if she came in here," I said. I thought I noticed his eyes get a little misty.

A few days later he came in for lunch. Same order—waffles with cherry vanilla ice cream. He ate. He paid. He was almost out the door when I shouted, "Sir! I'm always here and I'm very observant. What do you want me to do if that young lady shows up?"

He quickly walked back in, right up to the register. "I'll be very grateful if you'll ask her where her old man could reach her. Her name is Laurie; Laurie Franklin. And then call me, at my store or my house." He handed me a business card for Louie's Floors. He'd already penciled in his home number.

"Are you Louie?" I asked. I needed to know the situation; I'm good at situations, so I continue, "Are you Louie Franklin?"

"Yup," he responded, then stuck out his hand. Thick fingers, no ring, short nails, and a wristwatch with all the numerals on the clock face and an expandable wrist band.

"I'm Dot. Pleased to make your acquaintance." I liked his grip, but I had work to do. No time to play.

Sure enough, the next Sunday Louie showed up for breakfast. This time he ate slowly—perhaps on purpose—and soon all the other customers were gone. That's when I told him I was looking to re-tile the kitchen. It's not something I had planned, but the kitchen floor is old so it wasn't exactly a lie. I call it a good lie.

"Lemme take a look at it." And without waiting for an invitation, he jumped up and barged through the swinging doors.

As I watched, he paced the distance from the grill to the sink to the deep freeze, all the while counting his steps.

"It's a basic job, Miss Dot, don't let anybody take you for a ride. Shouldn't cost you an arm and a leg."

"How about you give me an estimate. I just want plain tile, not slippery, and not the kind that kills my feet when I'm standing and cooking for hours."

He wrote some numbers on a paper napkin, then asked, "When can I do this job? I'll need a good coupla hours."

"Early Sunday mornings, like now, are slow, and I close a bit before eight during the week, if you ever work at night. But, don't I have to pick out my tile so you can give me a price?"

"Don't worry, Blondie. It'll be good. You'll like it."

He was right, of course, and he still tells me not to worry and he still calls me Blondie.

WE'VE BEEN TOGETHER EVERY SUNDAY SINCE.

Louie comes here for lunch a few times a week, and I go over to his place after closing, a few evenings each week, and we call each other every morning when we wake up. Just to check, you know, that we both made it through the night. Not that anything is wrong with either of us. Louie is not a sick guy, and there is nothing wrong with me that a week in the Bahamas couldn't cure, but when you live alone you want someone to know if you drop dead in your sleep.

You'd think I'd be accustomed to being alone, because, truth be told, I've never had a regular, full-time companion. Not even a dog. I grew up right here, not only in this town, but in this diner. It's called Dan's Diner, after my dad. It should have been named Dan and Deb's Diner because my mother, Debbie, worked here just as many hours as did my father. If I wanted to speak to either of them I had to wake up before five-thirty in the morning—that's when they went to the market to buy their food supplies for the day. I came here after school whenever I dreaded going home to a house that echoed with emptiness. I could do my homework sitting in a back booth if it was slow, and it usually was slow between lunch and dinner shifts. (Come to think of it, it still is.) As soon as I could reach the register, I was working here, too. I've done everything from the front of the house to the back—greeted and seated, served, bussed, peeled carrots, and washed pots.

I didn't see my friends outside of school. Other girls had moms waiting with milk and cookies at 3 o'clock and I didn't want those girls or their mothers to gossip about me when they'd realize that no one was waiting for me in a warm kitchen with Ring Dings and Twinkies.

This diner has always been my second home. When you serve food you create community and when you create community you feel the love of a family. I needed that when my dad was diagnosed with cancer and I postponed going off to college. My plan was to defer for one year. As it happens, I deferred forever.

After Dad died I would pop into the diner whenever I was getting lost in sadness at home. As soon as I heard the clattering of spoons against coffee cups, and the clanking of knives and forks against the large dinner plates, I knew I'd be okay.

I planned to visit Lehigh University and check it out for the upcoming semester, even persuaded Mom to hire a temporary short-order cook and an extra waitress. I had it all organized: Mom would take off a couple of hours each day, attend to all the things she needed in relation to Dad's death. When she felt fully restored, she'd come back to the diner and I'd go off to school. Of course she'd return. She loved the place.

When Mom complained of headaches after dad passed away, I was sure they were caused by fatigue and grief. I was wrong. Everything changed on a Tuesday when Mom and I were driving home from appointments with the local bank manager, as well as with our lawyer and our accountant. We needed their help to change the ownership of the diner to Mom and me. I stayed strong for Mom, wiping away her tears at those meetings.

"You go on in and take a rest," I said, pulling up in front of our house. "I'll go check on the diner and bring home some food for dinner."

I picked up salad, burgers, fries, some chocolate pudding and two slices of seven-layer cake, deciding we would splurge on sweets to celebrate the completion of all the paperwork. I returned home, parked in front of our house, got out of the car and there was mom, standing there. Right where I had left her. I started to panic. "Mom, Mom, why are you still out here? Is somebody in there?"

She looked at me, a puzzled expression on her face. "Why are we here?" she asked.

I'm ashamed to admit that I didn't get it then; I blamed grief and exhaustion and thought that a good night's sleep was all she needed. When I went into work the next day I explained to curious customers that I was doing double shifts because Mom was sleeping so she "could get back to herself."

"What do you mean 'back to herself'?" asked Lucky, a steady customer back in the day.

I explained that I found Mom standing in front of the house and not going in.

Lucky frowned. "Besides being disoriented, what else is she confused about?"

I took a step away from Lucky's seat and loudly disagreed, "She's not disoriented; she's just tired. She's not confused, just a little forgetful."

Lucky convinced me to pay careful attention to mom's behavior. "When I come in next week for my usual lasagna I hope you'll be able to report that mom is improved," she said.

That week Mom forgot words—she called the paper napkins on the table "those white wipers," and when the doorbell chimed she said "the ringing announcer is at it again." I thought fresh air would help and insisted we take walks. When a neighbor greeted us Mom didn't say "hello," she didn't say, "I appreciate that you came to Dan's funeral." Instead she startled our neighbor, and me, too, when with a smile on her face she announced, "The man I married just left. He didn't say when he was coming back." A few days later I found a tube of her lipstick in the refrigerator.

These were serious symptoms and I should have known better, but Mom was sweet and kind and dressed herself and fed herself. She wasn't like those senile patients who don't recognize their family. I was certain this was temporary. How could I think it wasn't? I never heard of someone my age losing both parents, one after the other.

Lucky urged me to consult a neurologist. And that was the beginning of months of doctors' appointments, treatments, and finally hospice care. It wasn't too long before I was an orphan. An orphan with no extended family, not one living relative, and also no college degree. But I always had the diner.

Louie's growing-up years also revolved around a store. I know this because we have long talks every evening, sometimes for hours, either in person or on the phone. His grandfather started the busiest and best hardware store in the Iowa town where Louie grew up, eventually his dad took it over and then when Louie graduated from school he worked there, too. Louie's dad passed down to his son a great love for hardware stores and all that goes into them, and he also passed down a strong work ethic. Louie can talk about the store, the customers, and tools, power equipment, water heaters, and paint, all day long. The only subject he has trouble talking about is his daughter.

IT'S ONE OF THOSE COLD NEW JERSEY WINTER EVENINGS and we're in Louie's living room watching *Newhart* when a picture of a missing child flashes on the screen. Ah, an opportunity for me to broach the subject. "Did you get your daughter's picture on TV?"

"I tried," he replies, "but she was too old for TV and for the milk cartons." Then he shudders and looks straight at me. "Every day is rough for me, Dot. It's hard to sleep, my conscience bothers me. Ten times a day I ask myself, 'Did I screw up my kid?' Who knows? Maybe I did, maybe I didn't. And where the heck is she?"

I want to know the whole story and I want to ask about Laurie's mother, but his voice gets shaky and I don't want him to break down in front of me. He's a tough dude with an image to maintain. And it's all so fresh. So, I just let my eyes do the talking before we turn back to *Newhart*. Louie is quickly distracted by Dick and Joanna and their attempts to run the Stratford Inn. While he is laughing at the strange inn guests popping up on the TV screen, my thoughts are back to Laurie and her mother. Where is that mother? What happened to her? Is Louie a widower?

The snow continues and the ten o'clock news predicts we are in for a blizzard. Louie's house is warm and cozy. Nothing fancy, just regular. Old, plain furniture. Decorated by a man, but comfortable enough. Routes 1 and 9 are closed, and probably won't be plowed out until morning. I may be stuck here.

A few days ago Louie said, "Dot, there's so much I want to tell you but we never have time." Tonight's weather may provide the time. I'll find out if he's ready to spill his story.

Everyone says I'm a good listener. When you work in a diner you learn to listen. Some people pour their heart out to a shrink, others prefer a bartender or a food-server. The single customers, the lonely customers, the broken-hearted, are the ones who choose to sit at the counter. They don't want to sit at a booth, opposite an empty seat, nor do they want to go home to share a meal with memories.

At the counter I become their mother moving around, collecting ingredients, preparing the meal. I serve these lonely folks with the love they dream about or possibly once had. As soon as I place that platter in front of them, they talk. I know about their boss and I know about their wife. I know when they have a tough day at work and I know when their project wins an award.

It probably helps that I look like 'the little lady,' a mother figure from many a movie or television show. My blonde hair lends an air of cheerfulness to my appearance, my apron reminds them of Mom, and the fact that I'm short which bothered me when I was young, is now an asset. The men enjoy towering over me, it makes them feel more macho especially if they've had a hard day; and the few women who dare come in to a diner by themselves tend to be tough career women and they're never threatened by a short gal wearing an apron.

My listening skills are supreme. Lucky Louie.

CHAPTER FIVE

Louie

WE'RE RELAXING ON MY COUCH. THE RED AND BLUE PLAID is a bit worn, but it's a cozy place to sit and the heavy upholstery is good for a night like tonight. I turn off the TV so we can talk. With Dot close by, I'll be brave enough to say the truth and tolerate the sadness those words will bring.

I'm nervous. When I was a boy and something upset me I'd want to tell my mother about it, but I couldn't. She had no patience for unhappiness. 'Chin up,' she'd say and quickly change the subject.

Dot's nodding out; trying to keep her eyes open, but fatigue is taking over. While she's dozing I can't do my usual—slipping into the kitchen for my cherry vanilla ice cream—because she's leaning on my shoulder. Dot's eyelids flicker and soon open. "Louie, I had a sweet respite, thanks for your shoulder," she says as she stretches her arms above her head and sits up. "I'm ready to listen, if you're ready to talk," she says, "but you don't have to tell me anything you don't want to. You're under no obligation. If it's too painful to talk about Laurie, I'll understand."

This is just the encouragement I need. "There are sad parts to my story, Dot. I don't want to scare you away. The story starts with my wife. I married Suzanne and I loved her, and I protected her—for a while—until it all fell apart. I was too young to know what I was doing, and I listened to the wrong people, I was a fool. Damage was done."

Dot is attentive and interested. So far, so good.

"It started out as a sweet and normal married life. Suzanne and I went to work, came home to eat dinner with my folks, then watched a couple of television shows and went to bed. On the weekends we did our errands, helped around the house and we dreamed about our future.

"And then the future came. I was proud, my mother was thrilled, and my dad would break into a smile whenever we talked about the coming blessed event. Suzanne lost the habit of visiting her folks—she came from a very disturbed family, Dot, very disturbed. They didn't try to contact her; she didn't contact them. I assumed she was happy about getting pregnant; it was the next step of our lives. Maybe I assumed too much."

Dot is frowning. She says, "I don't know if I want to hear the rest of this."

I suggest we pause and I try to be a good host. "Let's break for food," is what I say; what I really mean is, let's break for ice cream. I've been living alone for quite some time. I'm not accustomed to normal food at normal meal times.

Dot is not her usual helpful self. This is a first; she's waiting for me to serve her. I do my best and take the ice cream out of the freezer, find spoons and bowls and bring it all over to her. She doesn't dig in. She's looking up at me expectantly.

"Oh? What? You want real food, too?" I ask.

She nods. I bring out crackers, cheese, some leftover chicken from the other night, and a banana, and set them out on the table. I hope that's enough, and I move with her from the couch to the table. I'm ready to begin telling her the worst part of my story, the words I've been unable to admit to anyone, even myself.

"Suzanne got very sick after Laurie was born and the doctor in our backward town did not know how to treat her. After many weeks of Suzanne getting worse and worse, he held a meeting with me and my parents and said Suzanne would need to live in a psychiatric hospital the rest of her life."

Dot says nothing but her eyes widen as she places her trembling fingertips against her lips. I tell her that a few days after our hospital meeting Mom announced, "It's time to forget about Suzanne. You heard what the doctor said. She's a mental case, and she'll probably get even worse. Laurie Sue deserves better. And so do you, my son."

Over and over I said, 'Mom, How can I forget my wife? That's Suzanne. I love her. She's my wife."

I explain to Dot that my mother was a tough woman. She ran our family. She also ran the store, even though my dad thought he did. Whenever we were not at work Dad and I would relax and chat and hang out with each other, but Mom never was the hang-out type. She was harsh and sharp and disciplined in everything she did, and she was always in charge, no matter the circumstance.

My mother had an answer for everything. "If you love this baby you will forget her. You will get on with your life.

Laurie Sue needs a mom—not just a dad and grandparents. A real honest-to-God mom."

Dot is suddenly hyper-alert. She perks up and says, "What?!? Your mother really wanted you to forget about your wife? She was serious?"

I know Dot, she's waiting for me to say, 'Of course I told my mother that was ridiculous.' Instead, I tell Dot the truth. My cheeks are burning, my throat is thick and with a husky voice I admit, "Yes, Mom was serious, and no, I didn't fight her. I was too weak."

I look at the wall, the ceiling, the light, anything but not Dot's eyes. I tell her how I repeatedly said, "But Mom, what about when she gets better? This is her home. I am her family."

Mom had a pat answer: "The doctor said she won't get better. Leave it to me."

It hurts to remember all this. I guess that's why I forgot about it all these years. I'm not proud; I know what I did was wrong.

My mother never let up; she reminded me every day that it was hopeless, Suzanne would never recover. I can still hear her saying, "this adorable little baby girl will have a mother in a locked hospital ward and that mother will not recognize her baby. Is that what you want for your daughter?"

Dot makes me feel even more ashamed when she asks, "I know your mother's plan was impossible for you because you're a responsible person and because you loved Suzanne. How was this resolved?"

I explain that my mother was a fast worker. I was stunned by her actions and it quickly became a done deal. She got an annulment for me, then legally changed our names— hers, mine, my father's, all from Franno to Franklin. She couldn't figure out how to change the baby's name, though, which was a more complicated procedure because we didn't have the actual birth certificate yet. The hospital or Bureau of Records had to send it and then we could apply to change it.

Before we left Iowa I went to the hospital to visit Suzanne many, many times. She was not at all herself, not the bride I married, and, anyway, she didn't want to see me. I asked a nurse on the floor, "Does my wife talk to anyone here? Does she walk in the halls with other patients? Is she crying very much?"

"'Nothing like that,' said the nurse. 'Your wife doesn't cry. She's silent and somber. She doesn't speak. Just stares into space. She hasn't connected with anyone—patient or doctor or nurse.'"

"Oh, Dot, I blame the doctors, the stupid doctors there, they gave up on her. Sometimes in life we don't know what it is that we don't know."

I can see that Dot cares, she's straining to keep listening, to keep her eyes open. It's late, way past her bedtime, but I can't stop, and I didn't get to Laurie, yet.

I explain that as soon as my folks got money from the bank for the store and signed up with a realtor to handle the sale of the house, we all moved across the country, here to New Jersey, to Truesdale. Me, my parents, and baby Laurie. I must have been in a daze all those months. I shoved Suzanne right out of my mind.

Dot has stopped eating and she's scrunching her nose up, moving her head back and forth, and looking confused she says, "But, Louie, you're the guy who's always in charge."

I have no answer. I'm shaking, wiping my forehead with the back of my hand, I see that Dot is shaking, too. Maybe from nerves, maybe from fatigue. I don't know how much more she can tolerate. It's after midnight and she's been up since before dawn. I'm grateful she hasn't bolted in horror.

It's snowing hard, a blizzard, they say. Dot won't be able to open the diner. Delivery trucks will never make it up Huntington Hill. No food, no business, no customers. No one in Huntington or in Truesdale will be able to get to work in the morning. The mayors will close the schools and the roads."

"Louie, I'm exhausted, but intrigued. Keep talking. I'm listening."

I drone on and on, relieving myself of years of unsaid words. I end my Suzanne memories by saying that everything we did was so Laurie would have a good life. I was convinced that to keep my baby safe I had to abandon Suzanne. "And now what? Where is her good life? Where is she?"

Overflowing with shame I wonder if Dot still respects me, if she still cares for me.

All our ice cream has long ago melted.

CHAPTER SIX

Dot

LOUIE IS TRYING TO CONVINCE ME THAT HE'S NOT A BAD person. He's telling me about money he provided for Suzanne if she should ever recover. He's telling me he truly did his best to understand what the doctors were telling him about his wife.

It's good for him to get this all out, but I don't know how good it is for me to listen to it. I'm trying my best. He's right, he's not a bad person. Now that I know what he's been through, I respect him more than ever. Nevertheless, he did something unimaginable. What else might he be capable of?

If he stays in that chair any longer his thoughts will crush him. I encourage him to stand. "Let's put on some music and walk to the window. We can look out at the falling snow, it's a glistening blanket."

Louie knows that although my customers like to listen to popular hits, and he likes to listen to jazz, I prefer classical music, so he bought me a cassette tape featuring my favorite Chopin pieces. In a few minutes we're at the large window, almost folding into each other, and gazing out at the smooth layer of pure, new snow while listening to a romantic piano concerto.

He's soothed now, and I'm settling down, too. His five-foot-eight body is plenty big compared to mine, and when we're together like this I feel safe and secure. His presence reassures me. Tonight, although I still feel protected, I suspect Mister I-Can-Take-Care-of-the-World might need some caretaking himself. I may become the designated caretaker. Surprisingly, that doesn't scare me. He's worth my staying.

Louie shifts his position and I realize he must soon sleep or at least lie down. In my fantasies—and I admit I do have Louie fantasies—Louie seduces me into his bedroom. I've thought of us cuddling and kissing. I've thought of us touching and teasing. I've thought of Louie strongly grasping my shoulders and suggesting we try out his new silk sheets. Obviously, none of that is happening tonight.

"Try going to sleep now. You need a good rest," I say, as I push open the door to his bedroom, which I've never before seen.

Not exactly the room of my dreams. This room is more like a teenage boy's hideout, or to be fair to Louie, the bachelor pad of a busy business owner. Yesterday's clothes are scattered across the floor, the bedsheets are rumpled, and an empty container of ice cream is on the night table next to a copy of last week's *TV Guide*. If I weren't so fond of Louie this might be a breaking point. I've ended relationships with several previous boyfriends because I couldn't tolerate their messiness. Something about Louie makes it easy for me to let things slide.

"Okay, Louie. Get yourself ready for bed. You deserve a good sleep," I say, wondering where I will spend the night. Too hazardous to drive home. Too hazardous to share this bed with him.

"Don't leave me, Blondie. Not now," he murmurs as he unties his shoes. His eyes are already closing when he adds, "And anyway, the streets aren't cleared yet. You need to stay here to be safe."

This guy, who's always concerned about me, and my safety, and my well-being, is ignoring the fact that I have no place to sleep. Did it slip his mind? Or, has his mind slipped because of this emotional evening?

I go back to the living room and decide the recliner is okay for one night, but how do I brush my teeth? And is there a T-shirt that I can use as pajamas? A blanket? I snoop around and discover other parts of Louie's house hitherto unknown—a laundry room and a powder room. Neither meets my standards, but I'm stranded here. My observations support what my mother used to tell me: men are at their worst when they are without a woman; women, on the other hand, are often at their best when without a man.

There's an alcove upstairs. It leads to a room with a door slightly ajar. Do I dare? Yes, I open it. Maybe I'll find nightclothes. Oh, this must be Laurie's room. It's a large bedroom with every space on every wall covered with a canvas. Large paintings, small paintings, landscapes, still lifes, modern abstracts—this is a museum. A deserted museum. A carelessly made bed, a chest of drawers, some shoes on the floor, and that's it. I bravely open the top drawer. Bingo! Tee shirts. I grab the top one and slip out the door. I've assumed this is Laurie's room, but come to think of it I saw nothing about school, nothing about a teen-age heart throb, nothing about friends, about music. No makeup, no mirrors, no books, no photos. Did she pack up everything that was important to her and take it all with her, wherever she may be?

Sleep comes quickly to me. I'm in the recliner and it's good enough. During the night I hear Louie snoring, which I can ignore. Then I hear him moaning. The moaning gets louder, much louder. I cannot ignore that, so once again I prove how daring I am. I enter Louie's bedroom. Thankfully, he's got pajama bottoms on. He is tossing himself around and whimpering some words. The only words I can make out are *stupid doc, stupid doc.*

I sit on the side of the bed and tell him over and over that all that was in the past, now he's in charge of himself. I gently stroke his face and comfort him by repeating, "You did your best." When he quiets down, I pat his back and he drifts off to sleep. I was right. He needs caretaking.

IN THE MORNING THE SNOWSTORM CONTINUES, AS DOES Louie's unease. I want to be helpful and this poor guy is suffering from memories. "Will it help you to talk some more about Suzanne?" A part of me hopes he says no. I'm eager to get back home and check on both my diner and my house.

"Nothing more to say about Suzanne," he says, "but I need to tell you about Laurie."

I'm in for it. He's back in talk mode. Sitting at the dining room table he looks well-rested. I, on the other hand, not so much. I doubt he notices the lack of makeup on my sleep-deprived face as he forges ahead with his story.

"We've had some tough times lately, me and Laurie. She didn't want to go to school for weeks at a time, and sometimes she didn't take a shower for a whole bunch of days and just stayed in her room. She cried a lot, a real lot. But teenagers do that, you know?"

While he's talking, he brings some soft rolls, butter, cream cheese, crackers, hardboiled eggs, and juice from the refrigerator to the dining room table. I'm relieved he's not asking me to prepare a cheese omelet or French toast or pancakes—that's also been a deal-breaker with some previous guys. More than once I've heard, *I don't have the experience that you do preparing meals. So why don't you try using my pots and pans? I bet you make a mean omelet.*

Louie continues, "Maybe I should have taken her to a shrink, but I didn't know she was planning to leave. I think she was influenced by some bad kids. Believe me there were plenty of bad kids lurking in her high school all the time. Every night on the news I hear about high school kids getting into car accidents, getting into drugs, drinking too much."

"How do you know she ran away?" I interrupt. I'm thinking that maybe she was kidnapped, God forbid.

"Oh, she called that first week. A couple of times. Wanted to tell me not to worry. The first day she told me she was having a sleepover. I was happy to know she had a friend. No friend ever showed up here at the house. 'I love you, Dad,' she said. 'I'll be back. Don't worry about me. I just need some time to figure things out.'

"I was stupid. I didn't ask her what she had to figure out. And I didn't ask her how much time she needed. At first, I thought she'd be gone for a day or two. It was after supper one day and she casually left for one of her usual evening walks. I pray that she's alive."

I can tell that he's holding back tears.

"Honestly, Dot, I don't know if she's dead or alive. That's a helluva thing to confess about your own kid, but it's true. The years of her growing up went by and I didn't realize I was not a good enough father."

I quickly come to his defense. "You love her; that's what counts," I say. It seems to me that Louie did a good job raising his daughter. I hope he realizes that some teenagers are going to do stupid things no matter how good their parents are, no matter how much their parents try. I wish he would stop talking now. It hurts me to hear the heartbreak in his voice.

He pauses and I think he's finished. He stands, walks to the refrigerator, opens the freezer and pulls out some cherry vanilla ice cream—for breakfast!—and another glass of orange juice. Now he's equipped to continue. I stand up to stretch, and walk across the room to the window and watch the blizzard that never stops.

I hope he'll give this a rest but no such luck. He calls, "Dot, I'm almost done. I like it when you're right here where I can see your pretty face, Blondie." He has me with 'pretty face,' and I return to my chair and he returns to his remembrances. He talks and talks, occasionally pausing to wipe his forehead, take a deep breath and get his bearings. When he finally seems finished I ask the one question that has been bothering me: "What did you tell her about her mother?"

"She never asked me about her mother, so I never said anything. It was my mom who decided it would be easier for Laurie if she thought her mother was permanently out of the picture. I call it a good lie. She told Laurie, "Sadly, your beloved mother died in childbirth.""

CHAPTER SEVEN

Laurie

THE DAYS GO BY. THE WEEKS GO BY. I DON'T KNOW HOW
many months, or maybe years, I've been here. Each day
rolls into the next when there's no contact with the outside world. I wouldn't know if our country was in a war; I
wouldn't know if there was an earthquake; I have no idea
what movies are popular. I've missed birthdays, TV shows,
holidays. Most days I like it here, but lately there are plenty
of days when I know that this life is too isolating for me
and sometimes too weird.

I've made up my mind.

I'm leaving.

Tomorrow, before breakfast.

This is not prison; there are no gates or bars. I'll walk
out in the morning before everyone is awake and call Dad
from a phone booth on the street. I hope I don't cry when
I hear his voice. Maybe he'll be the one to cry. He always
missed me when I was in Florida and I'd tease him because
when he'd see me after a long time apart, he'd get teary.

He'd say, "tears of happiness, my daughter, tears of happiness." I wonder if he'll say that when I call in the morning. I'm ready to hear his voice.

Along with some of my art supplies, I'm packing up a couple of my new outfits. Master says it's important that we look our best at all times, and it will take me a while to figure out what's trendy and what's not.

It's quiet. Sun just coming up. No one is here to say good-bye to, and it's better this way. No drama. No one trying to persuade me to stay. I'm on my way. Stepping out into the dawn is exhilarating, even though my eyes hurt from the glare of the rising sun. I've missed fresh air and I've missed the hum of activity from cars, buses, trucks.

I'd forgotten that many people start their day early in the morning. I see some moms walking young children to school. I see junior high school kids waiting for their school bus. There are many men and a couple of women, all carrying briefcases, waiting on the corner for the commuter bus to the city. There's a homeless man still sleeping—he's stretched out on a flattened refrigerator delivery box—in front of an office building. I see a guy on his bike, tossing the morning paper to his customers' doorways. There's a shopkeeper hauling a cart full of produce—fruits, vegetables—into his store, and there's a bakery that's just opening and several people are already lined up for their morning muffins.

It's joyful to walk. Now I'm passing a furniture store, and next there's a laundromat. And here's a GAP with jean jackets in the window. The stores are not yet open but I can window shop. I didn't realize how much I missed the freedom of walking wherever I want, whenever I want.

I'm taking long strides, I'm smiling. The air is crisp, the breeze on my skin is refreshing, and the street smells like a typical fall, back-to-school day. I purposely step on some leaves just to hear them crunch. I can see the pay-phone up ahead.

"Miss, stop right there!" A loud voice erupts behind me. Suddenly, there are two uniformed men next to me, one on each side.

"Don't move," says the guy on my right. "I'm Officer Barr, and we need to ask you a few questions."

"Are you talking to me? I didn't do anything. What do you want?" My knees are getting weak. I'm trembling.

"It's probably a misunderstanding. You'll be on your way in no time. We'll just check your backpack," says the other officer.

"Wait. What? Why?"

"We're part of motel security and we received a call that a young woman of your description stole some items. A light blue pants outfit, a yellow sweater, and also a small canvas and a watercolor palette, whatever that is. This will be over in a minute. Sorry we startled you. Just remove your backpack now and open it for us, please. Don't worry; you'll be right back on your way."

I do as I'm told. The motel security men are polite, and look surprised when they pull out my pantsuit.

I can hardly catch my breath as they quickly escort me through the streets and back to Master.

Master is agitated. He sternly asks, "What have you done? Who influenced you?"

"I was just going home. These are my clothes and my art supplies," I say. "This is not prison. I want to go home. You can't stop me."

Master signals to the motel security team. "Thanks for your help. You can go now," he says, as I watch him slip them each a twenty.

He looks at me. "I'm disappointed in you. You are one of my stars. No need to steal. No need to sneak away."

I thought I had made the right decision, but now I'm not so sure. I never want to disappoint Master. I want to go home to Dad, but I also want to help Master make the world a better place. Staying here, I know what to do and when to do it, even if I don't always like it. And I don't like it when I work in front of my easel from early morning until very late at night. I hardly get any sleep. But, if I go home I'll have to go back to school to get my diploma and high school drama will again be part of my life—the cliques, competitive girls, rowdy boys, hidden beer cans, speeding cars, cigarettes exchanged for homework.

Mixed-up thoughts confuse me and I hate confusion. I'll stay here and be good to Master. "I'm sorry. I'm sorry," I whimper to him.

"We can pretend this never happened," he says, "and as long as you are never again so foolish, I won't press criminal charges."

"Thank you. Thank you," I say as I sniffle. I promptly walk to my studio, resume painting and chanting, and in a few days all is forgiven if not forgotten.

I DIDN'T THINK IT WOULD COME TO THIS. I REMEMBER that second day, when Anna was helping me find my way around. I thought this might be my forever home. That morning as soon as I awakened, Anna told me the bedroom we had slept in will be my private room.

"There's no dresser," she said, "so keep your clothes on that second bed." She promised me she'd make sure I'd have a beautiful selection of new outfits.

She guided me back to Room 130, deposited me in the red chair, and quickly disappeared. That's when Master strutted in, studied my face, and declared, "Amelia, yes, Amelia will be your name. It suits you."

I was confused. "What? Don't you remember me? I'm Laurie. It's me. Laurie."

He then proceeded to sit upon his magnificent chair and resumed speaking as if I hadn't said a word. "Now let's get to work. Recite your mantra, Amelia.

I obeyed, saying my mantra three times. There's something about the way Master says things that makes us all listen to him. We are a family, we belong and we do as we're told.

"Now look at this money," he told me that day, as he pointed to the dollar bills on his desk, his gold bracelets jangling. "Every bill represents hard work. You will add to the pile with your hard work. But first you must study. You must study all the lessons I teach you. The more you learn and the more you study, the closer the world comes to becoming a peaceful, gentle place for everyone to enjoy."

He then told me the rules:

"Rule One: You will gaze at my hair whenever we are in the same room. You will repeat your mantra while observing my hair. While I speak, you study my hair and recite your mantra. You may say it softly, loudly, sometimes silently. You must say it."

I remember my face burning from the intensity of his eyes. *Is he serious,* I wondered? Yes, he is. He's determined that I stare at his head. This seemed peculiar to me, but maybe he knew something I didn't.

"Rule Two: Anna will bring you lovely clothes to wear. They will be your clothes for every day. You'll always remember that Master keeps you beautiful. No jewelry, no makeup, no trashy looks."

Anna has good taste and is always well-dressed. My grand-mother loved fine clothes. Maybe I am in the right place.

Master was booming at me from his throne, which is how I thought of that iron chair with its bright yellow cushions.

"Rule Three: All members of our group help one another. You will be helped, and you will help others. You will speak to group members only; outsiders do not have your best interests at heart. Beware of the kindness of outsiders. Beware of the kindness of strangers."

How could I meet an outsider? We're supposed to stay in this special wing of the hotel that's just for us. Anna and Tom told me that no one can come in here unless they're Master Academy students.

"Rule Four: No media—magazines, books, newspaper, television, radio, telephone, they can all be bad influences. I value your purity and will provide you with all the information you need."

I was okay with this. I'm not a great TV fan, and I'd done enough reading in school to last a lifetime.

"Rule Five: You will speak only when spoken to and answer any questions asked. You will not ask any questions."

I remember thinking this was not fair. My thoughts must have played out on my face, because Master continued:

"This is called 'contact functioning.' To make the world a better place it is best to not say anything until a person contacts you, with words. That shows that the person is ready to hear and absorb what you have to say. Eventually you will be able to begin conversations, but only after you're a Master Academy member for quite some time."

He leaned back in his chair. "Rule Six: When you are awakened in the morning, no matter how early it may be, you will immediately get up and get dressed and prepare for your day."

Remembering this now, I recall that I hadn't been so excited about life in a long time. I told myself that even though I'm scared, I'm looking forward to something. I'm not worrying about stupid teachers or incompetent bureaucrats at license departments. I asked myself: *Do I leave? Do I stay?* And I answered myself: *I'll decide tomorrow. Or next week.*

"That's all for today, Amelia. You can stop your chanting and begin studying for your GED. The GED prep book costs just twenty-two dollars. You can get that much money from about forty minutes in the street. Anna and Tom will show you how."

"The street? What?" I recall how puzzled I felt. And frightened. *Where were they sending me?*

In my memory I can clearly see Master as he presses the buzzer under his center desk drawer and then Tom appears in about thirty seconds. "You look pretty," he says as he picks up some notes from Master's desk and a large shopping bag. "Please follow me."

In a few minutes we are in Lyons Park and I'm holding a yellow basket that Tom pulled out of the shopping bag.

The basket was filled with hair ribbons. Some are bows, some are curled up, and all of them were either yellow or pink. As soon as anyone walked by, Tom stopped them and gave them a ribbon.

"This is for you," he said. "Watch. I'll tie it on your handbag right now, and you will be beautiful."

If it's a boy or a man, he suggested they give one to their wife or their mother or sister. Without missing a beat, Tom then added, "Five dollars will take care of your donation," and no one objects. Each person easily opened a wallet or handbag and out came a five-dollar bill.

Soon I had enough for my GED book and then some. But Tom was not finished.

"As long as people are strolling around, we stay here," he said. "Why don't you approach the teenagers and the kids, and I'll take care of the adults?"

He pointed to two little girls and their dad walking right in front of me. *If I don't act now, they'll be gone, and Tom will be disappointed.*

The girls liked the ribbons I selected for them. They're the curlicued pink ones that look like springtime. The dad said he wanted one for his wife, too, so I gave him a pink one that's not curled but beautifully stitched around the edges. He handed me a twenty, told me to keep the change.

Maybe I'm a born saleswoman.

We work until there's no one left to sell to. I managed to sell fifteen more ribbons. It's been a long time since I've had this good feeling. It's the way I felt when I won my first art contest—special. We walked back to the hotel and I was proud that I'm helping the entire Master Academy group.

Anna was waiting in our hotel room to talk to me. She wanted to be sure I understood all the rules. "Don't worry, Amelia," she says after a while. "You can complain to me if you are very tired. We've all become accustomed to the early wake-up routine, at first it's hard to start your day so early."

She tilted her head, and scrutinized mine. "You know, the name Amelia suits you. It means industrious and hard-working. Master always knows what he's doing when he changes names. I think you'll be like me one day and get a good match from Master. Tom and I are very happy with each other. We are going to be married in Wisconsin next month."

So they *are* a romantic couple—well, sort of. If I think about it, they do look like they belong together. I'm trying to figure out how to ask more about what happens if you don't want a match, but then my stomach growled. I'm hungry, but if I ask Anna where to get something to eat, I'll be initiating a conversation and that's against the rules.

Tom poked his head in just at the right time.. "Lunch is ready. Let's go into the cafeteria and talk about our plans for the rest of the day."

At lunch, I learned that I'm supposed to spend that afternoon studying with Master in Room 130.

At the appropriate time I walk through the winding hallway to get to #130. I tell myself I'm on a treasure hunt and the treasure is courage. I must gather all the courage I can find from my brain and from my body. Surprisingly I succeed—I knock on the door.

Once we're settled, Master in his yellow chair, me in the red one, he began.

"Welcome to Master Academy, Amelia. You did well with money collections today. I knew you would. I like

the way you and Anna and Tom get along, so they will not
leave for Wisconsin quite yet. Instead, they'll remain here
so you can work with them."

I dare not ask about their upcoming wedding. Are they
having a wedding? Do they have to postpone it because of
me, or will they be here for just a few extra days?

"Master Academy promotes a good and pure life. No
outside entanglements, no outside influences. Almost all
our members go from here in New Jersey to our farm
compound in Wisconsin. Many are married to each other,
some have babies, and all live righteously."

Master speaks with authority and certainty. I keep
my eyes on his hair when he's looking at me. Those are
my instructions. But whenever his eyes stray, I find mine
straying, too—to the bookshelves loaded with what
looks like psychology textbooks, to the desk covered in
money, to that framed photo of him hanging next to a
filing cabinet.

During those first few days Master would tell me about
other Master Academy students, and my thoughts would
go to Dad. I called him to let him know I'm staying with
Anna for a little while longer. I remind him that if I'm not
home he won't have to hurry home from work to be with
me. He worries that I eat alone too often. I've tried to
convince him that eating alone is okay with me. I showed
him a print of Edward Hopper's famous painting, *The
Nighthawks.* He was not impressed.

Master is still speaking. "Everyone puts their dollars on
this desk when they return from selling product. Some of
us make product, others buy their product from wholesal-
ers. Everyone has a skill or gift or talent that enhances our

community. I know that you are a fine artist. That's why I alerted Tom about you."

"You alerted Tom? Wait. How did you know that I paint? How did you know who I am? You knew my name?"

"I saw your watercolors on display at the Truesdale Town Hall and at the Elm Street Bank downtown. Unless there is someone else who has your old name, Laurie Franklin."

Now he's creeping me out. I thought he never went out because of bad weather or bad vibes or something. How did he know where I would go for a walk? Were Tom and Anna hunting for me all over town? Did they know I was Laurie when we met that first time?

I remember that Master was talking and talking. "You will paint, we will purchase all the supplies you request. My people tell me there's a craft store nearby. You will have all the time you need to create masterpieces. I know that outstanding ladies and gentlemen will want your paintings. You'll begin your painting regimen tomorrow morning right after breakfast."

Regimen? That doesn't sound like fun. He thinks I'm a fine artist. I suppose I am but I'm not sure what to do about telling him that I didn't win the county-wide art contest. I usually come in number 1 or number 2, but this year I didn't. I didn't win and it had nothing to do with my art or my talent; it was because this year students were on the judging panel. My name was signed on every one of my paintings so the kids I go to school with, who don't like me, who think I'm weird, would not vote for me even if they thought my artwork was the best. Those kids think I'm stuck up and snooty; they don't get that I try hard to talk, I really do. But I'm scared of saying the wrong thing, so I say nothing. The only time I'm not scared is when I have a paintbrush in my hand. *Maybe here my life will change.*

Master continues: "One of our newest members is an experienced salesman and he will be selling your work. Another member used to work for a large advertising company, a world-wide company, and he is right now in his room, preparing ads for 'Paintings by Amelia.' He came to Master Academy to lead a more authentic life; he's proud to be spreading kindness. We'll be selling to an upscale market and I will host some gallery openings in a new hotel."

Master is balanced like a king on his throne. He speaks and his back gets straighter, his neck longer, his head held higher. I remember experiencing the opposite and thinking: *My chest feels tight. Something's wrong with my breathing. I never had asthma, but I have it now. I have asthma today, I know it. I need asthma medicine.*

I need asthma medicine and I also need my GED. When Anna and Tom told me about Master Shekett they said I would be studying toward my diploma, not painting for money. It is flattering that people pay, but I want to be a high school graduate. And, what if my paintings aren't good enough? What if nobody buys them?

Master continues. "Living in our community is special, much more interesting than a lonely life with one parent who works all day."

"But I live with my dad," I say, pausing my chanting. Of course I'm going to stick up for my father.

"That's not really living. Here you belong to a group. You will be loved and nurtured and admired by everyone in the group. You may stop chanting now but do continue your gaze. My hair is important for the community. Every strand represents wealth. When I had a shaved head, we made no sales. With a short crew cut, we had some money, but the abundance appeared when my hair grew long.

"Blondes do better in life, Amelia, and I wish only the best for you. Blond hair brings out a woman's natural beauty. Anna will help you to become a blonde."

And with that, Master Shekett dismisses me.

I wandered back to my room and I didn't know what to do. *Blonde? What is that all about?* I'm thinking about Tom and Anna. They seem okay. They don't seem like they're out of their minds and yet they go along with whatever Master suggests. Why? Master probably is crazy, but maybe he's one of those eccentric geniuses I've heard about. I should make up my mind about leaving; it's time for a decision.

Why is life so hard? No matter where I am, I come up against stupid rules and now this place has too many rules for me. Change my name, sell in the park, change my hair color, no entertainment. My stomachache never goes away. I always have a headache. I wish I could blame all my troubles on a dysfunctional family but it's only me and Dad.

I remember the day that I told myself *today's the day I'll decide whether to stay or to leave.* I thought about it all that afternoon and then at the dinner table, while I'm still deciding, just finishing my chocolate pudding, Tom appears. He's wearing his usual preppy clothes and greets me with his usual smile, a smile that shows off his shiny white teeth.

"Hi, Laurie. I have a question for you. Do you know what art supplies you'll need for the next month or two? Can you give me a list of everything you'd like by tomorrow morning? Master told me to give you an unlimited expense account at the art supply shop."

I decided to stay.

I GOT USED TO LIVING IN THE HOTEL. EVERY ROOM IS THE same as every other room, except for Master's, which is larger, fancier, and smells like hair spray. All the hallways have frayed carpeting, but the eating area is clean and well maintained. The lighting is poor in many rooms but not my art studio. My studio has excellent artificial lighting because there's no natural light coming in. It's easy to feel comfortable around here because there's never anything new to get accustomed to.

When Master walks into a room, any room—the auditorium, the conference room, the cafeteria—I can tell he's arrived before I see him or hear him. His energy precedes him, He fills every space with his dynamic presence.

Master really does want to make the world a better place He wants every Academy member to be a calming influence on all the people they meet. He teaches us not to take anything personally when we are criticized, but instead to figure out why the person is critical of us. He says, *Analyze, don't personalize.* It's a good habit to get used to. It would have helped me in school when kids were mean to me.

I remember the day a girl in the cafeteria deliberately knocked my tray off the table and then walked away. I can see it now: I had noticed this girl before. She used to get into fights, punching, hair-pulling, scratching. She was often in the Dean's office and she was older than most of us, so she must have been held back in the early grades. My tray and all the food on it crashed to the floor. It was embarrassing; all conversations stopped. It was humiliating; everybody saw that I couldn't protect myself from a sketchy loser. Maybe someone else would have shouted at her or started a fight, but not me. I cried. Not loudly, but enough for tears to drip down my cheeks and onto the cafeteria table. I wouldn't have reacted like that if I analyzed before I personalized. I personalized by thinking she picked on me because she knew I was a disaster, and then I cried and felt sorry for myself. But if I'd analyzed, I would have realized that she was a kid who was flunking out of school. She was angry at the world and would have lashed out at anyone. It doesn't make what she did any better, but it would have made my reaction less personal, less intense.

Master gives us several lectures about how to analyze and not personalize. We practice that until it becomes a habit, an automatic response. Master sincerely believes he will make me a better person. He says he started making me a better person by changing me to be a blonde, which sounds stupid when I think about it. That's why I try not to think; thinking gives me a headache.

Master is a good man with a big heart who buys me all the art supplies I need. That's a good reason to stay here…I guess. Of course, at home I could buy supplies, too, but it always seemed like too much trouble to set up a real studio. Another reason to stay is because I have friends. Nice friends. People who care about me. People who agree with Master that our attitudes can make the world a better place.

The kids I see in the hallways seem nice. They're friendly and smile or nod at me, even the ones I don't know.

Master does not want me to get my GED. I bring it up again during our private study session. "First, Amelia, you must become adept at the rules. Please look at my hair. Focus your gaze on every hair on top of my head. Each strand is there for a purpose. You will soon understand the purpose. For as long as there is hair upon my head there will be dollars coming in. The dollars are from the ladies and gentlemen who appreciate your canvases."

My seascapes are soothing; the blue hues of the sky and of the water give off feelings of safety and security. Customers tell Master my seascapes make them feel rested and relaxed. "Gallery owners ask for your seascapes more than any other paintings," he says. I feel cheated. I don't have a seascape to look at, just the framed photo of Master. There are no windows in my studio, and sometimes I don't know if it's day or night.

More time passes. Life goes on. My name is now Amelia, my hair is now blonde, I have no permission to do anything except paint or chant. I always thought busy-ness is what I needed, but now I'm not so sure. I'd like to take a walk or go to a movie or go to a mall. I'd like to see my dad, too. No visitors are allowed here, and no phone calls, either. I know Dad's working hard and enjoying his work, but he might be lonely.

Every morning Master sweeps into my studio to talk to me and to watch me paint. At the beginning of my time here I was flattered because he knows more about art and about my paintings than my dad does. But now he takes up too much space in this small room and the firewood smell of his cologne wafts onto my canvas. "Good morning, Amelia. I'm here to give you today's wisdom. It will help you maintain your energy for painting."

The thing is, the wisdom that Master says he's giving me doesn't always seem wise. Sometimes it doesn't even make sense. "Look around you. Enemies are lurking," he says. He insists they are all around us, but the enemies he targets don't seem like enemies to me. Last week a new boy joined us and it turned out he had some books that he didn't turn in, like you're supposed to. Master found the books and yelled, "Get rid of these books. You may not keep them. They are part of the plot to corrupt you and other young people, They are part of the plot to break up Master Academy," he insisted. Later on that day I looked at those books. They were *Introduction to Calculus* and *Intermediate Calculus.*

I have doubts about the unique thoughts that Master is proud of. He thinks he's improving the world by teaching us innovative ideas and groundbreaking theories. Sorry, but his concepts are not original. Trying hard at things and being considerate and kind and thoughtful are not unique notions. When I was little, my dad taught me, "when in doubt, follow the rules." He didn't make a big deal out of being a good person.

Now I'm on my way to the lecture hall where Master is teaching a session about the Ten Commandments. "It's important to follow laws that have lasted for centuries," he says. "The Ten Commandments can guide you to have a righteous life." I know I'm not the only one sitting here thinking, *are you for real*? Two boys in the row ahead of me and Jenny, an older girl in my row, all wince. Of course we're skeptical. We're not permitted to have visitors here. How is that honoring our parents? And how come I must paint every day? Where is my day of rest? Afterward, Jenny says, "I hope you don't take this the wrong way and please never mention it to Master, but I wonder if calling him Master is the same as having another god or creating an idol." I don't say anything.

Everything is not perfect around here. There are older members who randomly punish some of the newer kids. At night, every so often, I hear a cascade of cries. I know that's wrong and that's when I want to leave, but in the morning everyone seems okay.

Walking back to my studio from the lecture I hear a commotion in the corridor. Oh, no. there's a paramedic racing toward the exit, pushing a stretcher. No one said anything about an incident or an accident and I'm not yet permitted to initiate a conversation so I have to guess. Does someone need help because they were harmed or is Master getting help for someone who is sick?

I may not have come from a regular family and I may not have been popular in school, but I do know it is not normal to say, "I will stay on the path," over and over and over. And it's not normal to never see a newspaper or TV or magazine. It's true I do have friends here. I do have people here who like me. It's reassuring to belong to a group and it's soothing to stick to routines and not have to make decisions. But, it's becoming more and more difficult to stay here. I want to get my diploma and then my driver's license. Master's teased-up, white-as-snow hair is gorgeous, but I don't want to look at it all day. Plus, I'm chewing my bottom lip way too often.

And, there's the hunger. Last night I dreamed about food. Today's meals had portions fit for a three-year-old. My stomach growls. Master is smart not to have televisions here. If he did, the food commercials would incite us to riot. Master says he doesn't want us to concentrate on the food, but instead on our mealtime conversation. We all know how to eat and speak at the same time. I think about a juicy pan-seared steak and about Dad's chicken parm. I think about mac and cheese. I think about Dad and grandpa and their ice cream.

WEEKS PASS, MONTHS PASS, AND AGAIN I WANT TO LEAVE. My heart is not in this. It takes me longer to finish each painting and when I mix my colors I sometimes am too hasty and don't come up with the best hue. Master is getting on my nerves again. I'm restless. I want to go outdoors. I want to know what year it is, what season it is. When I saw boots and snow shovels downstairs I wondered—is it the beginning of winter or the end? The days meld into each other. I'm tired, I'm sad, I'm done here…I think.

It doesn't take long for the change in my work to make its way to Master. One day he comes to my studio, his face mean, his eyes darting around, his fist in the air, and he's screaming, "My hair, my hair, I need every strand of hair! Amelia, gaze and chant, gaze and chant. You must gaze more. Chant more. Paint more. Paint faster. I know you can do it."

I have a brush in my hand, and yet I stop to gaze at his head. Yes, his hair is bright white, but so what? Am I a big jerk? Or is he a big jerk? Nobody else around here questions Master, so the jerk might be me.

There is a limit to how fast I can paint and still have my work come out good enough for people to buy. I tell Master I'm painting as fast as I can, but he says, "I know you can speed up. How do I know? Your dear, departed mother told me so. She comes to me. She talks to me. She tells me you must paint faster and faster."

I freeze. I can't believe what I'm hearing. "What? My mother is dead, deceased, she never talks to me or anyone else. She is dead. I don't know her. Even my father doesn't talk about her. He is respectful and never mentions her."

But Master is going on and on. "She is telling me you don't realize that there are enemies all around. She knows the world is a dangerous place and you are lucky to be here. Wait … I am listening to her … she is speaking now. Your dear departed mother cares about you, Amelia. She tells me you can paint faster and faster. She wants what is best for you."

My heart is out of control—too loud, too jumpy. Can Master hear it? My body is trembling. This is it. I can't tolerate anymore. I don't understand what's happening to me. I feel weak. I want to disappear. I'm sweating. My mother? Master gets messages from her and I don't? Is Master going crazy, or am I?

He continues, "Amelia, pay attention. Pay attention. Do not stop chanting. Keep it up, Amelia."

I chant, "I will stay on the path. I will stay on the path. I will…"

He says, "Speak up. I can barely hear you. My hair is thinning, Amelia, my hair is thinning." Master has become a desperate, frightened man, with a squeaky voice. He sounds like my Chatty Cathy doll from when I was four years old.

My voice is gone. Exhaustion takes over. My tears are flowing. I finally get it—I don't belong here.

Master is frowning and he looks worried too. When I used to be sad and stay home from school and cry a lot, Dad would look at me with this same kind of nervous face.

Master is saying, "Stop it, Amelia. I don't want to force you into The Isolation Room. You can paint. You can chant. You can gaze. I know you can, and your dear departed mother knows you can. Take a little break and shut off those tears. Go. Go to your room and meet me back here in the art studio in thirty minutes. Come back prepared to get to work. There are four more commissions waiting for you to fulfill."

But I don't come back in thirty minutes. I lie down in bed, and I don't get up, not even when Master comes himself to try and rouse me. I'm done with this life. If Anna and Tom were still here and not in Wisconsin I'd talk to them and perhaps feel better. If I had some of the money my paintings bring in I'd feel better, too. I'm done here.

When Master offers me food, I don't have the strength to eat. He tries to hide his alarm when I refuse steak, something we've never been offered. When I also refuse the carrot cake with whipped cream, it's apparent he's panicky about my health. He's looking from side to side, eyes darting, frantic to find a solution. He needs me.

Time passes. Minutes? Hours? Days? I don't know and I don't care. I sleep the sleep of a hibernating bear. A couple of new Master Academy girls are sent in to try to awaken me by standing me up, but my legs don't hold me. I want to shout, "I need to sleep!" but it comes out in a whisper. My eyes won't open.

I hear one of the new girls say to the other, "Amelia is sick. She needs a doctor." Maybe I do. I barely have strength to sit up. These girls are in awe of Master and the Master Academy. One says to the other, "Master is a turn-around expert and he will turn around Amelia. I heard him say she's ruining his reputation. You know, he's obligated to have certain paintings ready and she can't paint in bed."

So, he's not upset he might be ruining my life, just upset about his reputation. I squint open my eyes, to see the girl who is speaking. She's young, with braces on her teeth—like me, somebody at home cares about her. I'd like to tell her a thing or two. Plenty of good things happen here but also indentured servitude and unquestioning obedience are expected. I'd like to tell her that at first I liked the friends, the family-style dinners, the idea of a common goal. But, too much weird stuff is mixed in with that. I'd like to ask her if she's ready to not listen to music and not watch TV and to risk punishment if she dares to think for herself. My body may be slow but my brain is coming back. I must get out of here. I need to be in charge of myself.

Master's walking in. Standing ramrod straight, with a booming voice he insists, "Get up, Amelia, get up. I want to get you the best possible medical care. I've been thinking that your father must have the medical insurance information we need. We'll get that paperwork and arrange appointments with the finest doctors. Call him. I'll arrange for someone to help you walk to the car. Then Ben, our driver, will take you to pick up your insurance papers. They belong to you. Let's do this, Amelia. We are a team. We can do it."

He shows me a stack of brochures for 'Paintings by Amelia,' he offers me a chocolate cake with buttercream topping, and in a few days I have enough strength to walk—not far, and talk—not chant.

I rehearse a script that Master prepares and when I say it perfectly he permits me to use the phone that's apparently been hidden in his office.

"Dad? It's Amel . . . Laurie. It's me, Dad. Laurie. I'm going to come home to see you. Okay? I should arrive tomorrow, probably early evening."

Dad shouts through the phone. "Laurie, Laurie. Good to hear your voice, honey. Is this really you? Are you okay? Where are you?" He's hollering like a mad man. I can almost hear him jumping up and down.

I stay on script. "Dad, I'm okay. I'm coming to see you tomorrow evening. We'll talk then." He doesn't say anything about my weak voice.

Over and over he asks, 'how are you,' 'where are you,' and then he says he'll come pick me up. He asks, "What's the address, honey, I'll leave the house right now?"

I assure him I'll get there tomorrow and insist I must hang up. As I'm ending the call I hear him say, "Come for supper. You know the address. Same house. I'll start cooking now."

I guess Master heard Dad's enthusiasm because now he wants to accompany me, and he reminds me that this visit must be quick, we'll get what we need and be on our way. I'm not so sure about that. He insists I introduce him as my art teacher. I'm hesitant but he reminds me I've been painting all this time and teaching myself new techniques, so it's as if I've been in an art school. I don't lie to my father but this seems like a good lie.

BEN, OUR MASTER ACADEMY DRIVER, HELPS ME GET COM-fortable in the back seat. My eyes quickly close but I'm not fully asleep. I hear Master talking, "We must treat Amelia like gold. We'll quickly get her full medical coverage. Our income plunges every day she doesn't produce. As soon as possible we'll get her chanting again and painting again. I always knew Amelia would be a winner. Look at my hair—it's thicker and more masculine these days—all from her chanting.

"No one who knows me now, could guess how I used to be. I was shy and frightened. Today I'm the king. When the young ones throw that money on my desk, I know I'll never be shy and frightened again. I can buy the clothing and the jewelry that only rich people had back when I was coming up. And now I'm in charge. I will never hurt any of the young ones. I'm a good authority, unlike some of the sickos who I had to obey when I was young. I will save these lovely young ones, all of them."

I'm waking up, and Master is quick to tell me that even if Dad extends an invitation for a longer stay, even if he's attentive and loving, it is still kindness from the enemy. I'm getting a headache. I might want to stay home.

Looking out the car window is exciting. The streets are busy. Kids are playing. Their noises are happy noises, yelling, squealing, energetic sounds, schoolyard sounds. We pass cars filled with families. It amazes me that regular people are walking on a regular street. Surprisingly, the world has stayed the same. I'm insulted everything's been going on as it always did, but without me. We turn on to my street and I see our neighbor, Mr. Tobman. He's still driving his beat-up black Dodge Dart. We pass Leah, sitting on her front porch listening to music as usual, sounds like a Bob Dylan song. When we pull up to my house I'm surprised how close it is to where I've been all this time.

Ben drops us and takes off. The house looks the same. Drab gray siding, two stories, a dowdy little lawn out front, no flowers planted. When we moved in I told Dad I would take charge of planting flowers, but I never got around to it.

If I had the strength, I'd run right in to see him, but I'm too weak. I wish I could hang on to Master for balance, but I don't want to touch him. Not now, not ever.

I slowly make my way up the front steps, ring the bell, Master right behind me. The door opens and there is Dad. He looks the same. He's cute. His big smile and his dark hair are just as I remember. I guess I really did miss him because suddenly it's easy to breathe, a heavy load just flew off me.

Dad looks at me and seems puzzled. He's frowning. "Laurie, is that you? Who is this guy? What's going on? Are you okay?" Dad is confused. He hesitantly reaches out for me. "Come on in, honey. You, too, mister." Walking in I smell all the familiar kitchen smells of my life.

We hug. He holds me tight and doesn't let go until I pull away. I pull away because he's suffocating me with his strong squeezes. He looks at me again, asks if I'm wearing a wig, and before I can answer steers me toward the dining room. There's music playing. I forgot that Dad likes to listen to jazz. I think this is Miles Davis. There are balloons and streamers and a Welcome Home sign. The red tablecloth we use for special occasions is on the dining room table. Dad went all-out, but he's still looking at me funny. "You okay, Laurie? What's going on? Who is this man?"

"Please allow me to introduce myself, sir. I am Master Shekett," Master says as he extends his hand. "I am your daughter's art professor."

"Louie Franklin here." They shake hands and then dad continues. "Where did you folks meet up? Where have you been, Laurie? You know I was worried about you. Come, sit down. I have your favorite fried chicken and mac and cheese ready for you."

We sit. I'm famished; my appetite has suddenly reappeared. Dad is seated next to me and keeps looking at me, touching my face, clutching my arms, patting my fingers, and saying, "Wonderful. Wonderful. You're really home. You're back. This is good. This is good." He hugs me again, another tight, tight hug.

I don't want to be rude, but I'm starving. "Let's eat, I missed eating with you and I missed these yellow plates." It's true. It's a treat to see the plates that I've always known. Even holding the fork is familiar. The shape of it, the weight of it, the way the food glides into my mouth just right. The food warms me; I haven't been warmed in a long time. I eat and eat.

When Dad looks at me his face shines and his smile extends from ear to ear. Dad and Master make small talk. They discuss the weather, they talk about the neighborhood, they talk about my artwork, But then it doesn't go so well.

Master says, "Amelia is talented. Her paintings are spectacular."

Dad is confused. "Amelia?"

"Oh, that's what Master calls me," I explain.

"What? Your name is Laurie."

"I know. I know. And speaking of names I came home because I need my birth certificate, you know, the one that has the wrong name, so I can apply for insurance."

"What kind of insurance do you need? You're still on my policy from the business."

"You can see how she is run down," says Master, "and we want some important docs to take care of her."

Dad puts his arm around me and holds me in a way that makes eating difficult. He says, "Don't you worry, Mister Master, I can take care of my daughter plenty well. Always did. Always will. Laurie, I took care of you your whole life. I'm not stopping now."

Master says, "I can take care of her. I have doctors. I know what I'm doing."

"What? Who do you think you are? Don't interfere in my daughter's life. Don't you dare interfere in Laurie's life. She is Laurie, by the way, that's her name."

Master's body stiffens, his face is flushed and he's about to say something in response to Dad, but Dad beats him to it by bellowing, "Finish eating and then you can leave. Our conversation is over."

Nobody speaks. Dad's smile has disappeared, he's stopped eating, and he's staring at Master and watching him eat. It's too quiet. Finally Dad asks, "Again, where did you guys meet?"

I don't answer because I don't know what to say. and then dad stares at Master and says, "Mister, I changed my mind. Don't finish eating my food. Stop eating. You can leave right now. Your visit is over." Master takes another forkful of chicken and then another. Dad stands and shouts, "It's time for you to leave," pointing to the doorway.

Master doesn't move. Dad walks to him and says, " Get up. Stand. I will escort you out the door. Just who do you think you are?"

Master slowly puts his fork down, stands, but walks away from the door. "Who do I think I am? I am a very important leader. I am as good as you. I am as good as anyone. I'll match up with anyone you want." And then Master gets louder and louder. "I know right from wrong. I know exactly what I'm doing. Don't tell me when to leave. Don't you dare tell me what to do," he shouts.

I know how to calm him. Gazing at his hair, I softly chant. It works. He stops yelling.

But Dad's not finished. "You better get going right now and leave my daughter alone. I don't know what you're up to, mister, but whatever it is I don't want it. Get up and get out. Go now."

"I'm not leaving without Amelia," Master says, feet firmly planted as he stands next to the far wall.

"There's no Amelia here. Laurie is my daughter. Leave my premises or I call the cops."

"I can't leave without her. I need her," Master says, as he lunges toward me and attempts to pull me up from the chair and away from the table. Now that I've eaten a good hot meal I probably could resist him, but I'm not sure if I want to.

"Get your hands off my daughter!" Dad shouts, and pushes Master away from me.

Master takes a swing at Dad. Dad punches Master. Master falls against the table and then he loses his balance and slips to the floor. It's not a hard fall, but he gets up with some difficulty, puts his hands on top of his head, then screams, "My hair, my hair, what did you do to my hair?"

Dad yells, "Get out of this house right now!" and then looks at me and asks, "who is this lunatic?"

Master is stomping around the room, his nostrils flaring. He bangs into the wall. Dad reaches for the phone.

OFFICERS SPRINT UP OUR STEPS, DAD OPENS THE DOOR. "What seems to be the trouble?" the female officer asks.

"I can't get this monster to leave my house," Dad responds, pointing to Master.

"Please identify yourself. Are you the owner of this house? ID, please. And you, too, sir, your ID please"

I'm standing in the corner of the dining room wondering who to root for when the policewoman says, "Miss, we need your ID, too."

"I don't have a driver's license," I say.

She sternly orders me to immediately produce a passport or birth certificate.

Dad comes to my rescue. "I know where it is," Dad says. "She's my daughter. We live here. I'll run up and get it."

"I'll go with you," says the male officer.

Master is blundering around looking for his wallet. His hands are shaking. His eyes are blinking. I quietly try to soothe him. He calms down when I whisper-chant. The lady cop looks at me like I'm speaking in tongues.

Dad and the officer return, and now it's Dad's turn to look at me as if I'm nuts. "What the heck is wrong with you? What are you talking about? And, darn it, Laurie, take off that stupid wig."

"It's not a wig. My hair is bleached. I'm a blonde now."

"Officer," Dad says, "As you can see, I need to take care of my daughter. Please remove this man from my premises. He does not belong here."

The policewoman interrupts. "All three of you, come to the station." She looks at Master, then Dad, then me, and says, "Get going. Out the door. You, miss, sit in the front. The gentlemen will be in the back seat. Let's go. Get a move on."

It's my first time in a police station. It's not as scary as I expected, but it is shabby and I can smell stale cigarette smoke. It's dingy even though it's daytime and lights are on. The lady officer takes me into a small room with her. This room has flickering fluorescent lights so it's dingy only some of the time.

She's not so stern now. "I'm Officer Evans," she says. "What happened?"

"I came home to my dad, with my art teacher, and they got into a fight."

"What did they fight about?"

"Well, my dad wanted Master to leave."

"Master?"

"That's my art teacher, Master Shekett."

She looks puzzled. "Let me check that ID again," she says as she goes into the room next door where the other officer is talking to Dad and Master.

It takes her about ten minutes to return, and while she's gone I try to distract myself. I don't want to cry so I chant—it works. Finally, she returns and says, "You're free to go home with your dad. Jon Ligner will be detained here."

"Who?"

"Jon, the guy who had the fight with your father. We need to check his prints again."

The other cop walks in and seems apologetic. He says, "Come on. I'll drive you both back home. And don't invite criminals into your house anymore."

I have to set them straight. "Criminal? What? You are mistaken. He's going to change the world."

The cop looks at me strangely. I don't think he believes me, so I try again, "Master is not a criminal. He teaches people how to communicate so we'll have a harmonious world and can all live in peace."

Dad appears, wrapping an arm around me and leading me out the door and to the police car. I hold in my tears. This is one big blunder.

WE'RE SILENT IN THE CAR BUT AS SOON AS WE STEP OUT onto the sidewalk and start walking toward our front door, Dad looks at me and says, "I'm very glad you're home, honey, but you do have some explaining to do."

Before I have a chance to respond, a strange lady walks out of our front door.

"Louie, what happened? What happened? Are you okay?" yells the little lady as she flies down the steps.

"Dot, meet Laurie. Laurie, this is my friend Dot. Let's go inside to talk."

When did my dad get a friend? Why is she in our house? Does he have a roommate now?

We head toward the living room. I go to the couch, the plaid couch that Dad believes is fashionable, Dad dives into his brown leather recliner, and Dot lifts the overturned chair from the dining room floor and pulls it into the living room for herself. Before she sits, she straightens up the mess we left earlier—picks up the glasses from the floor, removes the dangling Welcome Home sign.

I hadn't realized how much I missed my comfy living room. My paintings are on the walls, and the hanging light fixture still has those pointy bulbs. The worn-out window shades are still there, still worn out.

Dad begins talking to the lady while we're settling ourselves. "I'm okay, Dot. Laurie here came home with a fella who's wanted by the police in two states. His prints came up right away. He's gone, so we can talk now."

"What do you mean he's gone?" I ask Dad.

"They're shipping him back where he came from. I think they said Wisconsin. He's got a record."

I stand. "I need to see him before he goes. I'll go with him. You don't understand. He needs me."

Dot looks from me to Dad and then back at me. She says, "Laurie, your father has been worried about you. Please, sit down, relax, let's talk."

"No. He needs me. I need him, too." I sit and explain to Dad and to Dot that Master's not a criminal. "What crime would he commit? He cares about people."

"That man is not a master, though he may be a monster, and his name is Jon Ligner," says Dad.

"I don't understand," I say. And then I start to cry. Really cry. Big, juicy tears.

Dot comes to sit at my side. This sweet blonde little lady, who I don't even know, puts her arm around me, nudges my head toward her shoulder, and strokes my hair. "It'll all work out," she says, pressing me into her warm body.

When I finally pull myself together, I wonder if I'm taking kindness from the enemy. Should I beware of Dot? She is an outsider, but then again, according to Master, so is Dad. I'm too tired to think about this so I just sit there.

I look around at the house, my house. It does feel good to be home. It might be a little shabbier than I remembered, but it's a familiar shabbiness. The kitchen drawer squeaks just like always, and the bookcase in the hallway looks like it's about to keel over, as it has for years. I'm more and more comfortable each minute.

Dad says, "Laurie, you're too skinny and too blonde. What the heck happened to you? Start at the beginning and explain yourself. You can say anything you want in front of Dot; she's good people."

"Does Dot live here, Dad?"

"No, no, not at all. We're friends from Dan's Diner. You know that place, in Huntington, right?"

Right now, I don't feel like I know anything. I don't even know where to begin. "Don't be mad at me, okay?" I whisper.

Dad nods. "Laurie, honey, I'm thankful you are here. I prayed for you to come home. I'm not mad at you. Tell me what's going on. Start from the beginning. From whatever made you leave here that day."

"Okay. Okay. Well, it all started when I met some nice kids, a little older than me. I met them when I was feeling bad because, don't be mad, Dad, well, you may not know it, Dad, but I didn't get my diploma. I didn't graduate. My teachers were mean to me. My so-called friends all dropped me. I felt like a big loser and these kids were older and they liked me. They let me be their friend. We went out for ice cream together. Then they introduced me to a group called Master Academy. It's led by Master Shekett. They all live in a nice motel just a couple of miles away and..."

Dad interrupts. "You've been only a couple of miles away all this time? Why didn't you come home?"

"I started to come home once, but it didn't work out. I thought about you, Dad, but I knew you were working and if I wasn't home you didn't have to worry about me and rush home from work." I look up at Dad. "That was wrong, huh? It sounds dumb now that I say it. I didn't get out much. Mostly I stayed in and painted. But don't feel sorry for me. I made friends and I hung out with nice people. I have good friends now, so that's why I want to go back there."

I explain that I loved feeling that my words, the way I spoke to people, could make a difference. My words could help Master create a new way of life for all mankind. And my artistic talent made it possible, too.

"We were all in it together," I say, "a whole bunch of us, and I loved that. Master taught us how to relate to people in a new way, a good way that could change the world. Everyone can lead lives that are more meaningful."

Dad is getting angry in that quiet way he has. He looks at Dot and says, "My life is meaningful already. How about yours?"

Dot answers, "I feed people every day. It doesn't get much more meaningful than that. But calm down, Louie, let's listen to everything Laurie has to say."

I tell them how much I liked the group of us sitting together at mealtime, same time every day, but I do reveal that sometimes there wasn't enough food, especially the last few weeks. I tell them about not getting enough sleep, and about my watercolors being sold at art galleries.

"And what is this business about walking on a path, and what about you being ill and needing special doctors?" Dad asks. I explain, and he shakes his head and looks serious and a little frightened, too, but he does chuckle when I tell them about Master's hair.

Dad looks surprised when Dot asks, "Laurie, are you depressed?"

"I don't know. I do know that I am dead tired. Is my bed still up in my room?"

"Yes, of course," says Dad.

"I don't know what I want. If I leave Master Academy I have nothing and I'm nobody."

Dot says, "Laurie, go up to bed. We'll all talk tomorrow. It's not a good idea to make important decisions when it's late and you're tired."

With that, she kisses me on the top of my head, and sends me on my way as if I were her little girl.

CHAPTER EIGHT

Dot

W<small>HEN</small> L<small>OUIE CALLED EARLIER TO TELL ME TO STOP IN</small> this evening, he was exuberant.

"Hey, Dot, amazing news! The kid's back. She called and she's coming home tonight."

I could hardly believe my ears. "Excellent! Where was she?" I had to know—was she kidnapped? Was she in another country? Was she in jail? Did she join a gang?

"I didn't ask her. I just said, 'Come for supper. I'll start cooking now.'"

That's typical Louie. He acts tough. Deep down he's a softie. I know that he worried about Laurie every day. But to her he says, "come for supper" and doesn't disclose his heartache.

"I didn't tell her about you," he said, "but I will. Don't be insulted, Blondie, I will."

When I got to his house the door was unlocked so I walked right in. Oh, my! The dining room is ransacked. Popped pink balloons and shreds of pink crepe paper litter the carpet. A "Welcome Home" banner waves crazily from the wall. Empty glasses are toppled here and there. Music repeats from the wall speakers, echoing in the cavernous living room, and the dining room chairs are overturned.

What happened? Did Laurie become insane while she was gone? Or, has there been a burglary?

I knew that if Louie were anywhere around I'd hear his booming voice and his jingling keys. He walks with strong heavy steps because he's usually wearing steel-tipped shoes. They go along with his checkered flannel shirts, and sturdy dungarees—no designer jeans for Louie Franklin.

Clearly, the house is empty. No sign of Louie or anybody else. No sign of a welcome home party except for some forlorn balloons and a tattered sign. The dining room looks like my diner after one of those unfortunate nights where half the clean-up staff calls in sick and the other half insists they must leave early to attend to a dying relative.

And then, as I was looking out the window wondering what to do, they pulled up—in a cop car, no less—and we found out just how lost Laurie's been this year. She may not have been far away physically, but it's clear she's been through the wringer. This scrawny girl, who is disheveled and has big bags under her eyes, looks nothing like the beautiful girl in the photo Louie showed me when we first met. She had curly dark hair in that photo, now she's blonde, and not a good bleach job. I watch as she exits the car, holding the car door for balance.

When I confirm that Laurie's securely in bed for the night, I go back to the living room. Louie's sitting in silence, but I don't join him. I need to keep moving to calm my nerves. I finish straightening up and prepare a snack for both of us—cheese and crackers along with cups of tea. I add a bag of pretzels and some red grapes. When Louie is settled and sipping his tea, I approach him and quietly say, "We need to talk."

"Oh, Blondie, not tonight. Too much has happened. Maybe tomorrow."

He's far too relaxed; he doesn't get it. I can't eat, I can't stay still, yet he's casually enjoying his food.

"No, Laurie's situation requires immediate attention. You need a plan of action."

"What d'ya mean? The kid's home. That's all that matters."

"Louie, pay attention to what she is saying. She wants to go back to be with that character." I hold myself back from adding, 'Pay attention to me. This is urgent.'

"He'll be in jail. Don't worry," Louie says while munching on a pretzel.

"That's not the point. Something is wrong with Laurie. Maybe physically, maybe psychologically, we need to find out. We don't know."

"Okay, okay. I'll make an appointment with her pediatrician. Or, do you think she needs a regular doc now that she's older? I was thinking she looks a little too skinny."

"Louie, you're not getting it. She's been brainwashed, and she's old enough to march herself right back there and there is nothing you can do to stop her. You need a plan."

He stops eating and finally looks at me. "What kind of a plan? What are you talking about?"

I can't stop pacing. "Face the facts, Louie. Your daughter has a new name and a new appearance. She has no ideas about her future, she has no high school diploma. Her only friends are in that cult. She…"

"Cult?" Louie is startled.

What was he thinking—that Laurie was at sleep-away camp? "Yes, a cult. Led by a criminal who insisted she stare at his hair. This is not an ordinary teenage thing, Louie. This is not a stage she's going through. Don't pretend it's okay and don't count on it getting fixed by itself. She has to get to a good place mentally and physically."

He is silent, then looks pleadingly at me. "Is this all my fault? I wasn't good as a single dad, right?"

"We have no time for blame. We need to figure out how to keep her away from those people she calls her friends. We also have to help her find a way to finish her education and get on a career path."

That's what I say. What I don't say is that maybe she has inherited her mother's tendency toward serious depression. And her maternal grandmother and uncle don't sound particularly stable or mentally healthy, either. It could be that we must head off a much more serious problem.

Louie looks up at me as if I know what I'm talking about. "Okay, what do we do first?" he asks.

I'm silent. I don't have an answer. I think. I concentrate. And then I admit, "I'm in way over my head."

We don't speak. Louie stands, walks to the refrigerator, and does his usual—opens the freezer and looks around. Predictably, he returns clutching a half-gallon container of cherry vanilla ice cream and a spoon.

Meanwhile, I try to determine the next step, scouring my mind for anyone I know who might have some experience to draw on when it comes to teenagers. Then I have it.

"I know someone who may be useful. She's a customer. Her name is Lucky—that's her real name.

Louie looks at me skeptically. "Lucky is a name like Master. Are you sure she's not a criminal, too?"

"She's an educational consultant," I say. "Just ... let me call her and we'll see what develops. I'm going home now, and I'll call her first thing in the morning. Your job is to keep Laurie here. Do *not* let her out of your sight."

He walks me to the door. "G'nite, Blondie. You're the best."

LUCKY'S BEEN COMING TO THE DINER FOREVER. SHE helped me when I was young and all alone in the world. She's a tall, thin, no-nonsense woman. She wears tailored suits, no jewelry, no makeup, and sensible shoes at all times. She seems capable and competent, or at least looks the part. As an educational consultant she works with young people who've gone astray or who have special needs. It's her job to figure out where they can get the best help for their situation, whether it's a psychological problem, academic situation, or a medical issue.

"Nice to hear from you," Lucky says when she answers. "How've you been? Last time we spoke you needed advice to get yourself out of a romance gone sour. Is this another one?"

"No, my love life is good for a change. I'm seeing a guy who is kind, and owns a business, and he's a decent soul.

We have a deep friendship and we're on our way to a deep romance, too. We're almost there. He's a good egg, and most of the time he's easy to be with, easy to please, and always easy on the eyes.

"It's his young adult daughter I need some help with. I'm worried about her. She's just returned home after being away in what seems to be a cult."

"Don't fret, Dot. As long she's already home the job is half done." Lucky continues, "I'm free tomorrow early afternoon. Do you want me to stop into the diner and we'll talk?"

In between lunch and dinner, the time when customers are sparse, Lucky pays me a visit. "Good to see you. The mellow aroma drew me right in, and now I hear the griddle sizzling," she says with a smile. I bribe her with lasagna and a fresh pot of coffee, and she begins to educate me.

"You and your guy didn't have to kidnap his kid, so you're a step ahead."

"Kidnap?"

"There are professional kidnappers who infiltrate a cult to pull out a member. Your gal is out, so you just need to determine how much deprogramming she needs. What's her name?"

"She's Laurie. Deprogramming? That sound mysterious."

"It's not a mystery, Dot. It's a way to help Laurie to adjust to life without the group she's just left. It's teaching her to think for herself and not automatically obey the rules of the cult. It's necessary for Laurie to realize that self-proclaimed leaders do not have all the answers to life, they're not automatically correct, and it is not necessary to obey them."

"How do we do that?" This sounds like a task for a hero, not for me or Louie.

"First step is to be sure she doesn't go back. I suggest removing her from the town where the cult is, so if she does try to return it will be difficult. Sometimes members of the group stay around even if the actual cult has disbanded. You want to buy time. The longer she's away from them, the more likely she'll stay away."

Lucky pauses to enjoy her lasagna, signals to a passing waiter that she needs a coffee refill, and then continues. "Cult leaders have a belief, an idea, and they are certain that this belief is the solution to their problems and the world's problems, too. They make it their mission to spread this unique idea to as many people as possible."

I am skeptical. "If it's a crazy idea why do people follow that leader? Is it only uneducated or simple people who join?"

"Many highly educated and even brilliant people join cults. These leaders are clever. They try to recruit people who are bright because they may be successful and have more money to donate, or may be well known and are good representatives if the media comes to call. Cult leaders create group spirit and group identity by using whatever appeals to their members. Sometimes it's a specific type of clothing; you've probably seen groups of hippie-looking people wearing orange robes or flowing capes."

"Actually, yes, at Newark airport I've seen some strange folks like that. I couldn't tell their ages and they didn't say anything to me, but I think they went over to some others to beg."

Lucky says, "Cult leaders convince their followers that the ideas they are promoting are making them superior to the rest of mankind. Not only do the leaders think their ideas are the best, they block access to any other ideas. They prevent contact with anyone who might be a source of outside information, even their families. Superiority is their goal; they are certain they know better than anyone not fortunate enough to be in their elite group."

"Okay … But, how do we protect Laurie now?"

"She needs psychotherapy and some deprogramming. I've heard about someone who might be right."

I'M EAGER TO GET TO LOUIE'S HOUSE AFTER I CLOSE. A part of me worries that he will have let Laurie leave, but thankfully, they are both at the dining room table when I arrive, plates empty, fruit bowl full, drinking glasses and paper napkins stacked. Laurie doesn't look as fatigued as she did. I hope she slept all day. I can see her prettiness under the strain. I wonder if she's suffering from malnutrition. The tee shirt she's wearing is hanging on her and her jeans are held up by a major belt.

I pull out a chair and seat myself. We chat, make small talk—I try to bring Laurie up to date on the television shows she's missed. Then I say, "I found out that there are professionals who can help. They—"

Laurie cuts me off, "I don't want to hear this. I don't need any help. I'm going back to my people."

Louie's face turns red, he stands and shouts, "Stop talking nonsense. I am your people. I am your father. You belong here with me."

I motion to Louie to sit back down and after a long minute he reluctantly does so.

In a controlled voice-of-reason tone I say, "Laurie, I understand you want to go back. It was a place where you were part of a group and you were recognized for your talent."

"That's right," she huffs. "That's why I need to go back. I'm glad you get it. You understand me."

"Think about this, Laurie," I say. "It may have been a good place for you for a while, but people change and now you might flourish even more in a different setting."

Laurie listens, remains silent, so I continue. "Laurie, there was a downside to it. It was led by a criminal."

She stands, and with her hands on her hips begins speaking in a tone that requires some energy. Good for her, she's recovering. "He never committed any crimes! Those cops don't know what they're talking about. Master Shekett is a good guy. I should know. I saw him every day."

I remain cool and collected and softly speak my mind. "Granted, he may have been kind and nice to you, but apparently he has a record. You told us he sometimes starved you, that he put innocent young people in isolation rooms. He forced you to change your appearance, change your name. Also, he didn't give you any of the money that your artwork brought in. Lots and lots of money went into his pocket, from your talent. It was not all good, Laurie."

"Yeah," she concedes. "I guess so, but it wasn't all bad, either."

She sits when I point to her chair. Maybe I should take her shopping tomorrow; I see her ribs. Or maybe she should spend a full day in the diner.

"Laurie, allow me to tell you what I learned from my friend Lucky. Listen to my ideas and then you can decide what you want to do."

No response.

"Deal?" I ask.

Laurie says nothing and I take that as a go-ahead.

"Lucky knows of someone who will show you how to sell your paintings *and* let you keep your profit. That person will also show you how to make friends who care about you, how to get your high school credentials, how to get into college, even help you get your driver's license. This person will help you prepare for a lifetime career. Maybe you will be an artist. Maybe an illustrator, maybe an art professor; you have many possibilities."

With an exasperated sigh Laurie says, "You don't understand. What about my friends? I need to see them again."

In my best take-charge boss-lady voice I say, "Let's get you straightened out and healthy and then you can decide who you want to see. You may want to check with a doctor to make sure you don't have malnutrition or anything else."

Laurie stares up at the ceiling and in a defeated monotone asks, "How long do you think it will take?"

"Honestly, I don't know."

She bravely looks at me, then abruptly stands. "I don't want to talk anymore. I'm going up to bed. I'm not making any promises."

That night, Louie and I try to make sense of all this. I tell him about Lucky's information.

"Lucky gave me the number of Doc Joan, a deprogrammer who happens to also be a psychotherapist-in-training. Lucky doesn't know her personally, but she suggested we give her a try. She's not around here, though. She's some-where in the Midwest."

Louie is adamant. "Laurie just came back. I'm not sending her to another state. That's ridiculous. No way," he shouts.

With sweetness and a smile I explain that if Laurie stays in the same town as her 'group' she'll be tempted to seek them out. He eventually nods in agreement, but next he gruffly asks, "How much is this going to set me back?"

Although his attitude is brusque, I'm glad he's not put-ting up a wall or leaving the room—his usual tactics when things are not going his way. When we disagree, which most often is about food he should or should not be eating, Louie listens to what I have to say, nods his head, says his piece, and then adds his famous phrase, "End of discus-sion," before walking away. The fact that none of that has happened this evening is encouraging.

"Never upset yourself over a problem that money can solve," I say firmly. "Do you want to make the call to Doc Joan, or do you want me to?"

CHAPTER NINE

Joan

THIS IS A DREAM COME TRUE. I'VE TAKEN WORKSHOPS about deprogramming and have already signed up a couple of girls who've left cults, and now I have a call to take care of another girl, this one coming from New Jersey, a state I've never before been to. I presume I'm skilled enough. I need the income. All my other careers have petered out. I'll fake it until I make it, and I know I'll make it.

I show up precisely as promised, several weeks after our initial phone call, at 8 a.m. The door is answered by a nice-looking guy.

"Come on in, Doctor. I'm Louie Franklin."

"Call me Joan," I say, and try to smile.

He's cute and I wish I could tell him that I deliberately underplay my appearance. When I'm meeting a new client I aim for plain and practical. I'm wearing a brown cardigan sweater and a dreary dress. The real Joan does have some style and can attract men—or at least attempts to. My granny glasses are small enough that you can see my dark eyes, and I wear no makeup other than my orange lipstick. I try my best, but I do know the truth: I have no beauty, I have no talent for attracting men, I don't even have my youthfulness anymore. I am on my way to becoming what my parents called an "old maid."

Louie explains that Dot is already at work at her diner and that Laurie is still asleep. We sit at the dining room table. A plain table in a plain room, no food smells, no fresh flowers, no bowls of candies or nuts. I fit right in when I open my no-frills black carry-on bag and pull out papers and booklets.

Parents are reassured if I tell them I've worked with someone like their child, so I say, "I'm happy to be back in New Jersey, some of my favorite clients are from this state. I look forward to meeting your daughter. It is your daughter who we are working with, correct?" I hesitate. I want to add, "You look too young to have a young adult daughter," but I won't give in to my urge to flirt.

"Yes, Laurie will be down as soon as she wakes up. She's been through a lot. For the last few weeks she's done nothing but sleep and eat. She was practically starved."

"I heard that she was missing for about a year or two. Is that right?"

"Yes, Doc. Go ahead and ask me whatever you want. I have no secrets. None at all. No secrets."

"Well that's good to hear," I say, thinking that he might be protesting too much.

"Louie—may I call you Louie? —when did you first suspect there was a problem with Laurie? What grade was she in when troubles began?"

Louie frowns. "What are you talking about? I had no problem with Laurie until she ran off."

He's speaking rapidly. It seems like he wants me to hurry and ask all the questions I've prepared so he can then put the last few years behind him. Sorry, Louie, I need to dig a little.

"Hmm. Dot seemed to recall you telling her that Laurie was sad and often isolated herself in her room, especially during her high school years."

"Yes, but you know teenagers have their moods."

Louie speaks with certainty. He barely moves while talking and shows no emotion.

"I see. Tell me a little more about that, please." I wonder if this man has any insight at all. Is everything acceptable to him?

"Well … it was after my parents moved away and then my mother died. Laurie was close to her. But Laurie wasn't bad. She just had crying jags and moped around a lot. You know, like teenagers do."

He's not being ironic. He believes what he says. "I see. So, you're saying that Laurie was displaying just normal adolescent moodiness."

"Yes, right."

"And what do you know about the cult she joined?"

"If it was a cult, it's probably not around anymore because the guy who ran it got arrested."

"I see. Do you know what attracted Laurie to that group?"

"Probably some high school kids who were bad influences. You know how kids are nowadays."

Louie is speaking like a reporter, not a parent. Most high school students do not join cults, even "nowadays." The few kids who do, often have serious unmet needs at home. He's not understanding how vulnerable and needy a child must be to join such a group.

I explain, "We need to get her away from the temptation. The cult is probably still there, as they rarely shut down upon loss of a leader. Cult higher-ups wish that the leader may leave so they can move into that position. Often a few vie for that one vacated place and sometimes a splinter group forms with one leader while another stays with the original group. Let's hope we get Laurie away from all this. Will she willingly spend a few weeks with me to explore other options?"

"Honestly, doc, I don't know. My kid is different these days."

Is he dense? Perhaps he doesn't understand the gravity of the situation. He's lucky his daughter returned. Many do not. And often those who do return need plenty of psychiatric care. Or is he just a dad in denial? I suspect this was a home where one rarely spoke of emotions. There's no room here for introspection. I must tread slowly with this guy. I wonder what the daughter is like.

"Louie, the first thing I'll do is remove her from this environment, take her on a vacation. Then while I'm with her we'll talk and talk and try to make sense out of all she has been through."

"She hasn't been through anything terrible except for this incident. Until she left, everything was okay."

Really now? Looking around I'm trying to find photos so we can talk about the family. No family photos. No photos of Laurie with friends. No photos of vacations or sports.

"I understand you brought up Laurie by yourself. How old was Laurie when her mother passed away?"

Louie looks down at his shoes. "Suzanne died in child-birth," he says softly.

"That must have been tough for you. How did you get through the early years?"

"My mother helped. We all lived together. It wasn't so bad. My parents and I decided not to talk about Suzanne. We didn't want a sad house."

I try to stay calm rather than show alarm. "I see. Louie, some of us believe that sadness is the appropriate response when there is a death. There are circumstances when a sad house is a healing house."

"That wouldn't have worked for us. My mother was careful to keep sadness away."

"I guess we'll talk about that some other time," I say. "Well, getting back to Laurie's vacation with me, I'll expose her to new ideas about her future and we'll plan a plan."

"Where is this vacation you keep talking about?" Louie asks. "And what new ideas do you have for my daughter? Nothing too nutty, please."

"I'm sorry. I thought Lucky would have told you. I have a Lodge in a midwestern suburb. We have accommodations for a few guests, a full kitchen with a part-time chef, a gym, and nearby transportation to several schools, colleges and workshop opportunities. Each guest has her own counselor who is with her all day, every day, for the weeks or months she's with us. I've arranged to be Laurie's counselor. A masseuse comes in when called, and an aerobics instructor too."

He doesn't ask any questions. He seems impressed with the chef and the gym; they'll soon be in place.

"I'll be getting my credentials any day now. Until a few months ago I was the owner of a rooming house. Now the rooming house has become a place for women who've lost their way."

Oh, no. Why did I mention this? He didn't ask, he doesn't care, what's wrong with me that I reveal what I want to keep secret?

He asks, "What happened to the rooming house, doc?"

With a sigh of relief I answer, "Oh, there were some issues with zoning. You know how bureaucracies are." This was a close call.

"Look, Doc, of course I want the best for my daughter. But, how much will this cost me? I'm not a wealthy man."

"My bookkeeper will contact you as soon as Laurie settles in and chooses her classes. I can assure you that no parent has ever regretted saying yes to this opportunity. We have payment plans if needed. You're putting your daughter on the road to a good life."

I hear rustling from the stairs. Laurie is shuffling down, sleep in her eyes, slippers on her feet.

"Good morning, honey," Louie says, sounding cheer-ful for the first time since I've been here.

Laurie would be pretty if she were healthy. She looks like she's been sleep-deprived, food-deprived, and perhaps under-stimulated, as well. Her blue eyes are excessive on her pale face. Her skin is dull and she moves sluggishly. This girl needs a hearty breakfast and strong coffee. And something for the black roots that are overtaking her blonde hair.

I stand to introduce myself. Laurie shakes my hand. "You're the lady from Dot, right? What are you going to do to me?"

"I'm not doing anything to you, Laurie. My plan is for us to get to know each other. How are you? Did you sleep well?"

"I'm okay."

"I'm glad to hear that. I'm here to be helpful to you."

Laurie rubs the sleepiness out of her eyes and she and I both sit. "Who said I need help?"

"Maybe you need some help in figuring out your plans for the future." She gives me a wary look so I quickly steer away from further conversation about her future and direct our conversation to the weather and New Jersey sport teams. We also talk about women's fashions. When Laurie seems comfortable with me I suggest, "Maybe you and I can take a little vacation together to relax and talk without any interruptions."

"Nobody's interrupting us here," she points out. "We could talk and get to know each other here in Truesdale."

"Yes, we could do that, but a change of scenery encourages new, creative ideas. Don't worry, it's not jail. You can return anytime you want. Let's give it a try. I actually have tickets for us for a flight out of Newark early this evening."

"What? I just got home. And where did you want us to go, anyway?"

"To my lodge. My car is parked at the airport and we'll drive directly there as soon as the plane lands, It's less than a one-hour drive."

"Your lodge?"

"Yes, it's a comfortable space, away from the distractions of city and suburban life. Just a place where we can talk and help you get your life back together."

Laurie stands up and shakes her head. "Let's not talk about this yet, okay? I need breakfast."

I encourage her to take her time and busy myself with my booklets and the papers that are in my bag. Interesting that Louie does not engage me in conversation now.

After oatmeal and cottage cheese and toast with strawberry jam and then two cups of black coffee, Laurie asks, "Are you sure I can leave your lodge anytime I want? At the … at the last place I went to, I couldn't leave whenever I wanted. They kind of made me stay."

"We're not like that, Laurie. There are two other young women at The Lodge now and they're also trying to figure out their future. You'll like them."

Laurie turns and stares out the window, chewing on her bottom lip. "I don't have any clothes to pack," she says finally. "I'm a different size than I was when I lived here, and I've been wearing stuff that was bought for me by my friend Anna."

"Please don't worry about your wardrobe. Within driving distance there are plenty of stores—and boutiques, too."

Laurie looks to Louie. "What do you think, Dad?"

Louie hesitates. "I don't know. I just got you back."

Laurie's biting her lower lip, moving her head side to side, and when she first opens her mouth says nothing. Then she states, "Oh, I hate this feeling of not knowing what to do. I like it when there are rules to follow and then I don't have to decide. Decisions confuse me. You know that, Dad."

"I know, Laurie, I know. I wanted you home so badly and now that you are here, I don't want to send you away." He moves to stand behind her and places a reassuring arm over her shoulders.

I need to be persuasive; I don't want to lose this. I remind them that this is a proven method of eliminating any negative effects from the cult, and this will assure that Laurie won't be tempted to leave again. I talk about some young people who never recover from time spent in a cult. I talk about how just a few months now can prevent a lifetime of tragedy.

Laurie looks at me skeptically, but I continue, "You never know how long the influence of the people from your past year will stay with you. You're at risk if you don't have a good intervention now. I know how to provide what you need. Don't miss this chance to guarantee a successful future." I look at Louie and add, "You don't want to cause Laurie a bigger problem, she must do this."

I see the pain in Louie's face: his brows are furrowed, he's shaking his head, yet he does man up. He walks around the table, looks squarely at his daughter, saying, "I don't want this, Laurie, believe me I don't, but it's for the best. When you come back, we'll make up for all our lost time. We can start over."

"Yes," I reassure her, and add, "Laurie, allow me to make this decision for you. Let's go."

When she looks at Louie again and he nods, and then she nods, I force myself to refrain from cheering. Even though this cute, single guy is sitting just a few feet from me I focus on the task ahead and remind myself that I am a professional and am not here for a social visit. Laurie will give me the chance to use the skills I've been learning. She needs stability and I can offer that. I need more income and she can offer that.

CHAPTER TEN

Suzie

THE FIRST TIME I SPOTTED HARRY HE HAD THAT FRAZ-zled, divorced-father look. Carrying a toddler over his shoulder, and holding another little boy by his hand, Harry was attempting to seat them and keep them reasonably quiet until their food was served. His tie was undone, his dark blonde hair a playing field for the youngest boy, and his classic facial features obliterated by a forehead scowl.

I was sitting one table away and luckily just happened to have a couple of kids' books with me. I was on my way home from my Children's Literature class, where I was learn-ing techniques of writing for the pre-school market. Picture books are big sellers and require just the right words to cap-ture a child's interest. It was my habit to stop at Joe's Coffee House for a quick bite after class. I was too tired to cook—on school nights I work the early shift at the drug store.

Harry did not have Cheerios nor any games or toys with him, and when the boys were finally buckled into their appropriate seats—high chair, booster seat—they needed some distraction. I held up the books I had and he smiled with relief but couldn't figure out how to come over to my table. The boys were in precarious positions and needed their dad's watchful eyes and strong arms, so I made a delivery. He tells me now that he invited me to join their table because he was immediately attracted to me. I suspect he simply welcomed another pair of hands.

When we started dating, I told him I'd been a pharmacy tech for a while and that was that. He assumed I got out of college, bummed around for a few years, and then settled into working at Drexler's Drugs. Sometimes even I believe that story.

But then one day, after we were married, I watched the new talk show, *The Oprah Winfrey Show*, that's produced here in Chicago and will soon go national, and it was all about being true to yourself.

When I told Harry that I'm taking another writing class at the ACA, that's the Academy of Creative Arts, I didn't specify that it's a memoir class. After all these years of secrecy this might be the way to reveal my past, and if I chicken out, I can say it's fiction. I've heard it said that truth is stranger than fiction. Will anyone believe my truth? What I went through is worthy of a soap opera or a TV show, but I chose to move on.

Harry and I have a good life. We get along well, we have friends, we have a lovely home—not extravagant, but a pleasure to come home to. I like Harry's two kids from his first marriage, and he likes that I don't want kids of my own. If only he knew.

Why am I stirring things up now? Maybe it's what Professor Milrod said on the first day of class: "Start anywhere you want. Writing your memoir helps you make sense out of your life. When you produce your memoir, you let your true self be known."

I need to make sense out of my life. It's time. I'm giving it a shot, Oprah. I'm giving it a shot. I may reveal my past to Harry…or not.

Professor Milrod, here is my mini-memoir, the story of Suzie Henderson:

I grew up in a crazy house with wacked parents and an autistic brother whom no one acknowledged as autistic. To be fair, maybe they hadn't yet classified autism as a disorder back then, and even if they had, word probably would not have reached our small town in Iowa. When I fell in love with the man of my dreams, I escaped. He earned a good living and all he wanted to do was make me happy. His parents had a solid marriage and their stability appealed to me. So, I married Louie Franno. We decided to have a family and he and his parents were thrilled when I got pregnant. I was thrilled most days. Some days I had my doubts about motherhood, but my mother-in-law said she'd help me.

I gave birth to a seven-pound, three-ounce little girl in December of 1964. We named her Laurie Sue. And then I got sick.

My brain betrayed me that very day. I felt it happen to me in the delivery room. I tried to smile—after all, I was happy to have a baby, a daughter, a family—but my lips wouldn't shape into a smile.

It took me more than a year to be able to smile again. By the time I could, I had lost everything—my husband, my baby, my home, my mind—everything.

That year was a blur of doctors and medications. Sometimes I fell asleep while they were speaking to me, so then they

prescribed heavy sleeping pills, thinking if I would get enough
rest during the night I'd be alert for our sessions. The trouble
with those pills was that I was groggy until the afternoon,
and those docs came early in the morning to do their talking.

The talking doctors asked me about my husband. Honestly,
those days I couldn't even remember his name. I knew we
loved each other but I forgot exactly who he was. The doctors
asked me about my parents and I did remember that they
were far from normal. The doctors nodded when I said that.
Now I realize that they assumed I had inherited the family
mental illness.

Then there was the doctor who wanted to analyze my
dreams. My dreams were messed up because of all the meds I
was taking. That doc got a kick out of my dreams—they were
gory and most of them took place in outer space. Years later,
when I got my hospital records, I found out that he diagnosed
me as someone who thought that she was an alien. He could
have asked me. As soon as he lowered my dosages of those
powerful pharmaceuticals my crazy dreams stopped.

The psychiatrists rotated through the unit and each one
offered a different bunch of medicines. The pills kept coming
and the doctors kept coming. "Backsliding" was one of their
favorite words. I later learned that every time my insurance
company threatened to suspend payment a doc would say I
was backsliding and in danger of catastrophe without continued psychiatric help. "Backsliding" was the magic word that
guaranteed continuous insurance payment.

No one ever suspected I might be on too much medication.
No one ever suspected I might respond to just one or two pills
and not seven, eight, and nine, which they usually prescribed
even though they never helped. And they made so many mis-

takes with my medications. When Lithium was giving me a side effect they took me off it and neglected to add a different mood stabilizer in its place. Not surprisingly, I had a manic episode and became enraged and violent. I yelled and cursed at nurses and other patients' visitors. I was so angry about everything and anything that one night I punched holes in the wall with my fist. Those feelings shocked me. My behavior shocked me. I am, by nature, respectful and polite. Finally, one of the nurses realized the error and paged a doctor to come to the floor and prescribe another medication to replace the Lithium. I was quickly back to my usual depressed self. Why? Why such incompetence?

One doctor suggested extreme exercise and then a dunking in cold water right afterward. It got me out of a deep vegetative depression, but then I became agitated. When he stopped prescribing that routine I became vegetative again. Yet, even in my vegetative state I was astute enough to figure out a solution that he didn't think of. I asked, "Why don't we try exercise alone and no water dunking?" And it worked!

That hospital unit was overcrowded and didn't seem like what I thought a hospital was supposed to be. It wasn't particularly clean—a haggard, bent-over man with an unlit cigarette hanging from his mouth swabbed the floors once or twice a week with murky water. It wasn't calming—the so-called TV room blasted cartoons from early morning until bedtime. It wasn't designed to keep spirits up—heavy shades were pulled down over the barred windows not only at night, but during the day, too. In all the months I was there I didn't see anyone recover. Sometimes a patient was sent home and we all cheered, but then a couple of weeks later that same patient would turn up again. Sometimes I saw patients fall, just sink to the floor, probably because they were weak. No staff ever noticed when patients skipped meals and returned their food tray untouched. Nobody cared. I thought I might never get out of there. Discharge was never mentioned until, astonishingly, I got lucky.

*O*NE DAY A *D*R. *P*ETERS CAME TO WORK AT THE HOSPITAL. *H*E *knew the latest neurological and psychiatric research and in a few months got me back on track with appropriate medication and several therapy sessions every week. The relief I felt when my brain started to work properly was immediate. I was strong again. I'd always known I was strong. It took strength to survive my childhood, where I was clearly neglected and witnessed what would now be called child abuse or child neglect against my brother. It took strength to go to college with no family support. It took strength to agree to marry Louie, who was my first and only boyfriend. I had never left Winter Falls, never been on a plane, and yet I made a life-long commitment. Strength had always been my friend, my constant companion.*

I was strong the day I left the hospital. Knowing my belongings were safe in a storage facility, I stepped right into the waiting van that was arranged to take me to the halfway house I would live in for several months. I left Suzanne in the hospital and emerged as Suzie. That name cheered me whenever I heard it, and it still does. It's a fun name. It's informal and yet substantial. Exactly how I want to be known.

The halfway house was the college dorm I never had. There were just four of us, all in our twenties, all recovering from an emotional breakdown or something like that. It seems that breakdowns or crackups, whatever they're called, come in different varieties. We shared our stories with Mrs. Shepp, the social worker who came to visit twice a week and she told us that we were proof that everyone falls apart in a distinctive manner and most everyone can recover.

I remember the day when all of us were sitting around the table and Shepp told me that I had a legitimate legal case if I wanted to sue. She said, "You were not treated with the standard of care for postpartum depression. You are a victim of medical malpractice."

I didn't know how to react. I felt rage burning throughout my body, but I also felt relief knowing I was correct all along about the incompetent doctors. Certainly I was shocked to know that everything I suffered should have, and could have, been avoided. Outraged and angered. I wondered: Do I cry out for justice? Weep for my lost year? Get back at everyone who mistreated me at the hospital?

We talked about what it would be like in court re-living my horrific hospitalization. Most of what I knew about court cases is from watching them on television and I was scared to put myself through hours of testimony. I thought about it for a few days and finally decided not to carry a grudge and not to bring negativity into my life. Oprah would probably agree with my decision. A lawsuit wouldn't give me back the year that I lost.

Instead, I would make each day count and I'd live life to the fullest. I wanted my recovery to be worth more than the dollars that a jury would give me; I wanted a good life, a full life, to be proof of my recovery.

The four of us in the halfway dorm, as we called it, helped each other. We updated our resumes, exchanged information *about vacant apartments, gave each other leads about jobs, and soon I was ready to enter the real world, use my professional skills, and build my life.*

I had no intention of finding my birth family. To me they were dead. I told the girls, "When I was young and easy to take care of, they were not capable of giving me attention, surely now when I am an adult with a serious life situation they would be more hindrance than help."

My dorm mates understood and agreed with my reluctance to contact my birth parents, but then they asked, "You will search for your baby girl, won't you?"

I told them, "Laurie Sue has good grandparents, a good father and, knowing Louie, probably by now a good mother, too. I doubt he could live without a wife. I don't want to intrude on Laurie Sue's life. I'm giving her the opportunity to grow up with a sane mother. I don't know if I've reached 100% sanity and I have no proof that I'll stay sane, either. People relapse all the time. I've caused enough distress for Louie, it's best I stay away."

Mrs. Shepp asked if I was certain. One of the other girls didn't believe I could carry that out. "Nobody could be that brave," she insisted. I pondered some more and honestly didn't think it took bravery. It was the right thing to do for Laurie Sue, for her new mother, for Louie, and for me, too. I needed a fresh start, and time to prepare myself for that fresh start.

Now, all these years later, I know I made the correct decision. Some days I wonder, "Am I supposed to feel traumatized without my daughter?" I don't. Other days I wonder if I'm guilty of not feeling guilty. I don't feel wicked at all. I did the right thing.

I used to wish someone, a Ms. X, would suddenly appear and say to me, "I gave birth to a baby who I never saw, and

I've had a good life. I'm not a bad person. I'm not maternally deficient. It simply was the wrong time and the wrong circumstance for me to mother a baby. The baby had a capable father."

When I wished for Ms. X it was a wish to know I'm not the only woman in the world to calmly proceed through life without her baby. In my mind, Ms. X would then add one of Louie's favorite expressions: "End of discussion."

Ms. X never did show up. But that's okay because lately my thinking is changing. These good years of marriage and love are convincing me that I am Ms. X. I've become my own role model, my own source of comfort and of common sense. I made the right decision back in the sixties. My daughter had a good father so she will have been well-loved and well cared for and that's all that matters.

My mini-memoir is complete. I fulfilled the assignment. Am I brave enough to show it to Harry? It wouldn't affect his love for me, I know that. But what if he thinks I should look for Laurie Sue? No, I don't want to complicate her life and I don't want to see her father. I don't want to be reminded of that dreadful year in the hospital.

Here you are, Professor Milrod. I've written my mini-memoir. It all takes place within one year, one literally crazy year. If I ever write a sequel to it, I'll write about Harry. But, until then, this is it.

CHAPTER ELEVEN

Laurie

MY EYES CLOSE THE SECOND THE PLANE TAKES OFF. I'M bravely holding back the tears that are threatening to roll down my cheeks any minute; one deep breath, then another. Planes remind me of my grandmother. I'm remembering how my grandmother would have treats for me. A deck of cards, a package of marshmallows, a pencil and notepads set up for tic- tac- toe. She would pop them out of her handbag when the plane took off and we'd be busy for our entire plane ride to Florida. Wherever I was, when I was with my grandmother, I was home. A part of me wants to tell Joan that I miss my grandmother and I want to tell her about the trips we used to take. But I do not want to take comfort from the enemy.

I hope I can quickly slide into a sleep and enjoy Grandma memories without worrying about trusting Joan. I suppose she's trustworthy, but her hair is tangled and short and a funny color—black with red in it when the light hits her head—and her smile seems phony, and her orange lipstick is garish. And she didn't pack any supplies for my airplane enjoyment.

I guess I did sleep. I hear a voice saying "Welcome to O'Hare. Enjoy yourself in Chicago." The passengers march off in an orderly fashion, but the airport is anything but orderly. Announcements are blaring, people are shouting, babies are crying. I quietly follow Joan to the parking garage. We pile our luggage into her station wagon and we're on the way to this place she keeps talking about, The Lodge.

Looking out the car window I see nothing but miles and miles of flat fields. Quite different than our congested New Jersey suburb. Much of the land I see is parched and brown, but there are also long stretches of crops. Acres of corn and then some low rows of greenery, probably soybeans. The sun is strong, and it feels much hotter here than in Jersey. I see farmhouses and remind myself that this really is the land of Grant Wood. I could stare at his painting *American Gothic* for hours. I'm always fascinated by the stoic old couple in that painting. In photos and in prints their long droopy faces match their stretched out farmhouse window. And I don't want to be mean, but they remind me of my neighbor Katie's basset hound. I wonder if the painting looks like that in real life. We're passing more land, more farmhouses. Yup, I'm in the Midwest.

Joan says we should grab a late dinner so we stop at a small roadside restaurant. There's country music playing, and many of the tables are empty; at home there's always a wait, and country is never an option. Surprisingly, the food is good enough.

Sitting across from Joan I get a good look at her uneven slightly stained teeth and her beady eyes which never blink. How do I know I'm not getting myself into another bizarre situation? Maybe Joan is another Master, and this lodge is another run-down hotel. What am I doing here? Where do I belong?

We pull up to The Lodge, a sprawling one-story building on a massive estate. The only time I ever saw this much empty land was when I played soccer in 5th grade. There are uninhibited flowers poking out of everything, every-where. Yellow blooms line the perimeter of the house, and the front porch is cluttered with pots bearing clumps of orange and red poppies. Also on the porch are a couple of white wicker rocking chairs.

I follow Joan through the wide front door and into a high-ceilinged room with dark wood paneling. There's a fireplace, two beige couches, two beige chairs. Baskets on end tables next to each chair are loaded with more flow-ers and some fruits—oranges, apples, bananas, and green grapes.

"Welcome to The Lodge, Laurie," Joan says as we enter. "I'm glad you're here. This is our main room, please help yourself to fruit whenever you'd like." She proudly gestures to the right then to the left, reeling off the names of rooms on each side of this house—kitchen, dining room, TV room, exercise room, library, and then a wing of bedrooms. She emphasizes the library and tells me its bookcases are filled with romance novels, mysteries, biographies, poetry books, and more. "Feel free to borrow as many books as you want, whenever you want. Now, though, I'll show you to your room."

After noticing the second-rate artwork on the hall-way walls, I'm surprised to see that my room is tastefully decorated—pale pink walls, white window shades, a floral bedspread and a down comforter folded at the end of the bed. There's a white desk, as well as a desk chair and chest of drawers that match the tan wood floor. A pink throw rug adds a pop of color.

Before Joan leaves she says, "We meet in the dining room at eight in the morning."

I unpack my small travel bag and admire the fancy white bathroom where I prepare for bed even though I know I won't sleep tonight. My thoughts scoot around my mind like gerbils on the exercise wheel we had in the science corner of my 3rd grade class. On the way back to bed, I notice a handwritten daily schedule as well as a list of program rules and regulations. Stupid, of course. The more I read that information, the more angry I become.

I must:

- Show up for all meals
- Stay in The Lodge or inform my counselor of my whereabouts
- Exercise daily
- Schedule daily talk with counselor
- Enroll in a school or 'betterment' program approved of by my counselor
- Do volunteer work approved by my counselor
- Make my bed every morning
- Refrain from playing loud music
- Refrain from speaking in a loud voice

Great. More rules to follow.

I'm mad at myself. I shut off the light and climb into bed, pulling the comforter over me. Why did I come here? I have a good home, a good bed, a good dad. This is not fair. I shouldn't have been encouraged to do this. Not fair. Why did I listen to them? How will I be able to check up on Master? Will my loneliness ever go away? Will I ever be a regular person? I'm back where I started.

SUNSHINE AWAKENS ME. MY WORRIES HAVE A WAY OF shrinking overnight. I'd like to tell someone that I'm feeling better now, but I never told anyone I was feeling bad. I make my way to the dining room, where two girls are already eating breakfast at the round wooden table. They're talking about a television show I've never heard of—a talk show called something like Opera. I'm not exactly sure because as soon as I walk in they shut up. I try not to bite my lip.

"Why can't I find a place to be at that has no rules? Wherever I go there are rules," I say as I take a seat at the table. When they just look at me and say nothing, I realize how strange I appear to them. And rude, too. "Oh, hi. I'm Laurie. Don't mind me. I'm just complaining to myself."

The girls, about my age, are Emily and Annette. Emily is beautiful, with wavy brown hair, big brown eyes, and high cheekbones. Annette is not so attractive. She's got a good smile but she's awkward, unkempt and speaks loudly.

I continue with my lament. "Meals at a certain time, one hour a day for exercise, compulsory talks with my counselor. This was supposed to be a rest. I can't believe I got talked into signing up for this."

"Deprogramming is hard work," Emily says. "Dr. Joan is an expert . . . or so my parents say."

Not only is Emily flawless in her appearance, she even eats flawlessly—she manages to enunciate clearly while chewing a roll.

"Well, I'm here because my parents forced me to come," Annette says. She's dripping tea on her shirt and making a mess on the table.

"Mine too," admits Emily. "I had no other place to go after The Musicians. And both mom and dad insisted I had to come here before I could go home."

"The Musicians?" I ask.

"Yes, that's the name of the group in Texas that I lived with for three years. It wasn't as bad as my parents think, except that they took all the money that people paid to hear me play the cello, and there were no visitors allowed."

That sounds familiar. "I painted," I say. "Like, a lot, for galleries. But Master got the money, not me."

"Master?"

"That's the name of the guy who ran our organization," I say, "but it's not, really. His real name is Jon." Not wanting to think about him I change the subject. "Anyway, here I am but I don't know if I'm staying."

"I've been here for three days," says Emily.

"And I'm a week into it," says Annette. "I don't want to return to Wonderland as much as I did at the beginning."

"Wow." I say. "Is Wonderland as pretty as it sounds?"

Annette seems to be figuring out what she wants to say to me. It's not such a hard question. While she hesitates,

I help myself to the food on the table. Interesting cheeses, plenty of fruit, some yogurt, sliced bread, and bagels, but not the Jersey kind. From the side shelf I bring over a hard-boiled egg and a glass of juice. It's tasty food, fresh and healthful. No sugary cereal, or six-hundred-calorie muffins. Although I need to gain some weight, I don't want to develop a sweet-tooth, so this seems right.

"Actually, at the beginning, Wonderland was beautiful," Annette says while I begin my breakfast. "They gave me pot to smoke and candy to eat and those were two things I could never have at home. But then the rules kicked in. Not like the rules you're complaining about here. These were rules about how to think, and who to talk to, and what to eat, and a hundred other things. They made me get high every day and sometimes made me take pills. It was getting worse by the day."

"So, how did you leave?"

"My parents tracked me down when I was at the beach with some members of my tribe—that's what we called our group. And my parents had Dr. Joan waiting in the wings. She swooped me to an airport and in no time I was here."

"What are the days like here?" I ask, peeling my egg. "Do we do things together or just with our counselors?"

"We have meals together, like now," Emily says. "But most days we each have activities and discussions and trips with our individual counselor. There's lots of planning about our future and how we will have a career and all that kind of thing. Joan and the other counselors encourage us to take classes and get certificates or other credentials. I'm studying music with a pretty famous musician."

"My parents thought we'd have daily exercise classes, but so far, nothing. That's a selling point to me," says Annette.

"I need to get my GED and my driver's license," I say. "Doc Joan said she could make that happen here. Do you think that's true?"

"Probably, yeah," says Emily.

We chat about other stuff. The neighborhoods we each grew up in, schools we went to, subjects we didn't like, college ideas. They talk about their parents; I talk about my dad. Neither of them comments about the missing mom.

When I get back to my room, Joan is standing in front of my door with a woman who introduces herself as Karen, a nurse who's come to give me a physical.

"Laurie, you have chosen a safe and nurturing place in which to heal," says Karen as she begins her medical examination. After some brief testing and some superficial conversation, she gives me the all clear. "Good food and sleep will quickly restore your health, Laurie. Good luck to you. This is the right place for you." And then she leaves. I'm not sure if she's a real nurse. She didn't look in my eyes or nose or throat, she just took my blood pressure and pulse. She didn't take my temperature. She didn't ask for proof of vaccinations, nor did she say anything about my weight, which I know is way too low. And she should have talked to me. Wouldn't she want to know if I was messed up? Wouldn't Joan need a double check to be sure she wasn't taking in a mad girl? I often think that a health exam should be an annual physical and an annual mental. When I mention that to Joan she says, "I wouldn't have wanted anyone exploring my mind when I was your age."

I remind Joan that she promised I could leave whenever I want. I tell her I'm thinking about it. "You can. But, since you are already here, why don't we talk a bit today and we'll decide about leaving tomorrow or the next day."

She kind of leads me into her private office in a separate wing of the Lodge, which also contains a private bedroom and bathroom. The office looks like Joan, a little cluttered, somewhat odd, and not too comfortable. There's only one couch, no chairs, so when we sit it's awkward to speak to each other. I twist to face her and she twists to face me.

"Laurie, can you tell me a little about the friends you made at Master's?"

"Well, there were a few nice kids there and they always made me feel popular. I especially liked Anna and Tom. I did have other friends, too, most of the kids knew me." Now I'm starting to miss them all. Coming here might not have been the right decision.

Joan asks, "Was that a familiar feeling for you or was it new for you to feel popular?"

I admit the truth. "I guess it was new. I didn't want to socialize too much in high school."

"I see. If we found a new situation where you could feel popular and at the same time work toward a goal that you choose, do you think you might give it a try? And it would be your goal, not one that someone else chooses for you."

"I guess," I say slowly.

"You seem unsure," she says.

I stare at the wall where Joan has hung several photos. There's one of a beautiful young woman with long strawberry-blonde hair. I wonder if she was ever a Lodge guest.

"I guess ... I guess I want to leave, and I want to stay," I say, and then realize what I've said describes a familiar feeling for me.

"It's normal to feel ambivalent," Joan explains. "It's good that you know your feelings. Feelings and needs determine our actions. Sigmund Freud, the great psychoanalyst, would be proud of you for admitting your ambivalence."

"What? Why is it good to be mixed up?" This confuses me. I like *yes* or *no,* not in between.

"It's complicated. Let's get on with our work, Laurie. Let's think about just one day at a time. There are three components to your program. First, we decide what and where you will study. Next, we decide where you will volunteer, because that is an important part of healing. And lastly we'll pick one immediate personal achievement for you to accomplish."

I listen carefully. "How long will all this take?" I have two immediate personal achievements to work toward—my GED and my driver's license.

"It depends upon how quickly we get started. Tomorrow will be relaxation time for you—walk around the grounds, talk to the other girls when they're free, get to know the ins and outs of The Lodge, and then we'll get down to work and determine a schedule."

Ambivalence is following me. Totally on my own I feel scared—I'm away from Dad and away from Master—and at the same time I feel grown up—I'm choosing what to eat, what to wear, what to read. I may not be making the best choices; I get mixed up a lot.

It's a relief when Joan finds me at breakfast the next morning and says, "Let's do some sight-seeing today and then we'll go shopping. When we return we can set you up with specific plans and a timetable. You need new clothes and I'd like you to experience Chicago at its best."

Here, there are no rules that forbid me to ask a question. "Joan, I'm wondering, is The Art Institute of Chicago still here? It's the famous museum with some of the best paintings in the world, right?"

"Yes, Laurie," says Joan, "trust me, you will get to see the finest art in the world. Which works are you particularly interested in?"

"Monet's *Water Lilies,* and Renoirs *Two Sisters?* And I think Van Gogh's *Self-Portrait,* is there, too."

Joan nods 'yes,' and I smile at the thought of seeing my favorites in real life.

Downtown Chicago lives up to its name as The Windy City. The sounds of the elevated trains, the busses, the taxis, the trucks, and the shrill car alarms make me want to skip sight-seeing and I try to persuade Joan to go directly to our destination, Marshall Field & Co.

Joan seems disappointed, but when she looks at my twitching eyes and trembling hands, she realizes I'm way out of my comfort zone.

Marshall Field & Co turns out to be a huge fancy store, and I'm sure I look like a kid at the circus as I gape at the displays. Joan encourages me to choose clothing I like. She doesn't interfere, but she also doesn't recommend. It's difficult at first; I'd become accustomed to Anna choosing my clothes and before Anna it was Grandma. Joan is helping me by not helping me, and soon I get the hang of it and I'm making fashion choices. I can do this ... I think.

I select several sweaters that a kindly saleslady tells me are part of the "special selling" program. Only later does Joan explain that that's Marshall Field's term for sale item. When I ask that same saleslady where we could find the shoe department, she says, "We do not have departments in Marshall Field & Co."

"What?"

"No, dear, we have sections. The shoe *section* is just down two levels."

Shopping is fun, but Joan tells me that the best is yet to come. She suggests that rather than promptly returning to The Lodge, we eat lunch in the Walnut Room.

"What's a walnut room?" I ask.

"It is the first restaurant to be situated inside a department store," she answers.

Upon entering, the gorgeous crystal chandeliers take my breath away. After years of plain suburban stores and many months of tacky hotel rooms, Marshall Field & Co is quite the experience for me. I notice other girls about my age having lunch with women who look to be about Joan's age. For a moment I pretend I'm on a mother-daughter shopping trip.

I feel normal and regular carrying my swag back to The Lodge. I show Emily and Annette my Jordache jeans and my Swatch watch. I think back to when I was in high school and I'd overhear girls talk about going to the mall together. I didn't understand how that could be a social activity, but now I do.

After dinner we join our counselors to discuss school plans. My smile is huge when Joan reports that I can take my GED at a testing site downtown, and once I pass I'll be eligible for admission to several nearby programs. I've been waiting for this kind of guidance forever.

Annette suggests I consider joining her at the Chicago Lycee where she is studying French language and culture. Emily suggests I learn to play an instrument at her music academy.

"I'll decide about classes after I have my GED," I say as I dash to the gym for my one hour of mandatory exercise. The truth is that I'm overwhelmed. After so many months of having no decisions to make, now there are too many.

While I'm working out, a thought occurs to me: I miss my paints. This is the longest I've gone without a brush in my hand for years.

Annette wants me to join her at her school program and Emily recommends I take classes at her academy. They both like me. Maybe Master changed me for the better, like he said he would. I can now attract friends.

The next morning at breakfast I ask Emily and Annette if they know where I can take art lessons. "There are painting classes at my music school, I think," says Emily. "There are always guys with paint-splattered shoes walking around."

Joan pops her head in from the main room. "Yes, the Academy of the Creative Arts (ACA) offers art, music, dance, and writing classes, too, and maybe even some other subjects that I don't know about."

She hurries to her office and grabs a catalog for me to browse. I can hardly believe it—there's a portraiture class taught by El Newman.

"Maybe I can get into that class," I say, pointing to the class description, and Joan beams. "El Newman's portraits always attract me, too. Those faces come alive and I feel like I know them and their personalities."

When it's time to take the GED, I show up where and when I'm supposed to, and even though I'm nervous, I answer all the questions and I have a good feeling when I'm done. The days waiting for the results to be mailed to me drag by, and some days I'm sure I failed. What would Master say if I told him I failed? Why do I care what Master thinks?

Finally, I'm notified that I am indeed a high school graduate. I call Dad to tell him and I tell everyone in The Lodge. The biggest bonus of passing is that Joan has arranged an interview appointment for me at the ACA.

THE ACA IS IN A MODERN WHITE BUILDING IN THE HEART of Chicago, The students span a range of ages. There are elderly retirees learning to sing and trying to paint landscapes; there are moms taking piano lessons and seriously studying interpretive dance while their kids are at school; there are young men studying guitar and ukulele; there are aspiring novelists and poets, as well as plenty of dramatic-looking folks hoping to become the next Meryl Streep or Henry Fonda.

"Everybody is nice," I report around the dinner table when I return from my interview. "I think it's because they're all from the Midwest. People are calm and pleasant around here. Is agreeableness a Midwestern habit?"

"Why do you ask?" Annette says. "Is disagreeableness a New Jersey habit?"

I don't answer. Probably because I'm not sure.

"Anyway, I need to go back to meet El Newman," I say. "I have no paintings here to show, so I have an appointment in two days to prove that I can paint."

I walk into the studio not knowing if El is a man or woman. I know the portraits, I know the floral watercolors and now I know the person. It's a welcome surprise to meet a pretty African-American lady with bold, deep black hair, and a smile defined by glowing pink lipstick. Looking into her soft brown eyes I'm assured that I'm in the right place, with the right teacher.

She doesn't talk much but directs me to a seat and immediately hands me a pencil and paper. She asks me to draw anything I want for two minutes. She has a lot to say after she seriously studies what I drew. It's a simple sketch and yet her comments are not so simple. I quickly learn that her gentle look is deceiving. She's a tough teacher and expects me to meet her high standards. From the work displayed in this studio it's apparent she gets all her students to paint their very best.

While she's speaking I hold my breath. I'm afraid her criticisms are letting me know I'm not good enough for her class. But then I hear, "You have what it takes, my dear," and I am overjoyed. It's one thing to be told my work is good by a customer who wants a blue painting to match her blue sofa, and quite another thing to hear El Newman tell me that I have talent.

Those few words from her stay with me all day. When I get back to The Lodge my shrieks of joy echo throughout the house as I dance from room to room sharing my good news.

When the day comes and it's time to get dressed for my first class, I put on my new jeans, a blue button-down shirt, and tie a sweatshirt around my waist. "I'm as well-groomed as Anna," I say, to nobody.

In the first five minutes of class, I learn how to create a pointy paintbrush by loading the bristles with water and just shaking the brush. Then, I learn that the studio needs low humidity, that a 16 x 20 canvas is ideal for a portrait, and that the eyes are the focal point of any portrait. And then we paint. The hour flies by.

"Your talent is apparent," says El Newman.

"Thank you, Ms. Newman," I say.

"Call me El, Laurie, please."

I can't believe I'm on a first-name basis with the great portrait painter. And then it gets even better, because El asks if I would like to join the watercolor group class that meets Tuesday and Thursday evenings.

I can barely answer; this is a dream come true. "I think so," I say, and then quickly correct myself and with a voice of certainty announce, "Yes, I would like to join."

"Good," she says. "You can begin this evening, if you're free."

I check with Joan and she agrees to pick me up at nine p.m.

I have a few hours to wait and I pace the halls. No class, no easel, no assignments, just me. I pace like a high school girl waiting for that special guy to call but scared he really will. I should probably go to the student lounge, but then I'd have to be social. Maybe I should phone my dad. No. I'll worry him and he'll tell me to come home.

These unexpected free hours give me a chance to be curious and sure enough my curiosity wanders to Master. Where is he? When will I get to see him? Has he been released to go back to Master Academy? Did they correct their mistake about him? Does he miss me? Is he making enough money now that I'm not there to paint? Does Master Academy still exist? Did Master really care about me, or just need my talent? How come I fell for it, if it wasn't about me as a person?

I think I know the answer. It's the same reason that I'm fascinated by portraits. Looking into someone's eyes, even if it's just part of a face on canvas or paper, is a connection. Why am I desperate for connections? Is everyone? Am I doomed to search forever? And what am I searching for?

The clock in the foyer tells me it's time for class to begin, but I'm not excited anymore. I can hardly drag myself into the studio, and when I do, I avoid eye contact with the instructor at the front of the room and with the students who each are setting up their easels. I inch over to my designated spot and remain motionless for the entire class, except when I bite my lip. I do not touch a paintbrush, pay no attention to the instructions, stay silent, and hastily leave the moment my watch says 8:55.

Joan is waiting in her station wagon. She smiles when I open the car door.

"You had quite a full day! I'm proud of you, and Emily and Annette and I are eager to hear all about it."

"Nothing to say," I huff.

Joan turns sideways so she can get a good look at me. It's a waste of her effort. I'm just staring straight ahead; I don't want to speak or smile. After a few moments she gives up, faces the windshield and drives. After a few minutes of silence she says, "I see. Things didn't go your way. We'll talk in the morning. It's okay to go right to your room when we arrive at the Lodge and I'll explain to Emily and Annette that you are sleepy."

Joan wants to talk to me and wants me to tell her everything, but I can't and I won't. I'm disappointed when I see how stiff she is; she sits up straight in the driver's seat and focuses on the road ahead. No soothing words, no sweetness ... not like Dad's friend Dot, who would be hugging me by now.

The car radio is playing Cyndi Lauper's "Girls Just Want to Have Fun."

Joan is waiting at the breakfast table in the morning.

"Laurie," she begins, "you had a tough day yesterday. When you're ready to talk about it you'll feel much better. I'm here to listen to whatever you have to say."

I look down at my plate and push my food around. I decide to tell her the truth. "I like the art class. It's that my memories are getting to me. I'm thinking about Master and worrying about him."

I avoid looking up at her and continue to butter my toast and to slice peaches into my cereal, as if this is not a big deal to confess.

Joan says, "I promise you, Laurie, when you finish your work here and you return home, you'll be free to do whatever you want. My goal is for you to think for yourself and make good choices."

I tell the truth again. "Maybe this sounds crazy, but I'm afraid that I might not want to go to Master Academy, but I'm also afraid I'll miss it too much if I don't go back. I do care about Master. He does need me. My chanting helps him. I hope he's okay....oh, I don't know."

"You don't need to know right now. Let's take one step at a time. Today we'll go back to ACA and find ways for you to become more comfortable there. You have a once in a lifetime opportunity with El Newman and you should take it."

"I know. I know. But when I have downtime, my mind goes right back to Master Academy and Master." That's when I remember that everyone knew my name. We ate our meals together. We listened to sometimes-boring lectures together. We were a group. And Master wanted the best for me.

Joan says, 'Let's meet on the porch in an hour. I have a plan."

When we arrive at ACA that afternoon, an academic counselor is there to meet us in the student lounge. This must have been Joan's plan. I don't know what she told him about me, but it couldn't have been good because as soon as we introduce ourselves he looks at me as if I'm breakable. He's wearing a suit and tie, which is a weird getup for this informal place, and when he speaks, he draws out every word.

"Laurie, your mom here tells me you need some encouragement."

I don't bother correcting him on the "mom" thing, and neither does Joan. He goes on to tell me that there are plenty of art books, magazines, and televisions to enjoy in the student lounge. I nod my head. I get it. I should change my personality and mingle. I hate mingling.

"You'll enjoy the communal tables. You'll meet other students," he drones on.

Joan butts in. "Laurie, this is an opportunity for you to work on your social skills while you wait for me to pick you up. Some days I'll bring paperwork with me and sit in the cafeteria doing my work while you are doing yours."

Now I'm really embarrassed and I'm glad she's not my mother.

Once the counselor guy is gone, Joan walks to the other end of the large room, and I'm alone at a table in the student lounge. This is probably some kind of therapy technique she learned in shrink school. I'm supposed to act as if I'm by myself but know that she's here for me in case I start to crack up. After quieting my nerves by taking deep breaths and then visualizing my favorite seascape painting, I'm feeling braver. I hate to admit it, but knowing Joan is close by is working. The longer I sit here, the more comfortable I feel. I might be okay in the lounge by myself next time...or the time after.

And I am okay. Thursday afternoon I enter the student lounge in an outfit I hope is befitting a Chicago artist. Stylish jeans and black high-heeled leather boots and a black turtleneck sweater. I'm not sure I'm ready to initiate a conversation, but I think I could hold my own if someone approaches me. I choose a seat at a large round table, making sure there are empty chairs on either side of me, which is what the counselor guy suggested. Several brochures are scattered around the table. I pick them up: *Write it Right* and *Music for the Masses*. I'm pretending to read and hoping a stranger will come along to assuage my loneliness. Just when I'm getting nervous that this is going to be high school all over again. a familiar Texas twang catches my attention.

I hear, "I practiced this piece for hours. Thank you for your kind words."

Yes, it's my housemate Emily. I let out a long breath and I can feel my heart rate slowing down. She's talking to several middle-aged women who apparently sat in on her music rehearsal and are now looking for seating. Emily notices me. She waves and soon they are all walking toward my table.

Emily thrusts her arm out and says, "This is my friend Laurie, everybody; she's an artist."

As usual I can't think of something clever to say. I smile nervously and hope that when I do say something I won't make a fool of myself. The ladies fit my idea of Midwestern folk. Not one looks like a theater person nor an avant-garde artiste. I hope none of them notices that I'm sweating.

They all take a seat, but no one is talking. It's unbelievable to me, but they seem relaxed and calm. Why aren't they worried about the silence? Are they waiting for me to speak? This is too nerve-wracking.

I'm saved when the woman in the tan pantsuit asks, "What kind of artist are you, Laurie? Do you paint still-lifes or are you more of a Jackson Pollock? By the way, I'm Irma."

"I work with watercolor and I'm studying portrait painting."

The woman with dark curly hair says, "I've always wanted someone to paint my portrait, or a portrait of me and my husband. Are there interminable hours of posing involved?" she asks, then adds, "Oh, I'm Suzie. I'm in the writing program here."

She looks like a nice lady. She's dressed casually yet with style. She has an open friendly face and she's asked a thoughtful question. "No, there's actually no posing. Some of the best portraits are painted from photos."

The third woman enters the conversation. "Hi Laurie, my name is Linda and I'm not sure what I'm here to study. I could listen to music all day and feel perfectly happy. But they don't let you hang out here unless you're a registered student, so I'm taking a photography workshop. It's fun but I'm not that good at it."

Suzie turns to Linda. "Maybe you'll come to my house and photograph me and my husband. He's eager to have more pictures of us to put in albums. When Laurie is ready to be a professional portrait painter she can use that image to paint our portrait."

"And I'll provide the background music while guests come to admire the portrait." says Emily.

"And I'll bring hor d'oeuvres," Irma says. She looks over to me and adds, "I'm part of the cooking program here."

These ladies are hospitable and warm. They encourage me, and Emily, too, to look for them before and after our classes. It's comforting to know that any time I'm here one of my new friends will be here, too.

Each time I'm with them I enjoy listening to their chitchat—they talk about everything—their families, what they watched on television last night, their problems, their most recent acquisition from the mall, the books they're reading, their latest accomplishment here at ACA.

In true Midwestern fashion, none of these polite ladies asks me why I'm living at the Lodge. I can tell they know a little bit about it, because Irma once said that the ads for The Lodge were attractive. Suzie added that she had seen them, too, and thought they were interesting and clever. The largest ads say that The Lodge is a healing place for young ladies. A few smaller ones say, "Lost? Find your true self," and "Begin again. Your new life awaits."

Listening to these ladies I'm reminded of conversations at Master Academy. They weren't conversations, at all. Master lectured and we were silent. Why did I think it was a good idea to listen to his tirades about how we, at the Academy, were more intelligent than the rest of the world?

These ACA ladies trust each other enough to complain, criticize, and say the truth about what might be bothering them. Suzie tells them about her trips with her husband. "When we travel I'm relieved because he stops obsessing about his ex-wife. At home, after the boys' weekends with us, Harry rants about her. He's never come to terms with the fact that she's not his ideal person." I continue to be shocked when Suzie, and the other ladies, too, admit, in public, that their lives are not perfect.

I notice that the others look to Suzie for advice. She's good at coming up with solutions. When Linda complained about her teenage daughter's messy room. Suzie gave her an idea that worked. She said not to insist that the daughter must get her room, which was in terrible disarray, immediately spotless. Instead, Suzie said, set a timer for ten minutes and tell her to clean until the timer rings and then stop until the next day. In a week the room was in good shape and, Suzie said, "most importantly the mother-daughter relationship bloomed."

Suzie gave interesting advice to Irma when Irma carped that her mother-in-law was critical of her cooking. Suzie said, "Don't argue, instead agree with her, tell her you want to improve your cooking, tell her you want your food to taste like hers, ask for her recipes." Irma thought that was absurd, but Suzie convinced her to go along with it. Sure enough, a couple of weeks later Irma reported, "my mother-in-law no longer says a word about my cooking and yet I didn't change anything. Same ingredients, same menu."

Suzie says that's because it takes two people to create a fight. If one doesn't fight back, the fight's over. "The way to a peaceful life is to join the resistance," she says. "Don't argue; agree. When the emotion is eliminated, common sense prevails." Suzie gives me so much to think about.

On a Tuesday evening, while I'm pleasantly chatting with my grown-up friends, I'm paged to the office. It's Joan phoning to say she's unable to pick me up after my class and she gives me the number of a taxi service. When I return to our table, the ladies won't hear of it.

"You are not that far from me," says Irma, "I'll drop you off."

"I'm even closer," insists Suzie, "I can easily drive you back."

Suzie's car is white and it has a sunroof—my dream car. That's not the only reason I'm glad to be driven by her. I had been looking for an opportunity to ask her about her writing. I wonder, does she write fiction? Poetry? Maybe she writes textbooks, she seems like the bookish type. There are several library books on the car's backseat, and paperbacks and magazines tossed amongst them.

I'm relaxed in Suzie's presence; she seems to have a calming influence on everybody. Yet, I'm too shy to ask about her writing. Instead, during the car ride I apologize. It's a habit I have. I apologize a lot because I know I'm a burden. "I'm sorry to impose on you. I know I should be driving myself, but I have to get my driver's license first. There's been a stupid problem with the paperwork and it's been a hassle with bureaucracy and red tape. It'll be the first thing I settle when I get back to New Jersey."

"Bureaucracy is ubiquitous," Suzie says agreeably, "you just have to deal with it."

"Yeah. It gets complicated. My birth certificate has some crazy last name on it instead of my name, Franklin, so I have to prove that I am me."

Suzie is all smiles. She's so easygoing she's not bothered by the messy back seat of the car, she's not bothered by detouring to drop me off, and she's not perturbed by traffic or honking horns.

She asks, "Can't you just go to the hospital you were born in and get a corrected copy?" Suzie's so optimistic.

"Not easy to pop into my birth hospital," I explain. "I wasn't born in New Jersey."

"Really? Where are you from?"

"Well, I consider myself from Jersey, but my dad moved us there when I was a baby. Actually, I was born in Iowa, Winter Falls, Iowa."

"Winter Falls? I know where that is. I ..." Silence.

I look at Suzie to see why she stopped speaking. Her smile has been displaced by a grimace and she now has a death grip on the steering wheel.

"You what? What do you mean? You know where Iowa is, or where Winter Falls is? What's wrong, Suzie?"

"Nothing, Laurie, dear," she says softly. She never called me 'dear' before.

She doesn't continue our conversation. Soon we're at The Lodge. "Thanks for the lift," I say as I leave the car.

Before I enter I look back to make sure she's okay. Usually, when we part ways at ACA she offers me candy or any other treat she might happen to have with her, and she always gives me a hearty 'goodbye, Laurie.' This time, nothing.

I see her behind the wheel but she's not driving. I think that's a tissue she's pressing to her face. She's just sitting there. What's happening to her? Why did she stop talking to me?

CHAPTER TWELVE

Suzie

AFTER LAST NIGHT'S ASTONISHING DRIVE WITH LOVELY Laurie my mind has been racing. Apparently my body, too. At breakfast, Harry asks, "Is something bothering you? You were flinging yourself around in your sleep."

My answer: "This coffee is too strong. Is there any more milk in the refrigerator?" Our conversation conveniently floats toward food and then to our plans for the evening. "Time for school, see you later," I say as I quickly place my cup in the sink, plant a kiss on Harry's cheek, and dash to the car.

In class my thoughts drift away from Russell Baker's autobiography and land directly on my dilemma. What's the right thing to do now? Am I blowing this up out of proportion? Am I being dramatic? I don't know for sure, not at all. This might be a coincidence; people have coincidences every day. And if it's not a coincidence, then what? Am I supposed to follow in the footsteps of those desperate mothers who have dramatic reunions with children they haven't seen for decades? Who would benefit from that?

I leave school earlier than usual; socializing in the student lounge has no appeal to me today. As I drive toward home I think about Harry. I am a happy person and he is a happy person. We have a good marriage. We love each other. We trust each other. What if he knew I was keeping a secret from him all these years? A big and important secret.

Today I need to take my alternative route. I've done this several times. I drive to the lake area, traffic is light, it's not yet dark, and if I'm lucky and find a good parking spot I won't have to leave the car to indulge my habit. Luck is with me and directly across the street from the new luxury condo I slip into a space that affords me a perfect view of the building's entrance.

I've read about perverted men who enjoy watching little boys play. Those guys stop at particular places, observe the action for a while, and then resume their regular life and regular routine; no harm done, they insist. I'm not a pervert, but I sit here, in my white car, and patiently wait until my desired targets appear. I need to see just one or two, and then my trust in myself and my judgment is restored.

Looking through the windshield I clearly see my first instance. She's a young mom crossing the street, holding her daughter's hand and with her other arm balancing a shopping bag brimming with groceries. She encourages the little girl to help her push open the door to the lobby. I observe and breathe a sigh of relief.

Following close behind is another mother/daughter duo. This daughter looks to be in her mid-teens. Perhaps because my sunroof is open I can hear that daughter's belligerent words to her mother. She's loudly complaining and ends her rant with, "Mom, you just don't understand." She's verging on hysteria. I observe, smile, and once again I know I'm okay.

I drive the rest of the way home pleased that I feel no envy, no sadness. I'm reassured that my decision all those years ago was the correct decision. I'm not envious of missing out on mother/daughter rites of passage. No need to destroy my stable life.

When you hit rock bottom, like I did, and you recover, like I did, you appreciate every day. When you know you suffered and landed on that bottom because of negligence and dereliction of duty, it's tempting to think about retaliating. But I decided, as soon as I started working again, that the best revenge is a life well-lived.

Harry and I definitely have lives well-lived. We enjoy every day. We go on vacations—last year to Paris for two weeks and also a three day weekend in New York City. We attend ball games at Wrigley Field and we appreciate the Art Institute—I can devote hours to the Renoirs. We spend many Sundays at the Adler Planetarium with the boys— they've become adept at identifying the constellations in the Night Sky exhibits. Each year I am stronger and more ambitious—taking classes, learning skills. I can sail a boat and I can speak fluent French—just because. Harry likes my energy and my pep, and I secretly relish the revenge.

Some people think a wife should tell her husband everything. I don't agree. Maybe one day I'll tell him only about Louie and leave out the part about Laurie Sue. An annulment is not a divorce; rather it's an eradication of the marriage. It calls the marriage a phony act that never really happened. It's as if I wasn't married at all, so when I told Harry I was never before married it was a good lie.

If Louie Franno were to show up at my doorstep today, I could handle his arrival. My love for him has faded. Oh, he's probably a good dad and a good businessman and a good husband, but he wasn't a good husband to me when it counted. He was as young and as limited as I was, way back then. We both didn't know how to do what the kids today are taught to do from an early age, communicate feelings. I've heard plenty of mothers say to their toddlers, 'use your words.' No one had ever said that to either of us.

Why did Louie run off with our baby? I suspect his mother somehow guided his actions. Just like we couldn't overpower my mother, we never could defy Louie's mother, either. Not that I wanted to. No, during those years I was relieved that an older woman was interested in my well-being. It's only in retrospect that I realize she controlled every aspect of everyone around her. Obviously, it was what I needed at that time. But did Louie need it? How does a young man break away if he has an infant and his wife is locked up in a hospital?

There's no chance that I could love him today. I've taken enough classes and read enough self-help books, and watched enough friends fall in and out of love, and watched enough Oprah, to know that you don't stay in love because of a good trait; even good character is not sufficient. You fall in love and stay in love because of the feelings that other person engenders in you.

If attributes alone were responsible for keeping couples together, people would get divorced whenever they meet someone with a quality they marvel at. "Oh, that man is taller, I'll go for him." Or, "That gal is wealthier. I need a divorce."

No, life doesn't work like that. Of course it's wonderful to be in a relationship with someone whom you admire and whom you respect. But, that's not enough. For long-lasting love you need that person to induce certain feelings in you. How that other person makes you feel creates the love, and then maintains that love.

I did the right thing by not searching after I was discharged. There is no chance of my having lingering love for Louie. Because of my memories of that terrible year, seeing Louie would not make me feel good, not at all. I'm not fearful of meeting him. I'd simply introduce him to Harry as an old boyfriend from my hometown

My house looks warm and cozy and I pull into the garage thinking about dinner, nothing else, and about Harry, nobody else. Enough procrastinating; time to walk in.

"Honey, I'm home."

He's in the kitchen. Always well dressed, even when cooking, he's in a light blue warm-up suit and clean white tee shirt. A crispy green salad topped with bright red tomato slices sparkles in the center of the table. Steam is rising from a pot on the stove.

"Suzie, good to see you. I've started dinner. The salad is done, but I left the dressing for you to make. The meatballs that you prepped last night are heating up. I'm just about to put the spaghetti in the boiling water. I'm glad you're home, Suzie. What kept you so long?"

I walk over to my handsome guy. He envelops me in his arms, his arms that tonight are radiating delicious food aromas. I'm so lucky.

CHAPTER THIRTEEN

Laurie

WE'RE WATCHING TELEVISION IN THE MAIN ROOM AND THE credits for M*A*S*H have just started to roll when Joan brings up the volunteer idea again. I had hoped she'd forgotten about it.

"You have two options at DuPage Hospital. You can work on Mondays in their gift shop, or Fridays, doing crafts projects with the kids in the Pediatrics unit."

"Is this mandatory? Maybe it's time for me to return home," I say flippantly, with one eye still on the TV screen. "And anyway if I'm working at the hospital I won't have enough free days for the ACA."

After those words come out of my mouth I realize I'm having a good time here at The Lodge. I'm not homesick for Dad, and my love for Master and my Master Academy pals has pretty much disappeared, or at least changed. Where will that love go now? It's still in me.

When I think about Tom and Anna I'm appreciative of the attention and the clothing, too, and I acknowledge that they did get me out of a deep rut. But they tricked me. They went looking for me that first evening at Lyons Park. Master needed an artist to sell paintings and I was it. That was a trick not a chance meeting.

Joan says that working teaches social skills and it also builds character because you have to show up even on days you don't want to. Okay, I give up. I nod to Joan, and say that I'll work in the gift shop. Why not? M*A*S*H has given me good vibes about medicine and doctors.

Gifts Galore is on the first floor of the hospital, and not only do they sell the usual—newspapers, magazines, candy bars, books, and balloons saying everything from "Get Well" to "It's a Boy!"—they also carry a full line of costume jewelry and hair accessories. I love all that fluff stuff.

I have a one-day orientation meant to teach me how to use the cash register and how to persuade visitors to buy multiple gifts for their hospitalized relatives and friends. My trainer, a young guy named Charlie, should have taken a lesson from Master. It's obvious that I know how to sell better than Charlie does.

I try my best to convert everyone who walks in here into a customer. I recommend books, ("Here's a terrific new Stephen King book. The hours in the hospital bed will fly by!"), I insist that all patients want to read *People* magazine, all new moms need balloons, and every female patient deserves a new ring and maybe a bracelet or two.

While working here I have a perpetual smile on my face and it's not phony. I think back to Master and the Academy. Did I ever smile? Did I feel happy when I was cooped up? I love selling; too bad I wasn't encouraged to sell my own paintings.

AT THE LODGE, ANNETTE, EMILY, AND JOAN WELCOME me back with some cupcakes they've just baked. "This is a perfect ending to a perfect day," I say, swiping one while inhaling the warm, sweet scent of vanilla and flopping into a chair.

Joan asks, "I take it you're enjoying your volunteer work?"

"Yes, yes. It makes me happy to know I'm good at something besides painting. Today I sold tons of balloons, books, a couple of headbands and a few watches, too. Everyone buys a Get-Well card when I show them the funny ones."

Annette comments, "It sounds like you are a born saleswoman."

"Master taught me everything I know about selling. It wasn't inborn," I say and then get embarrassed to have bragged. The Midwest is rubbing off on me.

Joan says, "People are not all black or all white, all good or all bad. Good people sometimes do bad things, bad people sometimes do good things."

Why did she have to bring this up? Now my mixed-up feelings about Master are coming back. "Night, all," I say, and dash away.

By the next day, when I return to ACA, Master is out of my thoughts and my three ladies are there to greet me at our table.

"You look lively today," Irma says.

Suzie adds, "Look at you, Laurie. You've got bounce in your step. And that's not easy considering you're wearing those heels. I love wearing heels, too, but I know most women aren't that comfortable in them."

"I'm with you," I say, holding up my foot for all to admire my heeled boots.

Linda asks, "So, what's making you so happy today? Falling in love?"

"No," I say. "It's my Monday volunteer job. I'm surrounded by sparkly jewelry in beautiful colors, and I like that. And I like convincing people to buy things. Yesterday I persuaded a new dad to buy his wife a pair of earrings as a thank you for going through labor. I told him all new mothers need a 'push' present."

"You're at DuPage Hospital, right?" asks Suzie.

"Yes, every Monday."

"I need a couple of gifts. Can I stop in even if I am not visiting a patient? DuPage is right near my house."

"Anyone can come into the gift shop. I'll be there next Monday."

I'm relieved Suzie is friendly again. I hope she does come to the shop.

IT'S MONDAY AND I SEE SUZIE IN THE HOSPITAL HALLWAY, walking toward the gift shop. Chicago is windy, especially in winter, and Suzie's curly hair has taken the brunt of that wind. I know about wind and curly hair; I'll suggest she buy a scarf.

Suzie sees me but she's standing motionless in the card aisle. She's watching me, actually gawking. Finally, she approaches me, but she doesn't explain her strange staring. She meanders a bit, nods at me, and walks to the jewelry case.

"Oh, look at these charm necklaces. You have them in so many colors, Laurie. They are lovely. What are they?"

"They're birthstones, made of cubic zirconia. That emerald-looking one is for May, and the red is July, ruby."

Suzie hesitates, takes a deep breath, and asks, "Laurie, which is your birthstone?"

"It's that bluish turquoise one. I'm in December."

I'm called away by a questioning customer. "Miss, may I make my own bouquet by mixing some of these flowers with those bright purple ones in the refrigerated showcase down the hall?"

By the time I return, Suzie is gone. She didn't buy anything, nor did she tell me she was leaving.

I have no time to fret about Suzie because I need to save all my emotional energy for Joan. I must convince her that getting my driver's license will be difficult and we'll want some extra help. After a relaxing dinner, my power of persuasion works and she promises to call tomorrow to schedule a Department of Motor Vehicle meeting with a supervisor.

We show up with the appropriate paperwork and bypass the waiting lines because of something, I don't know what, that Joan filled out. As I feared, supervisor Matthews has an obstacle and that's the name Franno. All of my mail and other ID say Franklin. Searching the birth records

Matthews comes up with a Laurie Sue Franno born on December 1st, 1964, in Winter Falls, Iowa.

I immediately pounce on him. "See, I knew it. They didn't know how to spell Franklin. That is me. That's my birthday and that's where I was born."

"I don't know about that," says Matthews. "This here paper says your father is Louis Franno and your mother is Suzanne Franno. No Franklin here. Were you always Franklin? Did you change your name?"

"I never changed my name. I'm a Franklin and so is my dad. Please, can't you just sign this, so I can get my license?"

"Sorry, miss. I must follow the law. Write to the hospital in Winter Falls and get a copy of the original birth certificate. Hospitals keep good records."

"But this is my original," I insist. My patience is running out. I feel my face getting hot, my heart is beating much too fast, and I can't stay still. My feet are itchy, I want to run. "Let's go, Joan, it's as bad here as in New Jersey."

While Joan bids goodbye to Matthews I sprint to the exit. When I'm calm in the car she suggests, "Let's call your dad this evening. Perhaps he knows something about this."

We do, and he does.

I explain what happened and he replies, "Oh ... well... um, Laurie...um... I never mentioned it to you but ...um... that used to be our name. It was my parents' name before we changed it to Franklin. No big mystery, just a name change. We all changed it."

He's talking crazy. Franklin's not our real name? "What? Why? Wait. Grandma and Grandpa Franklin, too? They changed their names, too? How come you never told me?"

I can't believe this. I've been lied to my whole life. I haven't had a headache or a stomachache in a long time, but now my head is pounding. This is crazy.

"It was so long ago. You were an infant and that's why they couldn't change your birth certificate. I think you had to be a certain age. I don't remember exactly. Take it easy, Laurie."

Why is Dad so calm? This is serious business. "Dad, if someone told you that you were really named Louie Frankenstein, wouldn't you be upset? How would you feel if you found out you were lied to your whole life?"

"Nobody lied to you, honey."

"Well, then it was a big secret, because I never knew."

"Laurie, now you know," he says firmly. "And I'll figure out how to get your birth certificate changed, too, and then you'll get your driving permit and everything will be fine."

"I guess. Do you have any proof that I was Franno? They don't want to give me my permit."

"It'll all work out, honey. I'll take care of it. How's everything else coming along? What does Doc Joan say about when you can come home?"

"Ask her yourself. She's right here. Hold on," I retort.

I throw the phone to Joan and run toward the safety of my room.

I hear Joan talking to Dad but I can't make out the words. As soon as she hangs up she knocks on my door, and then swings it open without waiting for an answer. I'm on my bed, a tissue box next to me, tears still spilling down my face.

"Difficult conversation?" asks Joan as she pulls the desk chair up to my bed.

"It's just confusing that I have two names—an old one and a new one and no one ever told me. That's odd."

I wonder if Joan remembers that I used to be Amelia. That's what makes this even more strange. I'm finally okay being Laurie and not Amelia and now I find out I'm really Laurie Franno.

"It is a bit odd." Joan pauses to think and then in a perky voice says, "Maybe people had trouble spelling Franno and your dad wanted a name more familiar."

"It was funny seeing my mother's name spelled out," I say.

Could there be more lies in my family? Is there a lie about my mother—was her name not really Suzanne? Now I'm being stupid, her name was on my birth certificate, my Franno birth certificate.

"Maybe your dad wanted to change it to have a new beginning after his wife's death. Too many painful memories for all of you with the old name."

Joan is hung up on my mother. She talks about her more than Dad does.

I explain that he never said it was painful for him. And I never knew her, so it wasn't painful for me. Still isn't. "Joan," I say, "I have no way to know what I missed." I cover my mouth to stifle a yawn.

"I see," says Joan. "You had your grandmother in your early years and then you had your dad and then your life at school, is that right?"

"Yeah, that's about right." I've stopped crying. Now I'm thinking. Thinking is not good for me.

Joan continues questioning me. "What about when you wanted to know something about your mother? Did they explain things to you, show you her pictures, tell you stories?"

"Dad said all the pictures got lost when we moved to New Jersey from Iowa, so we don't have any. Not even their wedding pictures. All I know is her name and that she had eyes like mine and hair like mine. I can blame her, or thank her, depending on the day, for my curly, curly hair."

"What about her family—you have another set of grand-parents and probably aunts and uncles and cousins?"

This is boring me. I lay down, move away the tissue box that I don't need any more, put my head on the pillow. "No. Dad said she had no family to speak of, whatever that means."

It's true. There's no trace of my mother.

"I see," says Joan. "Sometimes girls who grow up with-out a mom are curious about her—her likes, her dislikes, her habits."

"Not me. I've always been busy with school and with my artwork."

"Do you think you may have been attracted to Master's group because you felt something was missing in your life?"

Stupid question. I don't want to think about that at all. I quickly shout, "No!"

"I see. What about the days in high school when you were lonely and sad and perhaps truly depressed? Did you feel like you were suffering because you had no mom?"

"I never suffered," I snap. "I had bad days and bad moods just like all the other kids. And they had mothers."

"Laurie, were you serious when you told me you're not planning to find Master or look for the group when you leave here?"

Now that's a good question. That's why I'm here, right? Joan is on the right track. Because I have no mom, every-body assumes I am forever seeking something or someone.

All I wanted when I met Tom and Anna was to be popular and have friends. Maybe I thought I was missing something when I got involved with Master, but probably not. After all, I already had a father.

"I am serious about not looking for Master," I say slowly. I'm thinking about this and I mean it fully. "I'm serious about my painting now. And anyway, I wouldn't even know how to find Master if I wanted to."

"That's a good decision, Laurie. Your father said he would look into the name change and then come out here to spend a few days with you, and while he's here he'll help you to get that driving permit or license."

Joan stands up to leave and then adds, "He'll call to let you know when he's coming so give me a heads-up, please."

"Sure. And don't worry about me, Joan. My life is not a lie. A name change is a shock but it's not a tragedy. I'm over it."

Sometimes I think I'm more well-adjusted than Joan.

CHAPTER FOURTEEN

Suzie

"WELL, CAROL, WE'RE ON OUR WAY TO PRISON," I SAY AS I drive us onto the highway. "If Professor Milrod thought this was such a good idea, how come he's not heading to Milwaukee with us? Teaching memoir writing to criminals seems a little scary to me," I admit.

"Have you ever been to a prison?" she asks.

"No. You?"

"No. Never saw a prisoner, either." Carol pauses. "I'm terrified if you want to know the truth."

"Milrod promised they'd assign us non-violent inmates with high IQs, and he said we'll always have a guard nearby. I have Milrod's lesson plan and outline with me and I studied it last night."

"Me, too," says Carol.

"They just threw us into this assignment. I thought we'd have more preparation and training. Perhaps it's because we're older than most of the other students."

Carol says, "Too late to back out."

And so we drive.

Carol, like me, is in her mid-forties and trying to become a good writer. She's timid and doesn't speak much in class, so the only things I know about her are what I can surmise from her appearance. She's well-groomed, complete with makeup and nail polish, and her outfits have a corporate air.

She's so neat that I was hesitant to offer my car, for fear she'd look askance at the ragged upholstery, but she readily accepted. I was relieved when I picked her up and saw weather-worn furniture on her front porch and a lawn that could use a trim, and when she placed her luggage behind the passenger seat she didn't comment on the piles of papers and books in the back.

Some of my classmates are concerned about being away from their families for our two-week field-work internship. I, on the other hand, need this time. I have too much to think about and I need to think about it by myself. It's not Harry's dilemma; it's all mine, unless of course I decide to involve him. I'll do my thinking at the motel each night when I'm on my own, away from family.

Our motel is only a few minutes from the prison. We pass it just before the landscape changes from dairy farms, black-and-white cows and cornfields, to gloomy streets, decrepit urban buildings and finally a sign that announces the Men's State Prison. It's a two-story building; bricks dull brown, roof grey, windows painted black.

Following our written instructions, we enter through a metal door with a "Wisconsin Department of Corrections" sign hanging above it and then encounter our first locked gate. A frowning female guard checks our IDs, searches our bags, our pockets, even our shoes, then talks into her walkie-talkie and accompanies us through a second and then a third locked gate.

She walks several yards ahead of us. She is silent and seems angry. I'm puzzled and I think Carol is, too. She quietly asks me, "What did we get ourselves into?" The guard turns around and glares.

"Sorry, I didn't catch your name," I say, with forced cheerfulness.

"CO Barton," murmurs the guard.

"CO means correctional officer," Carol whispers to me.

Another glare.

We reach the end of a dim hallway redolent with the odor of uneaten meals, and then CO Barton announces, "There's your classroom. The MHT is in there, waiting for you."

"Mental health technician," Carol whispers.

Barton hurries back to her post and we meet a petite, dark-haired, dark-eyed ball of fire. She swiftly shakes hands with us and immediately begins her patter.

"Welcome, ladies. I'm Patti and I'll give you the lay of the land. I've done some writing exercises with my guys and they eat it up. They steer clear of trouble on writing days because they don't want to miss a class. I would keep doing it with them but these guys, the ones I've selected to be part of your class, need more than I can offer. They have important things to say and once they get their feelings out, they become new men. I know it sounds corny but it's true. So, as soon as I got the okay from the State, I knew I should call the ACA to get professional writers in here. Pleased to meet you. Any questions?"

"Any? About a million," replies Carol.

Patti stops to think. "Follow me to the staff cafeteria, and you can ask away while we get some chow." Patti does the best she can, considering that neither Carol nor I know enough to ask an intelligent question.

After lunch we shed our names. They say that for our protection we must maintain anonymity, so we are now Mrs. H. and Miss. P. We're introduced to the inmates we'll be working with. The guys are in their classroom seated on grey plastic chairs placed around a long industrial-looking table. They're wearing identical V-neck jumpsuits in navy, probably Polyester, and they all have white sneakers. Two of the six look like teenagers, although they might be in their early twenties. The other four are older, and one has pure white hair. Several have tattoos: hearts with names on their arms, a large bird on one guy's shoulder, and one of the younger ones has a tattoo on his neck.

Patti reminds the guys that they are privileged to have this opportunity and she expects them to do their homework and show up every day. Sitting in the back of the room is a man called a trusty. He's wearing the same blue uniform as the others, but his has pockets and in one pocket is a signaling device that is somehow connected to COs and guards throughout the prison.

"A trusty is an inmate granted special privileges because of his exemplary behavior," Patti explains. We learn that he's addressed not by name but as 'trusty,' and he will be sitting in on all classes and accompany us to the exit door at the end of each session.

Lessons begin. Students are eager for direction. These guys have had positive experiences with memoir writing classes. Memoir writing provides a legitimate way to talk/ write about yourself. You are expected to dig deep into your memory and then reveal all you have uncovered. Unlike teaching in a college classroom where students are accustomed to privacy and often are embarrassed to share early experiences, in the prison population students are hungry for attention. They have no illusions of privacy and they like to brag about their past exploits and to complain about their families.

To start, we ask each to list as many adjectives as they can to describe themselves. Enthusiasm fills the classroom as they scribble their words. They are so compliant that Carol asks, "Did you folks always follow orders so diligently?"

"No, ma'am," answers the boy with the neck tattoo. "But this writing stuff is real. It works."

Carol and I notice themes emerging after just a couple of days. The guys want to write about their inner lives, their traumas, and most of all, their parents, or lack thereof. Every day of the two-week program is fascinating. We prod the drug lord, the car jacker, the bank robber, and the scammers to recall pivotal moments.

We ask them:

What were you thinking when you planned the crime?
What were you feeling while you were doing the crime?
Has your thinking changed in any way? How? Why?

The "kids," as the older inmates call the younger ones, write about revenge. They committed crimes to get even.

The youngest one writes: *What was I thinking? I wanted to take away a stranger's car because I couldn't afford to buy one for myself. I would have stopped if I knew I could get a job that would pay me enough for a car. When I get out of here, I'll learn a trade. Maybe I'll be a writer ... whaddya think, teach? Can I make it as an author?*

His buddy, another "kid," begins his memoir by writing: *I got into too much trouble at school, so I was better off on the street, but then the street got bad, too. Trouble always found me. When you've got no one to protect you or show you the way, life is too hard. I'm into religion now. That's gonna do it for me when I get out. No more coveting. Know what I mean? That's a commandment.*

Whitey, the older inmate, does what many older, first-time memoirists do. He writes seven pages before he finally expresses what is most important to him.

I was abandoned by my mother, and my father was a mad man. I spent years and years searching for someone to tell me I was okay or at least good enough. When that didn't happen I wanted everyone to recognize me as a genius—people who knew me, and strangers, too. I wanted to make a name for myself. When that didn't happen I insisted everyone call me Master. I took advantage of young people. I don't mean in a dirty or smutty way. No. I just promised them a new way of life. I made them go by different names. I controlled their food. I controlled their appearance.

The prisoners go on for pages and pages explaining their choices, rationalizing their choices, and then finally they get to the meat of it. Their truth comes out, their secrets revealed, their fears examined.

A few pages later in his memoir, Whitey writes:

I met a girl who was like me. She had no mother. But, unlike me, she had a father who cared about her and protected her. He protected her from me. I thought I could take

care of her, but I was a stranger. Her father's devotion was
stronger than any devotion I ever saw and any devotion I
could give her. I have to admit it, it's true, his love, not
mine, is her birthright.

On the last day of class the students read their memoirs
aloud. Whitey's words reverberate in this cold room. His
voice is strong and sure and his fellow inmates pay attention when he speaks:

The loyalty I got from the young people I bamboozled
wasn't real. It was like my father's loyalty to me. It was phony.
He didn't care about me. But I did care about the young people
in my school, Master Academy. I wanted them to respect me
and treat me the way no one had ever treated me in my life.

One of the guys asks, "What were the girls like in your
school? Were they pretty?"

Whitey responds with sincerity. "I always kept my standards and my principles. When I was young I once had
the opportunity to take advantage of a young woman, a
woman who would do anything I wanted, but I left her and
warned her against hanging out with guys like me. It's true.
I never wanted to hurt anyone." He runs a hand through
his stark white hair. "Now that I'm locked up again I have
to learn how to change my ways. What am I learning? That
I should look for love and respect honestly. That's a tough
call. I'll try when I get out. No more shenanigans. I'll look
for a job, too. But will I succeed? I don't know."

"I've got a question," one of the older guys shouts to me
and Carol, at the end of the readings. "Can a person grow
up okay without a mother? Or with a bad mother?"

Carol promptly answers, "As long as a child has someone to believe in him, someone who cares about him, he

can grow up okay. Every child deserves to have someone whose face lights up when they see him."

These guys give me a jolt. They want their mothers to want them. These prisoners know the value of a good mother. My thoughts go to baby Laurie Sue. Did I harm her by not searching? No, I did the right thing, given the circumstances. No baby deserves a crazy mother. What if I had found my husband and my daughter too soon? What if I finally located them and then had to go into the hospital again? What if my brain started playing tricks on me again and I had sudden urges to cut myself?

I never knew good mothering. I try to bury thoughts of my childhood, but sometimes they intrude. Did I break down when I became a mother because I was afraid? Was I afraid I might inflict bad mothering on my innocent baby?

It's strange that Louie and I never talked about my family after we were married. They were dropped from our lives and we were okay with that. Nowadays, when I happen to see a person who has a disability I think about my brother. Is he still alive? If he is, who is taking care of him? Is he finally in a home where professionals are giving him what he needs? Was he ever properly examined and diagnosed? I do remember that Louie wanted to find help for him but we couldn't overpower my mother. I wonder, are my parents still alive? Do they wonder if I'm alive?

OUR FIELD WORK PROJECT ENDS ON A DREARY DAY, YET THE guys thank us for brightening their lives. Carol and I encourage our students to continue writing. "Write honestly. Say everything. You'll feel better after you write even if you never show your writing to anyone. Shame thrives in the dark."

The prisoners return to their routine with insight and hope for a future. Carol is proud of her accomplishment. She's happy. Me, not so much. I have questions. Sure, I'm proud and I know we did a good job and undoubtedly helped make significant changes in these guys, but I'm saddened by all the mother-talk.

"They all want the same thing," I muse on the drive south. "They wish for a mother, any mother. But isn't it enough to just have a father? Does it really all depend on the mother? Is that what it boils down to? Or maybe none of this matters. Maybe kids grow up just the way they are supposed to, no matter what the parents do?"

"Whoa, Suzie, what are you talking about?" Carol asks.

"Think about it, Carol. We know about men who abandon their families and the mom does a good job and the kids turn out okay. But what about kids growing up with just a dad and no mom? Do you think they turn out okay?"

Carol scoffs at that. "That would never happen. A man wouldn't bring up a child by himself. He'd bring the kid to his own mother or he'd quickly remarry. And anyway, moms don't leave their children."

I feel a lump in my throat and a sudden weakness throughout my body. It's an effort to speak. "Let's stop for a bit," I say to Carol. "I need a break."

"Okay," she replies, "there's a rest area coming up on the right."

I regain my composure in just a few minutes. I'm strong, but sometimes an unexpected comment overwhelms me and I need some recovery time. I tell Carol that I'd like to close my eyes to think and process all we've done at the prison. She's agreeable and I do close my eyes and think, but not about what we taught. My thoughts are going to that girl from The Lodge. The girl born on a December day in Winter Falls, Iowa. The girl who has dark curly hair. The girl whose name is Laurie. I'd like to believe she is well-adjusted and having a good life. But I ask myself, why is she living at The Lodge if she's well-adjusted? Did I cause her to have a difficult life, a life where she needs extra attention and extra help? Am I at fault? I thought I was doing the right thing.

Carol interrupts my thoughts. "Wow, Suzie, you really did take these guys to heart. Do you still need more time?"

I ignore her.

This Laurie girl is well cared for and seems as mature as any young lady I know. If there is inner turmoil she'll handle it, I hope, or get more help when she goes home. Her attendance at The Lodge is proof that her father is on top of things. My brief talks with her are probably useful, too. My sincerity is evident, it's real, I truly care about her. I hope she can tell that I have her best interest at heart.

Enough! Time to open my eyes.

We get back on the road but I can't control myself and continue to bombard Carol. "Carol," I say, "what if an emotionally strong man has a wife who dies or is very sick or runs away? That strong man would be okay raising the child, right?"

"I don't know, Suzie. Think about if the wife didn't die but was sick or something. Would she be able to have a good life without being with her child? I think mothers always return."

"I disagree," I say, "a strong woman is capable of living a good life without her child, especially if she knows her child is well cared for. Sometimes it may be better for the child to bond to someone who is capable of raising her or him, if the mother isn't."

"I suppose," says Carol. "But won't the kid want to search for the mom when he or she gets older or gets married or becomes a parent? Then what happens?"

It's hard for me to answer Carol's question. I've thought about this for years. With a shaky voice I answer, "A good mother, a psychologically mature mother, puts the child's needs ahead of her own. If the child searches and finds the mom, I'm sure the mom will have prepared for that day and she'll do just what she has rehearsed in her mind for years."

The words I speak sound so right. But what do I want? Have I prepared? And what if...what if...?

After dropping off Carol I head home, asking myself if I'm a psychologically mature mother, a mother who puts her child's needs first?

What are the needs of my daughter? Do I know? And what about the needs of Jason and Adam? I believe I'm focused on Harry's boys, my stepsons, whenever I am with them. But am I? Or am I thinking of the child I am not with?

Jason and Adam were preschoolers when Harry and I started dating. Those were the days when we'd play Chutes and Ladders, we'd read Dr. Seuss books, and we'd go for long walks along nature trails. Nowadays I look over their homework and listen to their accounts of teenage life. I have a feeling they tell me more than they tell their mother simply because they know I won't judge them. I believe a stepparent should treat a visiting stepchild as a guest, a loving and loved guest, but nevertheless a guest.

My father was never involved in our family conversations. He'd work on a jigsaw puzzle and pay no attention to the family drama playing out within feet of him. He didn't react to my mother, my brother, or me, and instead kept his head down as he inspected teeny puzzle pieces to decide which fit where. He had the ability to compartmentalize his life. A useful ability.

The boys will be coming here Saturday so I'll have the chance to test myself—can I be totally with them or will my thoughts wander to the girl at The Lodge?

HARRY AND I ARE ENJOYING A LEISURELY SATURDAY MORN-ing brunch, dawdling over our waffles and coffee, chatting about the boys' schedules, when we hear a car pull into our driveway. For an instant, but just an instant, I'm scared. Is my secret about to be exposed? No, that's ridiculous. And sure enough it's the boys' mother. She's delivering them much earlier than arranged. They're with us only on weekends and occasionally I envy Harry's ex-wife for getting to enjoy them all week.

"Suzie!" Adam shouts as he walks through the front door. "Guess what we did last night."

The hallway carpet is quickly covered with muddy footprints, and his jacket is dripping filthy water from where he's hung it on the coat rack in the foyer. He's carrying a red cooler. My envy for his mother has dissipated.

Jason is right behind him. "Don't be angry at us. Mom said you and Dad could handle this mess better than she could. We were on a fishing boat all night. It was fun, I caught bass."

Adam interrupts, "And I caught black crappie, which I'd never even heard of before last night. Anyway, I need my bed. Sorry for dripping all over the floor. I bet you wish you had daughters, huh?"

Both boys scoot upstairs before I can answer.

Harry lifts his head and turns to watch them as they dash. I see the love in his face. He's filled with kindness for those boys, and his smile is one of pride. And for a moment I slip and I visualize Louie gazing at Laurie Sue just like that.

Within fifteen minutes the boys are showered, and in their beds, Harry is cleaning up after them, and I am replaying Adam's words, *"I bet you wish you had daughters."* I hate when this happens. My brain is stuck on *daughters*. I gave birth to a daughter, but I don't have a daughter. She has a family—good dad, good grandparents, and knowing Louie's need for closeness, I'm sure a good mom. I've worked hard to become a strong woman. Am I strong enough?

Harry comes downstairs and we go into the backyard. It's a beautiful sunny day; the air is fresh, a couple of white clouds float lazily across the true-blue sky, a robin meanders over the grass, and we lounge in our comfy reclining chairs.

"I'm glad their mother didn't want them in the house after fishing. It gives us a few more hours with them this weekend," I say.

"Yes, but it's the same old story. She'll say she's depressed. She'll say she can't cope with the boys. She constantly says give her time, the depression will go away, and it does … until it comes back. She's just lazy; didn't want to clean up after them."

"Harry, it's okay. We can easily take care of this."

"But that's not the point. Her excuses are always the same and they're always total baloney."

I think, *Oh, dear husband, why are you so smug, so sure of yourself?* Aloud, I ask, "How do you know?"

"I know because I used to be married to her. I know because there were days she stayed in bed when she should've been caring for her sons; there were days when she yelled at me and at the boys only because she was irritable; and I know because I'm sure plenty of people try hard and overcome their depression or at least keep it to themselves. She lets everyone know her feelings because she wants sympathy."

I say nothing. I have no words. My beloved husband will never understand.

Harry spreads white zinc ointment over his nose, closes his eyes, and in minutes he's asleep.

I can't stop my thoughts, which go to Louie at times like this. Would he understand? Would he blame the mom? Both of my husbands have had good hearts, but when it comes to brains … sometimes I wonder. Louie was always sure of himself. He never thought there were things he didn't know. The way he saw the world was the way it was. He was limited but predictable. His mother is probably still bossing him around. There was nothing subtle about Louie. He made his presence known—no hesitancies, no ambiguities. He believed in his truth. End of discussion.

Harry, my handsome, six-foot sophisticate, is worldly and well-educated yet blames his ex for her depression. He should know better; but, alas, he doesn't.

When he awakens we have a good afternoon. He's a good guy, good dad, good husband, a person who's fun to be with and reliable and responsible. And he loves me. Is it fair for me to expect him to also be an expert in mental health?

Later, at the end of the day, comfortably sitting in our living room, he resumes talking about his ex. "Suzie, I know you must be annoyed at the boys' mother and I think I know why you don't say anything."

I'm startled and a little nervous. "Because I happen to have good manners?" I suggest.

"That, too, but years ago, when we were newly married, you told me that a married person should never say a word against any relative of their spouse. You've never said a word against any Henderson. I bet you won't criticize my ex, even if she deserves criticism, because she's the boys' mom. Am I right?"

Is he right? Yes and no. Yes, I wouldn't insult Jason and Adam's mom because she is their mom. He's right about that. But, no, that's not the only reason. The more important reason is that I won't condemn a person going through a depression. If only Harry knew my history. Could this be the time to broach it? Do I dare? Maybe. Slowly, gently, and with subtlety, I begin.

"Yes. I'm glad you remember that. It's true. Harry, And, I am particularly kind to people going through a depression."

"Well, you are a kind person. Always thinking of others."

"Harry, I've had personal experience with depression. I've been there. I know the suffering and I know that people need understanding not condemnation when they're depressed."

"I love you, Suzie girl," Harry says as he reaches to take my hand. "You're the best wife and the best step-mom ever. You're assuming she's really depressed, and I know she's not, she's just selfish. And when you say you've 'been there' I know you've never been like her. I know you all these years."

Do I argue with him? Do I insist I've struggled and suffered? Do I pound it into him that I went mad, that I had a breakdown? I don't think so. He just doesn't get it.

Harry goes on, "And you're the best aspiring author. How is that writing class coming along? When do I get to read what you're working on?"

My mind is racing. If I talk about ACA I might mention the portraiture student, the artist named Laurie. I might say she's from Winter Falls. That's ridiculous. There's nothing to worry about. I'll tell Harry she lives with her family in New Jersey. I'm letting my imagination override rational thinking, ...or not.

That brief memoir I wrote for Milrod's class turns out to be a helpful tool for me. Milrod told me I had some talent for writing and suggested I take pen in hand whenever I want to clarify something about my past. It's a good habit, recently a necessary habit.

At this moment I'm too emotional, too sensitive, and afraid that my past will come barreling out and roll right into this living room. It's time for me to practice my writing habit. When I write my thoughts and describe my feelings, anguish subsides, confusion dwindles. Putting my feelings on paper guarantees I won't be disturbed by my past, and I won't be tempted to talk and reveal inappropriate information. I want my father's knack to pop into my head because at this moment, when Harry is talking about his ex-wife's depression, my ability to compartmentalize is slipping away.

I finally respond to him. "Speaking about ACA, I'm going to do some homework while the boys are sleeping," and I hurry into my study. I must get my compartments in order.

CHAPTER FIFTEEN

Joan

I'M PROUD OF THE WORK I DO WITH THE GIRLS AT THE Lodge. My fellow students at the Chicago Psychotherapy Institute are not as skilled as I am. Several of my peers seem hesitant about their work. We're in the conference room waiting for our next class to begin and I'm happy to let them know that I'm quickly becoming an excellent deprogrammer. One of the fellows looks at me curiously so I explain, "I guess it's easy for me because I'm a natural at counseling."

A female classmate disagrees. "Remember, our professors have warned us that we don't yet have enough experience or training to advise people. We need another semester, at least, of psychological studies," she says. "We're not yet qualified to do deprogramming work or psychotherapy."

"And," adds another student, "we need to have completed our own personal psychotherapy sessions. I still have five more months to go. How about you, Joan?"

"Those professors are wrong," I tell them. "I quit my psychotherapy because I knew more than the therapist. And

Emily, Annette, and Laurie are doing very well, indeed."

I hear some gasps. One of the gaspers says, "What? You just used their names. You're never supposed to expose the identity of someone you're working with."

"Oh, that's not their real names. I changed them." I think to myself that this brash lie is for a good purpose, which is to get my point across, and anyway no one will ever meet these girls, so it doesn't matter, it's a good lie.

My fellow students are terribly rigid. The guy sitting across the table reminds me that I won't be fully credentialed without completing my personal therapy, and I won't be eligible for my doctor title until then.

I clack my spoon against a water glass to get everyone's attention and when they're all looking at me I explain, "I'm earning a good living without those formal diplomas. I won't say I'm proud of breaking rules, but I am proud that I'm not going along with every little rule. I have good judgment and I'd be foolish not to use it. The proof that I'm doing the right thing is that my three young ladies are in far better shape than when they first came to me."

No one says anything. I wonder if they're jealous of me. Today will be my last day here. I don't need more instruction, I know what I'm doing.

IT'S A LAZY DAY AT THE LODGE. WE'RE ALL HANGING OUT in the main room. I ask the girls for fashion critiques as I try on several outfits.

"Ladies, I may not be your age, but I still need to be attractive to the opposite sex. You never know when Mr. Right might show up."

Laurie is becoming the leader here; Annette and Emily tend to accept whatever she says as truth. I hope she doesn't influence them in a negative way about therapy, about life, and today about clothing. I want them to consider me a woman, not just a deprogrammer.

I needn't have worried. The girls aren't paying attention to me. Annette is rolling her eyes, and Emily makes a point of pulling a book from a nearby shelf to change the subject. "Joan, here's a book about food—recipes and menus. It looks good, Joan. Is it?"

I eye the book thoughtfully. "Cooking for a Crowd" is the title. I know it well. "No," I say, shaking my head "that's the book that gave me advice that didn't work. It's full of bad information."

This intrigues the girls. Laurie asks, "What kind of advice?"

"Yes," says Annette. "Maybe we can learn from your mistakes."

"Oh, girls," I say as I shrug my shoulders and make myself comfortable in the armchair. "I don't like to think about those days."

Of course, now all three are captivated. They huddle together on the floor, wide-eyed, looking up at me expectantly. They've settled in for a long story.

Laurie says, "You tell us to think and analyze all our feelings about the past. Aren't you going to take your own advice?"

"Hmm. You have a point, Laurie." Leave it to Laurie to be the most vocal and encourage the others to pry, too.

"I wasn't always a therapist. I wasn't always a professional. I was once a young woman on the verge of getting married. I had no career goals but I had dreams of a husband and travel and a home and a family. But that didn't work out and ...

"Who were you marrying?" asks Emily.

"Did you have an engagement ring?" asks Annette.

"Oh, girls, that's so far in my past. I was young and immature. I got involved with someone I didn't even know. I saw him in the street, he was handsome in his big cowboy hat, and I smiled at him. He smiled back and that was it."

"What do you mean *that was it*? You wanted to marry someone you didn't know?" Laurie seems shocked. I don't remind her that not long ago she ran off to live with strangers.

"Pretty much. We had a strong and sudden physical attraction. He told me he was a cowboy and returning to his ranch in two days, so why didn't I come with him? I didn't even know his name. I was naïve. No one had ever flirted with me before. I thought he was serious so I said, "I can't go anywhere with a man I'm not married to. And he said, 'Let's get married.'"

"I believed him. That's how dumb I was. I was far from my family, trying to make my way in a city where I knew no one. I was living in a rented room in a boarding house. I was lonely, very lonely. He told me to meet him at a bar that evening and I did. I thought it was cute that he was wearing that hat again. In fact, I called him Tex because of the hat. We flirted some more and then he said he loved me. No boy ever said that to me. Then he kissed me. No boy had ever kissed me. I asked if he was serious about us getting married and he just smiled. I took that for a 'yes.'

"Girls, understand that I was alone in the world. My family lived up in Maine and we weren't close at all. I left home very young and never looked back. My parents had no interest in being parents. They often were in legal trouble. They sometimes were in jail. They thought scamming the public, innocent people, was the way to earn a living. My goal was to get away from them."

It's embarrassing to talk about my parents. I don't like anyone to know how bad they were, just like when I was growing up I didn't want anyone to know me well, to become a friend, because then they would know who my parents were. My parents were known throughout our county. That's why I had no friends growing up and to this day I don't have friends. I missed out on learning that friend-making skill.

"I was so determined to have a new life that I told Tex I didn't need a wedding; City Hall would do as long as I had a white dress. He just smiled. He said he'd come by the next afternoon to plan our wedding and our life. I waited for him. And waited. He showed up at night, still smiling, still wearing his cowboy hat, and he said he was ready to 'pull out of town' in the morning. "What about our wedding?" I asked. When I told him I had bought a white dress, he looked at me with tender pity. He said, 'I won't touch you. I won't even ask you for a kiss. I have to move on. You're a good girl. Stay away from the likes of me.' And that was the end of Tex."

The girls look relieved, especially Laurie. "I'm glad," she said. "He could have been a murderer. He could have stolen from you. He could have raped you. This could have been a tragedy."

Now they're looking at me with pity. I won't tell them that he is still in my thoughts and dreams. They won't pity me if I tell them about my hidden stash. Should I tell the girls about the money I've made and saved? No, they're too young to understand.

Laurie, Annette, and Emily remain on the floor, waiting for more of a story from me. They're an enthusiastic audience so I continue. "I was able to buy this piece of real estate that we're living in right now—it was a big property that nobody else wanted. 'A white elephant' the real estate company called it. I planned to make it into a fancy hotel. I imagined a pool, a restaurant, nighttime entertainment, families coming for their annual vacation, couples coming for their honeymoon. But that vision required far more money than I had, so I settled on making it into a guesthouse. I was going to be the cook and that book, Emily, was going to teach me everything I needed to know. But it didn't. My inn flopped."

"Oh, no," says Annette, "that's terrible. Were the recipes too hard to follow?"

"Was it because you weren't a good cook?" asks Emily.

"I bet it was because you didn't have a good sales team," Laurie says. "Even the best businesses fail if the public doesn't get to know about them. 'Bombard the public,' is what I learned from my sales rep at Master Academy."

"You had a sales rep?" asks Annette.

"I had a sales team. They represented my paintings, but I didn't get to meet the people who bought them, and I never got the money from them, either."

Laurie could easily dominate this discussion so I swiftly continue my story. "Girls, let me tell you what I did when I realized the inn wasn't going to make it."

"You cried?" asked Annette

"No. Well, maybe once. It flopped because the building needed thousands of dollars in repair to meet the standards of an inn. So, I studied to become a real estate agent. But I wasn't very good. I made money but my boss, the real estate broker, didn't like me. Clients complained to him that I was brusque."

The three girls look at each other, each with a hint of a smile. They think I don't notice. I see everything.

"Tell us more," goads Emily.

I explain to them that walking into other people's houses was not for me. "I rushed prospective buyers in and out of properties. I had no patience," I say.

I leave it at that. No need to tell them that the cozy living rooms, the bedrooms full of love, the nurturing kitchens—those rooms all taunted me. I couldn't bear witnessing strangers living the life I deserve.

"Next, I started doing this—counseling, deprogramming. I went to a school that taught me enough to get started and here I am. I'm proud of what I've made of myself."

Laurie seems bewildered. "But how did you learn about Dr. Freud? Didn't you need years and years of school?"

"Oh, I read tons of books. I know Freud better than most shrinks know Freud," I say. The truth is that all the years that I was living alone and isolated, the library was my place of refuge and psychology books helped me understand my family and myself.

Annette and Emily look at each other with raised eyebrows. I'm relieved when Laurie totally changes the subject.

"There's a portrait competition coming up, and El Newman thinks if I put my mind to it and paint every day,

I have a good chance of being one of the winners."

Ah, this is a good opportunity for me to reinforce a lesson to the girls. After all, it's me, not Laurie, who is in charge here. "Goals are good. ACA is good for you, Laurie. Not only to upgrade your talent, but also to increase your friendships and your social skills. Are you still friendly with the women you met that first time you were in the student lounge?"

"Yes. We hang out together during breaks. One of them, though, is away on a field work assignment. She had to take two weeks off from work to go to Milwaukee. She told us that she's part of a team that's teaching memoir writing to prisoners. They say it helps with their mental health to write their life story. They reflect on their lives and then they begin writing their memoir. Sounds stupid, right?"

Annette and Emily listen attentively when Laurie speaks. I don't want them to be influenced by her ideas which are contrary to proven theories. I immediately interject, "No, it sounds like a worthwhile program. Self-reflection and self-analysis are important skills. They create emotional maturity and psychological well-being."

Laurie counters with "Please, Joan, stop talking to us like a professor, and anyway that's probably not true. Self-reflection a good thing? Really? I never thought of it that way. I get too sad if I think too much, so I keep myself busy. I don't want to be a deep thinker."

"Well," I begin, "in my training as a counselor I learned that..."

Laurie interrupts, "Please don't get all professional with us. I like you much better when we just plain talk. I don't need fancy therapy. Our regular talks and discussions are good enough for me, without all the psychological words."

"Your dad said the same thing to me on the phone. He said he didn't sign up for therapy. But the thing is, according to all the experts, there are some topics that must be discussed."

"I thought *you* were the expert, Joan. Isn't that why I'm here? Aren't you a doctor, even if you're not yet official? You know, I don't care about your title. I don't care if you're a psychiatrist or a psychotherapist or a ferry boat captain."

"Okay, Laurie, you win. No self-reflection. No introspection. Yes, I am the expert around here." I proudly stand and smile at these three lovely young women. "I'm going back to my bedroom to try on a few more outfits and then to get ready for bed. Let's drop this discussion. We'll talk again tomorrow. Good night, girls."

CHAPTER SIXTEEN

Laurie

As soon as Joan walks away, Annette turns to us with worry on her face. "Why did my parents think Joan was so great? She only went to school to learn enough to get started. Maybe this lodge business will flop, too."

"Maybe it's already flopped and we don't know it," Emily says, as she studies the cookbook that started this conversation.

"You're right. I don't see the masseuse she promised us. I don't see the hundreds of girls lining up to live here," says Annette. "And she told us an aerobics instructor was here. Did you ever see that instructor, Laurie?"

"No," I say, "but she did get each of us to stay away from our groups and she did get us all into a school program. And she does know about Freud." I feel like I should stick up for Joan a little bit. She means well. She's not Master.

Annette says, "Her psychology talks are silly. She thinks she knows what's going on inside my head. I don't even know what's going on in my head."

"That's the point," says Emily. "We're here to learn what makes us tick."

"I want to learn that from a real psychotherapist. Not from Joan. She's good at some things but she thinks she knows everything," I say.

"Should we tell our parents? They're paying a lot of money for us to be here," says Annette.

"Not me," I say, "I simply don't listen to Joan when her ideas are silly, and that's how I can put up with her. She wanted me to have goals and my newest goal is to finish this program and be gone."

"True about silly ideas," says Annette. "She told me to book a tour to Paris as soon as my semester at the Lycee is finished."

"What's wrong with that?" asks Emily.

"She said she should accompany me, to make sure I wouldn't get tangled up in the Wonderlands again or something else. Of course, my parents would be paying for her airfare, hotel, everything."

"If you and your parents agreed, who would be here, running The Lodge?" asks Emily.

We all think about this for several seconds.

"Maybe that's why her businesses flop. She doesn't plan ahead," I say.

Suddenly, a cry comes from Joan's wing of the house, a sound like someone is in pain. The three of us rush out of the main room and are about to knock on her office door when the noise gets louder. She's not crying—she's yelling.

"Who is in there with her? I didn't see anyone come in," says Emily.

"Shh, listen," says Annette.

We hear Joan repeating to herself, over and over, louder and louder. She's shouting, *Tex, Tex. Tex.*

"Oh my gosh, she's yelling at herself. Come on, we need to get away from her," I say, and we rush back to the main room.

We look at each other as we sit on the edge of our seats and finally Annette suggests that we attempt to find out more about Joan. The Lodge is not Master Academy, it's not The Musicians, it's not Wonderland, but it does appear to be run by someone who is a little bit off and maybe not qualified to be in charge of a deprogramming establishment.

"Let's do some Nancy Drew sleuthing," I suggest. "On Wednesday, when Joan goes shopping and none of us have classes let's see what we can find out."

I'm good at organizing and I give them each a task. Emily should research the town business area and make appointments with either the Chamber of Commerce or whatever business credentialing place she can find. With her beautiful face, she'll be welcome anywhere. Annette could be our defender if we have to argue with anyone. She'll help us gain access to whatever we might need, or maybe just figure out what we will need and what we should do. My job is to find a way to get us into town. The bus schedule doesn't work for us, so I look for a car service to pick us up. My other job is to understand what information I want to find. I feel something is off about Joan, something is not right, but I don't know how to identify that something.

On Wednesday we search for Joan's name as we walk around downtown, but don't find a trace of her. In fact, it takes us a while to find a trace of downtown. Rural and suburban are mixed together here, it's not like there's one solid business district. The Chamber of Commerce is of no use—the office manager is not swayed by Emily and seems annoyed that we stopped in. We pop into the library to do research, but soon realize we're not such good researchers.

"There's City Hall," says Emily, pointing to a gray, squat two-story building with engraved letters above the double doorway. "Let's see what we can discover in there."

Sure enough, records at City Hall tell us Joan is truly the owner of The Lodge, that she has voted in the last elections, and that she pays her taxes. That relieves us. It's some proof that she is an upstanding citizen, I think. I notice a strange notation on her ownership deed, though.

"Look, girls, come here. This says that Joan insists upon paying her taxes in cash. Why would they record that information? Why would they care how she pays, as long as she does pay?"

Annette says, "Maybe she's a secret drug dealer. In Wonderland every dealer had loads of cash but no checking account."

Emily says, "Everyone has a checking account."

Maybe we're on to something but what are we proving, anyway? I ask the girls, "Are we being too Nancy Drewish?"

We start laughing at ourselves and then we notice secretaries looking up from their desks and giving us dirty looks. We take the hint and laugh all the way to the sidewalk and then we laugh some more. Annette says, "I haven't had so much fun in a long time." Emily and I agree. I admit to myself that this is new for me. I truly am enjoying myself. I'm not painting or drawing; I'm with friends and I'm having fun. We laugh our way down the street and then across another street and soon we're at a small grocery store.

"Let's pig-out," says Annette. We buy tons of junk food and hope we can get to The Lodge and stash it away before Joan returns. In the taxi on the way back we agree to stop snooping. We remind ourselves that we each know what it's like to be in a place with no freedom. Here, at The Lodge, we can leave anytime we want, we have enough to eat, and we're making progress in our chosen fields. It's not all bad.

I say, "Let's make a promise that we'll make the best of our time here and we will immediately tell the others if we come across anything too disturbing about Joan."

I don't know why, but that makes us burst into giggles again, the driver turns around to see if we're okay, and we just laugh some more. Annette says, "I feel like I'm in high school, but come to think of it, I never laughed in high school."

"Me, neither," says Emily. They both look at me. I nod my head in agreement and in a few seconds the three of us are giggling again.

"I'm glad we're returning to The Lodge. It's our temporary home and Joan is our temporary, imperfect mother," I say.

Annette adds, "And we are three imperfect sisters."

THE NEXT DAY I'M BACK AT ACA, AND BUSILY PAINTING my dad's portrait. I work on it all day. The shading, the shadows, the reflected light, the tints and colors, the angles; there's much to think about and that's good for me. I'd rather not think about Joan.

Today El stops at my easel for quite some time. "It's coming along beautifully, your colors are perfect, and you've captured his eyes," she says. "I'm impressed that you have the endurance to work at this so many hours each week."

I smile, thank her, and do not mention that this schedule is nothing compared to my workload last year. This is more like a vacation.

El is purposeful and strides into a room ready to let you know what's on her mind. You can tell she's an artist just by her clothes. One of the workshop students told me they were expensive, although at first glance they look like rags, but artistic rags. El wears bright colors that most people would think clash with each other, and yet she is the epitome of style when wearing an orange tee shirt with pink slacks and a red shawl. Her socks are usually purple.

"At the rate you're going," she says, "you'll certainly be finished in time to enter this year's ACA portrait contest."

And I do finish. And I do enter.

The competition is daunting and for the couple of weeks that the judges deliberate I'm worried. I title my portrait, *Dad Louie*. Out of the thirty-six entries there will be only two prizes and one honorable mention.

While waiting for the judging to occur I distract myself by hanging out with Annette and Emily. We play some games—mostly Jotto and Clue -and we go for walks, too. We're always on the lookout for something weird about Joan, but so far not much to report. Once, when I walked into the main room she quickly covered up whatever she was writing—it looked like a letter—with a blank sheet of paper. I'm not sure that was weird, though. Could be she wanted to protect the privacy of the person she was writing to.

Hooray! Today's announcement: *Laurie Franklin, Honorable Mention for portrait* Dad Louie. *You and your portrait, and as many guests as you wish, are invited to the ACA awards ceremony next month.*

Everyone I invite wants to come. Emily and Annette, Joan, Dad, and my three ACA ladies. Irma and Linda ask if food will be served, and Suzie asks if "the subject of the portrait" will be coming.

I wasn't sure about inviting Dot. Dad hasn't talked about her in a while, but I hope that she's still part of his life and that they're more than just friends. I decide to go ahead and send her an invite, too. She's played an important role in my life, even though I barely know her. I wouldn't be at The Lodge or have had the chance to study with El if Dot hadn't found Joan.

Dad explains he'll come for the ceremony, but not any earlier. "Sorry, honey, I want to visit you as soon as possible, but right now I'm bogged down with work. Everybody in town is replacing floors, ripping out carpeting, discovering ceramic tile, and I can't get away this week. But soon, I promise, I'll be there. I love you."

Rather than leave the portrait in the studio, I get it framed and bring it to the Lodge, where it brightens up the main room. Emily remarks that now she'll know exactly who my dad is as soon as he steps into the auditorium.

"Let's go shopping," suggests Annette. "We should buy new outfits to wear to the award ceremony."

It's fun to go with the girls—this is my community, my family, my friends. I belong. We do lots of talking and lots of laughing on our shopping trip, and that easy camaraderie is still with us when we return to The Lodge. We make ourselves comfortable and listen to Emily telling us crazy stories about The Musicians. As she's talking I realize that I've been listening to music playing in the background for weeks and it hasn't bothered me. I may not love it and probably wouldn't miss it if it were not playing, but I haven't cried once from music. I smile to myself while she tells us, "Their music was amazing. It was the glue that held us all together. Except when it was used to torture us."

Annette and I each pop up from the floor where we were lounging. "Torture? What do you mean?" I ask.

Annette says, 'You're kidding. Music can't torture."

Emily says, "Not kidding, but maybe not true torture. Take it easy. Take a seat. I'll explain."

Annette and I each choose a chair and a pillow and give Emily our attention. She gets a far-away look in her eyes and says, "You know how music changes your mood? The way restaurants play certain music to make you order more and eat more, and malls pipe in other types of music to get you to spend more?"

Annette interjects, "Is there music to take away your appetite?"

Emily ignores her and continues. "The Musicians used good music in a good way to make us bond and have feelings of togetherness. But they also used music in a bad way to make us fear for our lives."

I want to know how that could happen, it seems impossible. "What do you mean, fear for your life?"

"You know how in scary movies they have minor chords playing to create suspense? That's what they would do if one of our members showed a hint of not obeying. They would have the scariest music coming from every speaker in the building. After a while I think it changes your brain. It made us scared that any minute we were going to witness something horrible. It was as if a catastrophe was waiting for us—a fire, a fight. We all became paranoid. One day I seriously thought the ceiling was about to fall on us. One by one, we turned into obedient slaves just to get that music to stop."

Annette adds, "I once heard that the CIA, or some other groups like that, use certain music as part of their torture for prisoners."

"I could believe that," says Emily. "Imagine hearing unbearable loud music for hours on end. You don't hear the lyrics after a while; everything sounds like noise. There's no safe space in your mind to escape to so you lose the ability to think. There's no way to prepare yourself for that kind of psychological torture, and it's physical torture, too, because the volume is ear-splitting." Emily goes on to tell us that she believes that if her musical talent had been recognized and nurtured at home, she wouldn't have jumped at the chance to join the Musicians.

Even though I don't like to look back, that comment made me wonder what my life would be like if I had been at a specialized art high school.

Emily and Annette have become my true friends. We talk, we laugh, sometimes we cry. We enjoy telling each other about our cult experiences and the weirdos we lived with. It took courage for me to finally admit that I lived in a cult for almost two years. I called a man, who might have been a criminal, *Master*., I stared at his hair and I chanted to his hair. I never went outdoors because I had to paint from early morning to late at night, Master sold my paintings and kept all the money.

They asked why I stayed and why I left. I'm still pondering those questions.

We talk about our families. I tell them about Dad and I tell them about my grandmother, too. Annette remarks that it sounds like she kind of was my mother, and I think about that. She asks, "What would your life be like now if your grandma was still alive? Would you have joined Master's group if grandma was around?"

This is precisely why I don't like to look back. There's no point.

Annette stacked up some metal moving trunks in the middle of the main room. That's our stage for modeling. When I model my new clothes for Joan, I'm proud I've regained most of the pounds that were starved off me at Master Academy. I now look regular not freaky. As I try on my selections I think about how I shopped. It was easy for me to pile up garments to take into the fitting room. I do notice that maybe El is influencing me without my knowing it. These new clothes are bright colors—cerise, lime green, violet—and are more artsy and whimsical than anything I've ever worn. It was not that long ago that I wanted to look tailored, like Anna. Now I just want to look like me—with perhaps a hint of El.

"Girls, you've motivated me," Joan says when she joins us. "I'm going to do even more shopping. We'll be having guests and I want to represent the Lodge in a positive way. Oh, Laurie, your dad called. He'll definitely be here for the awards dinner. By the way, Laurie, does he favor a particular color? Does he go for women with a business-office look? A casual look?"

I never thought of my dad caring about women's clothes, or caring about women, for that matter. I don't know what to say to Joan and look to Emily for help. She immediately saves me by changing the subject.

"I can't wait to see your dad's expression when he arrives and looks at his portrait!"

Joan scowls at the change of subject. "I hope my new outfits won't be too youthful," she says. "I don't want to make you girls jealous."

We don't know if she's serious or kidding. All three of us stifle our giggles and Annette relieves the awkwardness by asking if my friends from the ACA are coming.

"Yep," I say. "Each of them has responded. They're all coming."

CHAPTER SEVENTEEN

Louie

LAURIE'S HOME, BUT SHE'S NOT. WHEN SHE WAS MISSING, the house was empty and hollow, now it's still empty, but I feel some hope for our future. I'm still sad, though, because Chicago is a big and strange city, far from Truesdale.

I'm assuming Doc Joan knows what she's doing, and Laurie will return in a good mood and with a good head on her shoulders. When she called to invite me to a ceremony at the art school she's been going to, she was excited about it and I heard happiness in her voice for the first time in years. Maybe it'll stick. And that's why I'm on my way to Chicago, even though I have loads of work waiting, a couple of customers wanting their floors done yesterday, and a contractor and a decorator each begging me to 'squeeze in' their special client.

I'd feel better if Dot were coming with me. I'm accustomed to seeing her almost every day. I count on her and her advice, more and more. She's loaded with common sense.

On my way to the airport I stop at the diner to say goodbye. I bypass the hostess and walk straight into the kitchen. Dot always manages to keep chaos under control. Today she's quietly coaching the new waitress, inspecting an outgoing platter and encouraging the guy who's learning to slice tomatoes using a new-fangled knife. I stand and watch in awe. Dot sees me, smiles and signals that I should wait at a booth in back.

Her boss-lady attitude softens and she is her regular sweet self as soon as she joins me. We don't sit, I have no time. She gives me last-minute instructions: "Take pictures, Louie. Remember, it's important for Laurie that you are there for her and that she knows you are proud of her. An award ceremony is a big deal."

"I know. I know. I wish you could come with me."

"I can't get good coverage these days. You know that. But you'll be back before you know it and Laurie may be coming back with you, too."

"I hope so. But you never know about Doc Joan. She may want to keep Laurie longer. I hope she knows what she's doing."

I do have some concern about the Doc. She seemed a little strange but then again most shrinks are a little strange. I did a marble floor for a child psychiatrist who did not own a television, and I did a custom wood plank floor for a behaviorist, whatever that is, who painted all his ceilings black. Shiny black, not matte, but nevertheless black, in his office.

My rental car is waiting for me, thanks to Dot, and I drive from the airport directly to The Lodge. The grounds are well-maintained, and the place is impressive from the outside, at least. Lots of land; I know I'm not in Truesdale.

Joan greets me at the door and ushers me into a large room. Nice furnishings and solid, good quality flooring. Maybe she does know what she's doing.

Joan is wearing an outfit that I'd never expect a role model for young ladies to be wearing. Maybe I'm old-fashioned, but for my way of thinking too much is showing.

Surprisingly, Laurie is not here.

"Laurie is helping to set up chairs and tables at ACA," Joan explains and then takes a seat on a large beige couch. "We have a couple of hours before we need to leave for the awards ceremony, so let's use our time wisely. Come sit here next to me; time to relax from your plane trip now. Let's talk." She pats the seat next to her.

She's getting me agitated. "I want to see Laurie." I'm talking too loud, but I need to see Laurie.

"Sit down, Louie. We should talk. Let's start with you helping me understand the name change. I suspect there is more to it than Laurie was told."

Is she still hung up on that name change? Why? "Now you sound like Laurie, making a big deal about nothing," I say. "It was just a name change. Perfectly legal. People do it every day."

I don't want to sit. I want to leave. Joan reaches for my hand and practically pushes me down on to the couch. She's strong and I'm shocked by her forcefulness.

"Please, I want to help your daughter. She's ready to take the next step toward maturity, but I'm at a loss to figure out why she's cut off from her feelings. Did she learn to hide her feelings because you hide yours?"

What is this all about? Where is this coming from? Does Joan think that Laurie and I play hide-and-seek with our emotions?

"Oh, come on, Joan. Don't make everything into a federal case. I'm a working man, I don't stare at my bellybutton all day and I don't analyze everything. There's no sense in going over old events. I don't look back; I look forward. Please, stop this kind of talk."

Joan ignores my pleas.

"How did Laurie handle the death of her grandmother? Sometimes thoughts about a prior death are stirred up when there is another death. When your mother died did Laurie talk about her own mother? Did she ask you questions about her mother's death or about her mother's life?"

"We don't talk like that in our house, Joan. We take care of business. Laurie never knew her mother. There's nothing for her to say."

"But you knew her mother. You loved her, right?"

"Of course I loved Suzanne. I still do. I never remarried. I . . . I can't talk about this anymore. Let's get ready to go, now." I move forward, about to stand, when she leans close to me and overpowers me with her eyes.

"Not so fast, Louie," she insists. "What can you tell me that will help me better understand Laurie?"

"Stop it. I'm not your patient. I don't want to be therapized. Laurie's fine. She'll come back home and life will go on."

"Louie, I must reveal to you that Laurie is wooden. She throws herself into her painting, which is a good thing, but she has no interest in trying to understand herself. Remember, she did join a cult. What was she looking for? Please, help me figure this out, Louie. We need to get Laurie on the right track for the rest of her life."

"And talking about my wife will help Laurie? I don't get it."

"Tell me about Suzanne. Her life, her death. This is urgent. Where is she buried? Do you visit the cemetery with Laurie? Talk to me, Louie. Trust me, Louie. I know what I'm doing."

She wants me to trust her. She dresses like a floozie. She's charging me a ton of money. She wants to hear about my life, not my daughter's. She wants to hear about my wife, who I never talk about and never think about. And now she's bullying me, and for some strange reason I'm letting her.

My voice is losing its power. The words are coming out in hoarse whispers. "It's not like that, Joan."

"Then what is it like?"

"Joan, she's gone. Isn't that enough to say? It's enough for me. I'm getting upset. Stop this."

Joan moves closer to me on the couch. I can feel her breath; her face is practically touching mine. Her eyes are piercing me. She says, "It's okay to get upset. Allow yourself to feel your feelings. This can be easy, Louie, just tell me the truth."

"I can't," I rasp, and attempt to look away. This is too intense. I want to run. I need to escape. "Sometimes a lie becomes the truth. Sometimes good lies are true enough. A good lie can hurt or help. Drop this, Doc, drop it, before it hurts."

"Louie, you've been a good dad. You brought up a girl all by yourself. Now that girl needs some help to get to her next stage of development. Say the truth. Secrets and lies cause problems, serious problems."

I'm losing my strength. My hands feel clammy; I'm sweating. I look down and see that my right fist is clenched, and I didn't even know it. My left hand is rubbing my chest. My chest hurts; not heart-attack hurt, not indigestion hurt, but surrender hurt. "Drop it. You're playing with dynamite," I croak.

"This is the time to talk, Louie. I'm listening," she says, as if I haven't spoken.

I expect a therapist to be soothing, but Joan is scaring me. Her tone is cruel. Her voice makes me wince. This is not good for me. I hear my pulse in my ears.

"Hush," I say. It's not in me to tell a woman to *shut up.*

It's obvious she wants me to say something, but I can't speak. I have no voice and I'm immobilized on the couch. My heart hurts. There's no way out of this. Joan is not bigger than I am, yet her presence immobilizes me.

"Just breathe," she says, as she inches away from me.

My mind tells me to make a run for it. My body does not obey.

She continues tormenting me. "Just breathe and speak. I know what I'm doing. This is for Laurie, for her complete recovery."

Her brutality wanes and slowly my voice returns. "If I tell you, do you have to tell it to Laurie? I can't let her know."

All these years it's been easy to say nothing about this. Easy not to think about it. Easy to keep a secret. And now, with this wild woman confronting me, I am compelled to reveal everything.

"Know what? And speak up; I can barely hear you." Joan is shouting.

I can't say the words, even though, for a moment, I thought I wanted to. "I'm done, Doc." I try to stand but stumble back onto the couch.

Joan places a heavy hand on my shoulder. "Speak the truth, Louie, speak the truth. Your words will help me work with Laurie. Your words will save Laurie. It's your obligation to save your daughter."

I close my eyes, press my chin to my chest, and hug my elbows to get some relief. It works. I can say the words. I whisper in disgrace, "She didn't die. She's in a hospital. She went crazy."

Joan shudders. Her little beady eyes are bulging out of her head.

I manage to stand up. I'm looking at the door but can barely shuffle toward it. I'm shaking all over. Another step, another inch.

"Louie, what are you doing? Where are you going?"

"I can't see Laurie. I can't stay here. I'm going back to the airport. I need to go home. Don't try to stop me. Take care of my girl, please, take good care of my girl."

I failed. I know I failed. I thought I was a family man. I'm not. I'm a fake. How can I live with myself? I've ruined my family. Agonizing sadness overtakes me.

Slowly, I will myself to walk. My gait is unsteady, but I make it out the door and wobble toward my rental car. Joan is following close behind shouting, "Come back. Why are you leaving?"

I turn to face her. "Because I've lost my ability to lie."

CHAPTER EIGHTEEN

Laurie

DAD WILL BE WALKING IN ANY MINUTE. I WONDER WHAT he'll say when he sees his portrait. I'm proud to do something for him, especially something that makes him look so cute. He really is a good dad. He hasn't held it against me that I ran off, and he's still paying for The Lodge. I hope he'll be proud of me today. I'm wearing a new green outfit that's kind of sophisticated, and pretty, too. He'll be relieved that I'm not skin and bones anymore. The ACA building makes a good impression—he'll see that his tuition money is well spent. He'll also see the excellent paintings on the wall—proof that the instruction here is superb.

Everyone except Dad is already here. I see El, all the portrait class students, Annette and Emily, my three ACA ladies. And of course, many ACA students from other departments. They're all seated, munching on carrot sticks, enjoying cheese cubes and crackers, sipping lemonade, and I can tell they're happy for me and the other prize winners. And, amazingly, I feel happy, too. I stop to chat with my guests. I notice that Suzie and I are both wearing pumps—high heels that most women shun for everyday wear. I tell her that they are my most comfortable shoes and she says they are for her, too.

I hope I don't embarrass Dad in front of everyone when I run to greet him with hugs and kisses, but that's my best way to show love and appreciation. Any minute now.

Dad Louie is perched on a wooden easel next to the other prize-winning paintings. They're each covered with a blue velvet cloth that will be removed during the actual ceremony.

I keep looking toward the doorway and then I step out into the hall. Where are Dad and Joan? They should have been here already. I wait as long as I can—until I hear the beginning rumblings of a microphone.

"Welcome everyone," says the ACA dean as he opens the program.

The audience listens respectfully and then there's an interlude of music. What begins as a quiet instrumental quickly develops into the enthusiastic theme from Rocky, *Gonna Fly Now.* The guests are spirited and lively in their seats. Then another speech, this one from a ceramics major who is encouraging students to consider ACA's sculpture program. I'm barely listening to the words, instead I'm focusing on the entryway. Where's Dad? Wishing doesn't bring him into view. He's not in the auditorium when the dean says, "Honorable mention, portrait category, goes to Laurie Franklin. Laurie, please step up and tell us about your watercolor."

I self-confidently walk up to the stage; no one can see that my palms are sweaty. "My portrait is called *Dad Louie* and it is a portrait of my father, who should be arriving here any minute." I hide my disappointment behind a smile.

I remove the blue cloth and the audience claps. I hear whistles and hoots from the avant-garde artistes who've become my buddies, and then amid the noise and commotion there is a sudden gasp. Everyone, including me, turns to scan the room to identify the person who made that piercing sound.

Irma and Linda have closed in around Suzie and are murmuring to her. Linda takes Suzie by the hand, pulls her up, and carefully ushers her out into the hallway. This is strange.

The audience settles down, I continue my presentation—about ACA, about El Newman, about watercolors, and I finish just as Joan enters the auditorium. I'm surprised to see she's wearing a revealing two-piece outfit, short skirt and low-neck top, more appropriate for a much younger woman. But, that's not what most surprises me. She's alone. Where is Dad?

As soon as the program is over, I corner her at the lemonade table. "What happened? Where's my dad?" I ask.

"He became ill as soon as he arrived from the airport. He didn't want to infect you and he said he'd be back as soon as he feels better, probably in a week or two."

"What? A week or two? I don't get it. Where is he now? I want to see him. Will he be okay? I want him to see his portrait." She must be mistaken. He wouldn't come all this way and then leave. My hands start to tremble. This can't be true.

"He's on his way to the airport to catch a return flight. He didn't want to waste any time. The sooner he sees his doctor, the sooner he'll get well and come on back to see you."

"Oh, no, what do you think is wrong? Will he be okay? Why didn't he come in for just a minute?" I ask. I can't remember the last time Dad was sick. I think of him as germ-proof. Why would he rush home? Wouldn't he want to see me? There are doctors in Chicago. This news gets me chewing on my bottom lip. I hate that habit.

"Do you think he has something serious?" I ask Joan as we walk out into the lounge area. I spot Suzie and Linda sitting on a couch in the corner and my scary thoughts subside a bit.

"I'm sorry we're out here" says Linda. "Suzie wasn't feeling well. But we did see your portrait. It's outstanding." Suzie doesn't look like herself. She's clenching her teeth and her face looks old.

"Joan just told me my dad had to return to New Jersey. He suddenly took ill. Maybe you're coming down with the same thing, Suzie. I hope not. It was something bad. He had to turn right around and go home."

Suzie's face unclenches and she noticeably exhales. I wonder if she's been upset by the unfamiliarity of our lounge area today. Usually paint-smeared artists, instrument-carting musicians, sweet-smelling pastry chefs, and writers laden down with books, are crowding each table. Today's decorum is startlingly different. Conversations are quiet, the only fragrance I detect is from fancy guests' perfume, and there seems to be an unwritten dress code that even the student activists are obeying.

The four of us sit together, and while the three of them make small talk my mind goes back to my dad. "Joan, was he very sick when he got off the plane? What do you think is wrong with him?"

Joan replies, "Sometimes people react physically when they are emotionally upset."

Suzie squirms in her seat.

I don't understand. "Why would he be emotionally upset? Did I upset him because I made a big deal about the name change? Do you think he could still be disturbed about that?"

Suzie excitedly asks, "Oh, was your name not always Laurie?"

Before I can answer, Joan speaks: "No, Laurie, you did not cause your dad to leave. Maybe he picked up a virus in the plane, on the way here. Or, something may have been bothering him; something unpleasant, perhaps."

I look at Linda and Suzie to explain. "Joan thinks everything is psychological. Even a virus. Right, Joan? You think we should all talk about everything and say our feelings and we should think about the past, even if that makes us sad."

"Well, yes," says Joan, in her self-righteous tone. "Freud said that the events we deliberately don't talk about will come back to haunt us, so we're better off expressing our feelings, talking about our memories, and not keeping our emotions bottled up."

Suzie fidgets, takes an exasperated breath, looks squarely at me and in a quiet, conspiratorial tone says, "Laurie, Freud was not always right."

"I beg to disagree," says Joan, glaring at Suzie. "Freud is still relevant. My work is based on his ideas. The truth must be told. I encourage Laurie to express her feelings in words; that way she won't get sick."

"Joan," I ask, "are you telling me that my dad got sick from feelings? That's crazy."

"It's possible," says Joan, in a snooty way.

Suzie moves closer to me and says, "I'm sure your father will quickly recover." Her words, spoken with kindness, immediately calm me.

Did Dad and Joan talk to each other before he felt sick? Did she say things to him that made him sick? Did she prod him into saying things so ridiculous that he made himself sick? Now I'm starting to think like Dr. Freud. This is stupid.

Suzie turns to me and with a look of tenderness puts her arm around my shoulders. "You do need to become aware of your feelings, Laurie, dear, but you have no obligation to share them. Just be sure you're telling the truth to yourself, know the truth in your heart."

I try to be polite to Suzie. "I don't usually go for this kind of talk. But you're giving me something to think about...I guess."

I wonder, do I really know the truth in my heart? I doubt it. The truth about what, anyway? What am I supposed to look for in my heart? Today I'm disappointed about Dad not being here and I'm nervous about him, too. Those are my feelings. I felt a little better when I told my friends that Dad did something weird, really weird—he traveled all this way and then turned around.

Suzie's observing me so closely I wonder if she's reading my mind. "I'm glad you're thinking about this," she says. "It's important for you to understand that when you feel something, even something bad, something negative, something strong, it's a feeling that belongs to you. It's a message from your brain and your heart."

She's making sense, I guess. I'm lucky because I know how to make myself feel good. I immerse myself in an art project and my bad feelings fade. If I let myself feel what's happening and don't whisk away those feelings, Suzie says I might be able to understand what's going on deep down. Do I want to? Where is deep down and how do I locate it? I'm nervous about looking inside myself, I don't want to find something that's shoved away for good reason. What if the next time I'm upset I do discover the deep reason why I feel that way? What if I know exactly what's bothering me, and what if there's nothing I can do about it? See, I know this is stupid. I will never look within.

Suzie lets go of me, stands, and in a clear voice, loud enough for Joan to hear, says, "Whenever you have a strong physical reaction to something, pause for a moment and try to guess what your body is telling you."

This type of psychological talking scares me, although Suzie does give the best advice of anybody I know. No, maybe Dad's friend Dot is just as good an advice-giver. Suzie said something to me last week that's the same as something Dot told me when I first met her. They both said, "Be careful who you choose for friends. You will turn into your friends." I'd like to turn into Suzie one day. She's level-headed, she's energetic, and she's kind-hearted. I'd be her, but without the psychology stuff.

Joan's listening to everything Suzie's telling me. Joan is not a comforting advice-giver. Here she goes, butting-in with more of her Freud talk. "That's right, Laurie, remember to say your feelings and tell the truth. No secrets."

I can tell that Suzie doesn't like what Joan is saying. Probably doesn't like Joan, altogether. It's obvious that these two ladies are mad at each other. I think they both want to be my Dr. Freud. Suzie moves toward Joan and says, "There's information, secrets, if you will, that I'll take to my grave, and that's acceptable. It's not a sign of psychological problems, it's just my way of having a good life."

"Are you sure about that?" asks Joan, pulling herself up and placing her hands on her hips.

"Yes, I'm sure," Suzie says, with a phony, stiff smile on her face. Linda watches Suzie, then turns to me, and then she looks toward Joan. She shakes her head while saying, "I didn't know The Lodge was so psychological." Shrugging in disbelief she happily makes her way back into the award area, refreshments still being served.

I wish these ladies, Joan and Suzie, had other people to think about. Why me? I ask them, "Why are you both worried about me?"

Joan answers, "Oh, Laurie, I wonder what would happen if you allowed yourself to ask questions about your past. To acknowledge that you might want something that you don't have."

I don't know why she's saying this. She knows I'm not the type who looks back. She and Suzie listen while I clarify, "I have no experience, no practice, in talking about feelings. It's just not my thing."

Joan smiles. "That's good insight, Laurie, it's a beginning." She thinks she's done her job because I mentioned the word *feelings,* so she excuses herself and walks back into the crowd, probably to chat up one of the men.

I stand and don't know what to do. Should I talk to Suzie or follow Joan and Linda into the party room? Suzie makes that decision for me. "Let's walk and talk," she suggests, while hooking her arm through mine. She wants to comfort me, I guess.

As we walk in the school's courtyard she asks if I ever have the opportunity to talk about serious topics when I'm home with my family. I say no, and explain, "Maybe it's because I'm an only child. No sister, no brother."

She's quiet. She wants me to say more. I add, "Also, no mother, and a dad who expresses his deepest emotions only when he's in the hardware store. If emotions start to emerge in our house, he runs for his ice cream to swallow them away." Suzie doesn't see the humor in that.

She seems unsteady on her feet and lurches a little, then catches herself. She's still holding on to me but now it's for her balance, not for my comfort like it was.

She asks if I wish for a larger family. I say, "I wouldn't want a sibling; I like being the center of Dad's attention. Maybe I'd wish for my grandparents to still be alive and to still live with us. Even after they moved to Florida, I had Grandma for vacations. She seemed to know what would be coming next in my life and she'd prepare me, the way a mother would prepare a daughter."

Suzie is hanging on my every word. She's listening so intently that if I didn't know better, I'd think she's mistaken me for a professor and is searching for hidden meanings. She removes her arm from my elbow and places it across my back, gently pushing me toward her. We're both wearing heels, mine a little higher than hers; we're now about the same height. We're so close that I can smell her shampoo—it's Prell.

There's a small table and sitting area up ahead. We hurriedly claim two chairs before the throngs emerge. We sit and enjoy the sunny day while faintly hearing the music. Suzie is gazing at me the way I used to gaze at Master's hair.

I can tell that she's truly interested in me because when she finally stops inspecting my face she asks questions about my life. She says, "Many girls your age wish for some things that they don't have. Or, they wish their life had taken a different path. What has disappointed you, Laurie? What do you wish for?"

"If I've had any disappointments, they mostly have to do with school. The kids were immature and inconsiderate. I didn't fit in with the nerdy ones, I didn't fit in with the athletes, I was not a preppy, and there was no group of artists to join."

We're quiet for a few minutes and then Suzie tells me that she enjoys my company and anytime I'd like to discuss anything with her—even a personal situation—she's available. I thank her and then say that I need to go back inside. "I have to collect my portrait and some other items."

She stops me from fully standing and says, "Laurie, dear, before we part, please tell me how your life has been. Has it been difficult? What are you missing? What are you wishing for?"

Now she's peering into my eyes trying to find some answers. She's waiting for me to delve within, but that's not me. "Suzie, I have no deep, dark secrets. Everybody knows what I want. I want my driver's license and then a car."

CHAPTER NINETEEN

Dot

"LOUIE, I DIDN'T EXPECT YOU TO COME BACK SO SOON. Are you okay?" I ask. He has shambled into the diner. He's bedraggled. His shirt is wrinkled and untucked. He's slouching. Does he have 5-pound weights in each shoe?

"You must have had a bad flight. You look exhausted. You okay? Is Laurie with you?"

"No, Dot, Laurie's not with me. And I'm not okay. I had to get away. I'll go sit in the back. Ask one of the wait staff to bring me some cherry vanilla, please, when you have a minute, and then when the customers leave, we can talk. Take your time. No hurry."

Louie sits, eats, waits. Finally, after I close, doors locked, I make my way to the back booth. He does not offer his usual embrace and loud "Howdy." He remains seated. He remains silent.

"What happened? Is it Laurie? What's wrong with her?" I ask.

Louie eats the last spoonful of his ice cream. He won't meet my eyes.

"I missed the award dinner," he says softly. "I abandoned my daughter."

"What? What happened? Plane problem? Did you get to Chicago?"

He looks up at me and now he's raising his voice: "Oh, I did. I got there and I saw your pal Doc Joan and she ruined my life." His energy is returning. He's frenzied and shouting and trying to catch his breath as he repeats, "I'm ruined. I'm ruined."

I move to the other side of the booth to sit next to him. Placing my arm on top of his, I gently pat his hand and then, when his breathing seems steady, I insist he tell me what happened.

"I'm done, Blondie. I screwed up big time."

This is not my Louie. My Louie is a tough guy. This Louie seems defeated. "Did you have a fight with Laurie?"

"No. I never got to see her. On the plane back I had a fight with myself. I made a mess of Laurie. I did it. I caused her problems."

"Louie, you gave her a good life. What are you talking about?"

"I ruined my daughter and I probably ruined her mother back in Winter Falls, too. It's over. I'm done. It's too late for me. I failed the two people in my life I was supposed to protect."

He pulls away from me and slides to the end of the seat, his back touching the wall. When he finally has the courage to look at me, he reminds me of a little boy lost in a crowded aisle of the A&P.

"You know, Dot, sometimes I believe Suzanne really did die in childbirth. I believe that lie. She might be rotting in a nursing home or she might have died all alone.

And it's my fault. Doc Joan says Laurie is like a robot and she has no authentic feelings. 'Wooden' is the word the doc said. I don't even know what that means but it sounds right. Why else would she run away? Why else would she take up with that criminal? The kid gets hooked up with a criminal and it's all because I told a lie." He puts his head down on the table. "I thought it was good enough. A good secret. A good lie. I'm done, Blondie, I'm done. I just want to sleep. Sleep and never wake up."

"Louie, you have to get past all this. What happened? Did Doc Joan do something to you? Did she block you from seeing Laurie? Did she use a crazy therapy on you? What did she say to you? Tell me."

He looks up at me embarrassedly. "She told me the truth would make me free. No. The truth is killing me."

I'm apprehensive. He wouldn't reveal his secret to Joan, would he? "You didn't tell her about Suzanne, did you?

"Yup."

"Did she tell Laurie?"

"She said she wouldn't tell Laurie. I can't face Laurie now. I can't even face myself."

I wish I knew how to make this better for Louie. He's hurting and he's right, it's because of Joan. I hope I'm not giving him wrong advice when I say, "I'm no shrink, but I know you have to get yourself going. You must get over this. Everybody makes mistakes in life. We have to find out what to do next. You'll be okay. You'll get better. We just need some guidance, some advice."

"Dot, I'm not promising I can get over this. I don't know what to do about Laurie. I ruined her and probably her mother, too."

I'm thinking that if Louie gets himself back to work he will get over this, but I don't know how to help him right now. We're quiet, looking at each other and listening to the lyrics of the song coming from the wall speakers. Ironically, the song is Barry Manilow's, "I Made it Through the Rain." "Louie," I say, "hear these words. You, too, can be the survivor successfully overcoming hardship. Go home, Louie, go home and take a shower, go to sleep, and I'll come over in the morning. I'll have an answer. You know me. I always come up with answers. And Laurie is not ruined."

I don't tell Louie that I'm scared. I don't know Joan. Will she keep her word? Or, will she tell Laurie that her 'dead' mother is alive?

I RING LOUIE'S DOORBELL AT 7 A.M. THE NEXT MORNING. After closing last night I called the family therapist who has an office directly across the street from my diner. I've often helped him out in a pinch—his coffee machine wasn't working and he needed his daily caffeine fix so I sent it over, and more than once he's asked me to prepare a roast beef sandwich that he could run in and nab in the few minutes between patients, so when I asked for quick advice he agreed to listen to my story at the end of his day.

He said, "For the best resolution it's important that your friend go back there. If he goes immediately he'll quickly recover, it will work out. He should speak to his daughter and tell her the truth—that he's fearful he has messed her up."

When I give Louie the advice, he says, "That sounds right. Talking to Laurie will help me. I can leave here anytime. I'm not working. I can't answer my phone. I can't sleep; I'm losing my business, and that's not all I'm losing. I'm also losing my mind."

He's too emotionally fragile to do this alone. I'm tempted to close the diner for a couple of days; this is urgent, but I've never done that and don't want to start a precedent.

"I'm going with you," I say. "Please, Louie, have patience. Take care of yourself and I'll make the arrangements for everything. We'll go soon. Don't worry, Louie, we got this."

Before I leave to get to work, even though it's morning, and even though I am a witness in his kitchen, Louie opens the freezer. He has no shame. In minutes he's savoring the cold vanilla flavor and the luscious cherries. He slowly feeds himself, directly from the half-gallon container. The smooth, silky texture flowing into his mouth gives him comfort. The sweet, creamy taste probably reminds him of happier days, he's calm and he's almost smiling. Louie's inner struggle is on hold while he eats ice cream.

It takes me 24 hours to put together a crew of workers who will keep us open and do what needs to be done. They may not do everything according to my methods, they may seat customers in a way that favors one waitress over another, they may delay serving the salad until the entrée is ready, they may not be swift at refilling water glasses, but Dan's Diner will stay in business in Huntington while I take care of business in Chicago.

THE FLIGHT IS UNEVENTFUL. HERE WE ARE AND I'M impressed with this lodge. I'm in a good mood. Whenever Louie and I take a ride, no matter where we're going, it feels good to be next to him. It feels like we belong together. The outside of this place is huge, the grounds never end. It's green and fresh looking, flowers all around. Inside is not bad, either. Louie barges in—that's my guy, already showing signs he's returning to his ways. Doc Joan doesn't seem to be here. As soon as we're indoors, Louie excuses himself and finds his way into Laurie's room, where she lights up when she sees him.

"I was worried about you," she says as they hug. "The first time I called, you sounded sleepy so we couldn't talk, but the second time I called you said you were too busy to talk, so I assumed you were recovered. What was it, anyway?" Laurie pulls back, looks at her dad, and says, "You look like you always do, so you're healthy now, right? I hope Joan is not mad. She likes to know when guests arrive so she can be here with them. She's out this morning."

I remain near the doorway and just peek in. Laurie can't see me from where she is and I don't want to intrude on the father-daughter relationship, but I do want to be sure Louie has himself under control.

"Honey, I love you," he says, as he sits himself on Laurie's unmade bed. "I'm sorry I wasn't there for your award show. I've been having a tough time. Not feeling so good. I'm sorry, Laurie. I know it's all my fault."

"What are you talking about? What's your fault? Come on, Dad. I'll show you the portrait I did."

"Laurie, first sit down here on the bed next to me."

Laurie does as she's told. She looks puzzled.

He begins, "I need to explain to you that everything I did was for us. It was my job to take care of you and I did. It was my duty, but I did it the wrong way. I could have got other opinions, but I was looking at things only one way, Grandma's way. Maybe there were other ways, but I didn't know about them. I always thought I should keep going no matter what. But now, I don't know. Now I don't know how to keep going."

Laurie puts her head on his shoulder. "Dad, what are you talking about? Don't be so upset that you missed my art show; I'm over it. I'm over the name change thing, too. We can go to Winter Falls together."

"Tell me, Laurie, was I a good enough father?"

"What kind of a question is that? Of course, you were, and you still are."

"But, then, why did you leave for all those months?"

"Oh, Dad, that had nothing to do with you. Just forget about it. I don't think about Master and the others anymore. I'm over them."

"Was it bad, honey, that we never talked about …about your … your mother?"

"Oh, come on, Dad. It wasn't bad. I never knew her, so I never missed her. And I don't like to talk about sad topics anyway. I'm not like Joan and her psychology lectures. Let's go to see your portrait now."

Laurie bounds up and pulls Louie with her. She's full of life; he lumbers behind.

I meet them as they enter the main room. "Oh, Dot, hello. I was hoping you were here, too. Great to see you!" She gives me a warm hug and then asks, "Want to see the portrait I painted? Come on."

"Yes, of course. How are you, Laurie? It's been a while since we've seen each other. You are looking just lovely."

The three of us walk toward the fireplace and there on a sturdy easel is Laurie's watercolor portrait of her father. She certainly is a talented artist. This painting is proof that Louie was a good dad. Love oozes out of every brushstroke. An artist who had blame in her heart could never paint a portrait like this. I hope Louie can see that.

A heavily made-up woman with a messy hairdo and wearing a tight black sweater and a pair of shiny black slacks walks into the main room. She startles when she sees us.

"Oh," she says as she approaches. "You have another person with you. I didn't know Louie had a lady friend. Are you his girlfriend?"

I don't answer that question because it is rude, and also because I don't know the answer. Laurie then introduces me to the woman. She is Joan. I look at her and wonder why Lucky thinks she's a good match for Laurie.

We move on to closely inspect the portrait, we *ooh* and *ahh* and Laurie beams when Louie smiles and says, "Hey, that does look like me. Not bad, Laurie. I'm a good-looking guy, if I may say so myself."

Perhaps I've been worrying for nothing; a flattering portrait is enough to get Louie back to himself.

Joan adds to the compliments and then suggests we each choose a comfortable chair. She then manages to turn the adoring amateur art critics into unwilling participants of a psychotherapy group.

In a serious tone, as if she's addressing a criminal jury, Joan asks "What do you see in that portrait, Louie? What do your eyes tell you about yourself?"

"Oh, come on, Joan, give a guy a break. I'm here to enjoy my daughter not to psychoanalyze my face or my eyes."

"If you ask me," says Joan, "those eyes are trying to say something. Maybe those eyes have something to communicate, maybe they . . ."

I've had enough. I disrupt this conversation. "Maybe it's time for Louie to take good care of himself and get some rest."

With that, I usher Louie away and encourage him to take a snooze on Laurie's bed.

When he is asleep I hesitantly return to the main room. I'm not sure what Joan will spring at me next. I'm surprised at her forthrightness—or is it just plain bad manners? When Laurie steps away to chat with her friend Annette, I sit next to Joan and truthfully respond to her "girlfriend" question.

"Louie is faithful to Suzanne. There is no girlfriend," I say, then lower my voice to a whisper. "You and I are the only ones who know that Suzanne may still be alive. That is, assuming you didn't say anything to Laurie."

"No, of course I wouldn't want to traumatize that poor girl. But her father should find a way to tell her the truth, don't you think?"

"I'm not a therapist so I don't really know."

Joan stiffens with haughtiness and says, "Well, I am a therapist and I do know. Laurie should know the truth and the sooner the better."

Joan certainly is staunch. I try to loosen her up. "I don't think Louie is ready for that task. He's very shaken now."

"If he won't tell her then I will. It is important for her recovery that there be no secrets," says Joan in her unwavering way.

"You are very sure of yourself, aren't you? Does everyone in the mental health field agree with you? Aren't there some counselors who would leave well enough alone?"

"But Laurie is not well," is Joan's quick retort.

"Bringing up this subject has disturbed Louie. Won't the same thing happen to Laurie?"

"We'll soon find out," is her smug answer.

I need some relief from Joan's talk, and from her unblinking eyes, too. I think she might be a crackpot and I'm hoping she has not harmed Laurie in any way. Clearly, she's harmed Louie. This is definitely the end of my asking Lucky for advice. I wonder if I should call Lucky from here to suggest Joan should be reported to some professional association. Laurie wanders back toward us and I don't want to make a scene.

I change the subject. "Let's eat when Louie awakens," I suggest. "Perhaps we can find a nearby place to go to. We haven't eaten since New Jersey."

"I know a nifty diner," says Joan, who assumes she's invited.

WE SLIDE ONTO THE RED VINYL SEATS IN THE BACK ROOM of the Essen Diner. I love to eat at other people's diners, and I can tell that this is my kind of place: A booth, a Formica tabletop bounded by shiny chrome, a miniature jukebox on the table, the requisite metal napkin dispenser, small plastic bowl filled with packets of sugar and packets of sugar substitutes, a plastic ketchup bottle, and a saltshaker.

We order and Joan doesn't wait to be served before diving in. "Don't you have something to say to your daughter?" she asks Louie.

Louie says, "Maybe later, Joan. Take it easy."

"Maybe now, Louie. It's time to come clean. No more lies. No more secrets."

I glare at Joan.

Laurie asks, "What's going on? What are you talking about?"

Joan responds, "Your dad needs to explain some things to you. I can get him started."

"What things?" asks Laurie.

Joan ignores her. "Laurie," she says, "it seems to me that during your high school years you may have suffered from depression."

I'm as surprised as Louie is. Why is she mentioning depression? Why is she making this a medical conference?

We're both relieved when Laurie says slowly, "Okay. And if I was depressed some days why is it a big deal now?"

"It is a big deal," says Joan. "It's a big deal because there is a genetic component to mental illness. If you come from a family where someone's suffered through a major depression, or any other psychiatric illness, you should know about it. Just like you'd want to know if heart conditions ran in your family."

"Okay. If you say so," Laurie shrugs, then looks to me, clearly confused.

"Let's take a break from conversation and start eating," I say, as the waitress arrives with our orders. Lamb shank, Shrimp Newburgh, sirloin steak done just right, pork chops, and each dish accompanied by a Jell-O salad with walnuts—not what we'd find on a New Jersey menu, and the presentation is not quite up to my diner's standards, but the waitress is charming and after the first few bites we all agree the food is tasty.

Laurie plays with her shrimp, doesn't eat much of her sides, and instead continues the conversation with Joan. "I don't get it. Why are you picking on me and why are you picking on my dad?"

Joan commands Louie. "Louie, say the truth! Secrets are poison."

Louie begins to stand. "Let's go, Dot," he says to me, and is annoyed when I remain seated. "Why are you still sitting? Let's get out of here."

Laurie leans across the table to confront Joan, practically nose-to-nose, and says, "Look what you're doing to my dad. My father doesn't lie to me, so stop telling him to say the truth. He always tells the truth. Your talk about depression is getting all of us depressed. Look what you are doing to him, he can't even eat his dinner, and I've lost my appetite, too."

Laurie turns to Louie and to me, deliberately excluding Joan. "I appreciate that you came all this way and I'm sorry to do this to you but I need to leave here. Joan is getting on my nerves and I must take a break from her. I'm really sorry. I love you both so much. Thank you for coming. I'll see you back at The Lodge. I promise we'll have plenty of time together tomorrow." She frees herself from the booth and bolts toward the exit. At the door she looks back and shouts, "Sorry, again, Dad. We'll catch up tomorrow, I promise."

"Where are you going?" yells Joan. "Come back, Laurie, come back."

Laurie turns toward us, sneers at Joan, and says, "I'm going where I feel comfortable. I'm calling my ladies. They're at the student lounge at ACA right now."

We watch Laurie sail out the door and I convince Louie to sit and resume eating. I whisper comments to him every so often and I do not include Joan in our conversation.

But, before dessert, Joan starts in on Louie for the umpteenth time. "Do you know if Laurie's mother is alive? You told me she became mentally ill. Did she get better? Where is she? Your neglect of your wife has a deep effect on your daughter. Your daughter can't feel love if you have broken her bond with her mother."

I won't let this continue. "Stop it, Joan, stop it right now. Louie has a heart of gold. He raised that girl to the best of his ability. How dare you come along and doubt his love." I then signal the waitress. "Some cherry vanilla ice cream for the gentleman, please."

CHAPTER TWENTY

Laurie

I DECIDE TO CALL A CAB. IT'S EMPOWERING TO DO THAT and to know I have enough money in my wallet to give a good tip, too. I'm grateful for Dad. The conversations we've had lately mean the world to me. Even though we probably didn't talk about the things Joan has in mind, I don't care because Dad has hugged me and told me he loved me more times than I could count.

It's true that thinking is not my favorite activity, but I would like to understand Joan's obsession with secrets and lies, and now mental illness and depression, too. What could she want from my dad? She insists he's got something to tell me.

He's not one to tell me if there's something serious on his mind. He's not the serious type, especially now that his father is gone. I can still remember when years ago I would hear him discussing important things with my grandfather. After dinner they talked about money and business and sometimes Grandpa would urge Dad to go out and have a social life. He would say, "You're only young once." Eavesdropping, I would wonder why he thought my dad was young.

All those years Dad never did have a social life. Now that he's not so young it looks like he has one with Dot. Could the secret be that he did have a secret social life years ago? Could Dot be an old girlfriend who just became public now? Maybe she used to be married. But Joan wouldn't know that. Could Dad be having serious financial trouble? Are we running out of money because of the expense of The Lodge? Joan might know if that were the situation. Does Dad have a secret illness? Joan wouldn't know that.

Even though Dad doesn't talk about his emotions, it's apparent that he's happiest when he's planning a project for a customer. When is he unhappy? I have no clue. Maybe never. Was he unhappy when his parents moved away? He never mentioned it. When his parents died? Probably, but he didn't say anything to me.

Enough thinking; we've arrived and I'm out of the cab in a second and dash right through the doorway. Energy fills this building. Lively melodies from the music students, bright paintings from the artists, tantalizing aromas from the chefs; creativity abounds. I see that my ladies are at our usual table and I'm feeling healed already.

I walk toward them and see Linda aiming her camera at Irma and at Suzie. "Don't smile," she says, "just talk to each other. Look into each other's eyes while you speak. That's it. Now look up at me for a second. Perfect. Got it."

Irma's passing around a tray loaded with her newest concoction—a cinnamon roll baked with maple syrup and pecans, and Suzie is talking about her experience with prisoners. "I met some nice men. Yes, they did bad things. But still they were nice, they were sincere, and I believe some of them will become law abiding."

"How can you be sure?" asks Emily. Coming from the music studio, she's arrived at the table the same time as I.

"There are no guarantees," says Suzie, "but writing about their life and reflecting on their experiences does give them understanding." She smiles at me and Emily. "Take a seat, both of you are just in time to hear me tell everyone about my prisoners."

"Were you scared of them?" asks Linda, as she packs up her camera and all its equipment.

"Nothing scary about them, and anyway, we always had a bodyguard kind of guy with us. I know we did a good job because one of the inmates liked the writing class so much that he wants to become a writer."

"Did they write about their crimes?" Linda asks. "Do you have information that the police might want now?"

Suzie answers with her usual sweet yet authoritative voice. "You're a serious reader, Linda, and you love your mystery stories, but remember I was their writing instructor, not their lawyer. They wrote honestly about their lives and their feelings." When Suzie criticizes it sounds like a compliment and her smile never goes away.

"Feelings? Suzie, Joan would love your job. She's big into feelings," I say.

I turn to Irma and quip, "Your goodies are giving me feelings—happy, contented feelings—thank you."

Suzie tells us about one of the older guys who talked about growing up with an inferiority complex because of terrible parents. "Did he murder his parents?" Irma asks.

"No. Nothing like that. Nothing violent. This guy honestly admitted that the only way he could feel good about himself was when young people called him a master. He forced kids to pretend to worship him."

I've been only been half-listening, enjoying the normalcy of being back at this table, but that last comment startles me. I am quickly alert. "What? Wait. Where was the prison?" I ask with a shaky voice. "Was it in Wisconsin?"

"Yes, in Milwaukee."

"How old was this old guy? Did he have white hair?"

Suzie's eyes widen with surprise. "Yes. Good guess. The other inmates called him Whitey."

I'm finished with Master and with all the people there. But, if I could see him one more time and know that he's somehow managing his life, I would feel much better about myself. I did leave him unexpectedly and that really wasn't fair. I was one of the few who was able to relax him. And he did count on me for money. I know I'm done with Master. But, still.

I try to hide my excitement and coolly ask, "Are you going back there, again? I'd like to see a prison. Maybe I could go with you."

"No. I finished my internship, so I won't be going back." Suzie shakes her head back and forth in concern and adds, "Believe me, you wouldn't want to go there."

"Enough prison talk," says Linda. "When are you girls done in Chicago? I hope you're not gone before I have a chance to develop these photos and give them to you as mementos. Just in case, I'll take your home mailing address." She has a slip of paper that she hands me and I pass it on to Emily after I jot down my New Jersey information.

I answer first. "I think I'm done. I'm feeling better than ever, I'm not in danger of going back to my group, and it's time to leave because Doc Joan is too harsh to me and to my dad. She bosses him around and wants him to tell me things."

"What does she want him to tell you?" asks Linda.

"I don't know, and I don't care. What he tells me is none of her business."

Linda says, "Well ... she is a therapist."

I'm tempted to inform Linda that Joan may not be a real therapist, but I don't want to get into that. Instead I say, "I'm healthy enough. I already have plans for when I get back home. I'll get my license and get a car and then I'll look for a job. She shouldn't be worrying about me. I can earn a living by painting portraits; a small living, but people will pay me."

Suzie wants to know more. "What do you think Joan is bugging your dad about? What topic?"

"Oh, something about some secrets or lies. I don't really know. She likes to talk psychology stuff and it's way too confusing for me. She makes a big deal about everything."

Suzie is into this. "Are you curious about the secrets?" she asks in a voice overflowing with curiosity.

"No. Secrets remind me of high school with all the nasty girls."

I think back to my high school days. Those secrets were never important to me. They were ways to make some kids feel bad and other kids feel like big shots. And in my days away at Master Academy there were secrets there, too. Anna and Tom never told me that they were sent out to find me. I thought they just saw me and liked me. Secrets

are stupid. Joan likes to dwell on things to make herself
feel like a big shot. She gets stuck on one topic and tries to
psychoanalyze it forever.

To change the subject I ask Suzie, "In that prison you
went to, can anyone just come in to visit an inmate?"

"No, of course not. Why are you so interested in prison life?"

"Oh, nothing. I'm just thinking that the prisoners probably get lonely."

I WAS RIGHT—I EASILY GET A LIFT BACK TO THE LODGE.
My ladies are always accommodating. When I walk in, I
see Joan flipping through a copy of *Romance Magazine*.
That's a peculiar choice for her but I don't say anything.
She waves to me as if nothing happened during our dinner.

I sit on the couch and ask her, "Where are my dad
and Dot?"

"They went to the motel down the road. They said
they'll come by in the morning."

"Was my Dad okay?"

Joan looks up with nastiness imprinted on her face. "Yes.
His lady friend takes good care of him."

"Joan, my ACA mamas didn't get me upset. Not for
one minute. Why can't you and I get along like that? Stop
telling my dad how to talk to me, I know you, you want
him to talk to me like a shrink. He's a grown up; he knows
what to say to his daughter."

"Oh, Laurie," says Joan as she pulls her chair closer to
the couch. "Life is not so simple. Sometimes we have to be

ruthless to get at the truth. The truth may be painful, may be brutal, but it must be exposed"

"That sounds cruel. Did Freud tell you that?" I snipe.

"Well, yes, he does espouse saying everything."

I just might say everything to Joan right now. Instead I mind my manners and change the subject.

I pick up one of the many brochures that Joan has floating around the main room. They're from various hotels, motels, lodges, and resorts. She insists new guests will come if The Lodge is as beautiful as the photos in these booklets. I suggest, "We might be able to drum up some new business if we go to the prison my friend Suzie worked at for her internship. Remember? I told you about it, it's in Milwaukee. Do you think we can get in? Do you think we can visit prisoners? It might be interesting. You always want me to be interested in new things, right?" I don't think a men's prison will get Joan new business, so I call it a prison, not a men's prison. Joan is money hungry and asks me to get the contact information from Suzie.

"Perhaps we'll take a drive one day next week, after your dad leaves. You're right. It'll be a good opportunity for you to see something new and it will be a learning experience for both of us. In the worst case, you and I will have plenty of time to talk in the car and that's a good thing."

I knew she'd think it's a good thing. Whenever my grandma wanted to talk to me about something serious or tell me something important, she would say, "Let's take a drive, Laurie." When we were in the car, trapped with each other, but not facing each other, she'd bring up a topic such as my homework habits or "my maturing body," as she put it. Awkwardness would be gone by the time we reached our destination and then we could look at each other without embarrassment. It worked every time.

THE NEXT DAY IS WARM AND PLEASANTLY SUNLIT. I WALK with Dad and Dot away from The Lodge and away from Joan. They had been meeting with her on their own so I don't think it rude to exclude her. I proudly announce, "I can't remember the last time I had a headache or a stomach ache or a 'can't-get-out of-bed' day."

Dad says, "I noticed you smiling, fooling around with your friends, enjoying music. It's all good, honey."

Dot asks if my new-found serenity—she doesn't say happiness—is from hanging around with women. She names Joan, Emily, Annette, and then adds, 'and those three women from your school and your art teacher, too." Could be.

It was a good visit all around, and within one week after Dad and Dot return to New Jersey, Joan secures two visitor applications. We're both approved to come to the prison. Sunday is visiting day and prisoners can spend thirty minutes in the supervised guest area. Wisconsin here we come. We've been warned that up until the last minute it's possible that prisoners' visiting privileges may be revoked, but since we don't have a definite person in mind to visit probably the trip won't be for naught if that happens—even if some are punished there will be others allowed to get visitors.

Eagerly, we get going. I'm trying not to get my hopes up, but that doesn't work. In the car I confess. "Joan, I have something to say."

"Sure, Laurie, I'm listening."

"Well, you always stress honesty and no secrets. This is not exactly a secret."

"Laurie, you can say anything to me."

"I hope you won't be mad at me. No. Never mind. It's nothing."

Joan just keeps driving, her eyes on the road. After a few minutes of silence she says, "I told you all about the things I've done wrong in my life. You can tell me anything. There's nothing you can say that will change our relationship."

Before I lose my nerve I swiftly say, "I want to go to the prison because I think that there's a prisoner there who I might know."

"Really? And who would that be?" asks Joan.

"It's Master," I say in a rush of words. "But I promise I don't want to do anything with Master Academy anymore. I just wonder where he ended up. I promise I'm not interested in re-connecting."

It's a long stretch before Joan speaks again.

"Thanks for your honesty. We'll soon find out. This is a good test to determine if you really are finished with that part of your life. You've made progress in my Lodge program, so if it is Master, how will you respond if he tries to persuade you to return to his lifestyle?"

"First of all, Master Academy was shut down. And secondly, I like my life better now. I like having a future that's more than just turning out art for Master to sell. I'm done with him, but I don't want you to think bad of him. He was decent and good most of the time."

"It's probably not him, anyway," says Joan, "so we have nothing to worry about."

We've followed the instructions on the Visitor forms, we're both wearing long sleeves and show no bare skin. We've been prepared for our car to be searched, but we are surprised when they search us, too. Gross.

We are led around a corner to a long hallway. Sitting on the floor, in front of a door, is a guy who could either be a prisoner or a guard or a downtrodden vagrant. He doesn't look up when we pass. His eyes are closed and his head is bent forward. If he had a guitar in his lap I'd think he was Picasso's *The Old Guitarist* come to life.

Finally, we're escorted to the guest area. Four prisoners at a time are permitted to enter for "social visit," an afternoon where guests can visit a select group of non-violent offenders. Four prisoners walk in and sit on a bench. Joan and I are directed to a bench opposite them.

There is a glass barrier between us, but the person in charge of the visiting program assures us that we can speak in normal tones and our voices will be heard. Joan immediately tests this out. "Hello. How do you do? I'm Joan, a therapist from the Chicago area. Don't worry, I'm not here to be a therapist. And this is my friend, Laurie. And your names are…?"

The four young men introduce themselves and smile at me. They're looking at me, checking me out the way high school boys do. It's been a long time since male attention. I wish it wasn't from guys who are locked up.

Joan tries again, "I have a lodge. It's like a spa. If you know a young woman, perhaps your sister or a neighbor from home, who is looking for a getaway to try out a new way of life, well that's what we do at The Lodge."

They are still ignoring her, preferring to look at me. So I ask, "Where is Jon?"

"No Jon here, ma'am."

I try again. "You know, the older man with white hair."

"Oh, you mean Whitey. He doesn't like to come out to visitors. He's not so social. We guys like to meet new people. Whitey doesn't."

Devon, the only one whose name I remember, finally pays some attention to Joan. He asks, "He your man?"

"I don't know any prisoners," says Joan. She stiffens and adds, "I'm a therapist."

I look pleadingly at Devon. "Can you ask Whitey to come out? Tell him Amelia's here."

"No, I don't think so. If I go back, I won't be able to come out again."

I persist. "Please. Do it as a favor to me. We came all this way. Please."

"I thought your name was Laurie," says Devon at the same time that Joan asks me who Amelia is.

What?!? When I was pouring my heart out to Joan was she not listening? I did tell her during more than one of our many talk sessions that I had been called Amelia. I can't believe this. She forgot such an important bit of information. I can't look at her. Suzie would be proud of me because I know why I'm feeling strong negative feelings.

I implore Devon again. Finally, he relents, giving me a wink as he leaves. Joan makes odd small talk with the other men while I continue to look at the door and at the wall clock. What if it's really him? What if it's not? What if it is and then our time is up before he arrives? I wait and I worry.

And then he appears. His tag says Jon Ligner, and other than his hair being boldly white he barely resembles the Master I knew and almost loved. What happened to his handsomeness, his haughty presence? He used to be vibrant and vigorous, he's now gaunt and moves in slow-motion. He keeps his head down as he sluggishly puts himself into the chair across from us.

When he finally looks up, he ignores me completely; his eyes widen in disbelief at Joan. "Hello, ma'am. Thank you for visiting. I'm Jon, although the guys call me Whitey. I appreciate that you made the trip here."

Sitting up straighter as she introduces herself, Joan smiles broadly. "And what would you like me to call you, sir? You do have pure white hair. It's no wonder they call you Whitey. Your hair is a sight to behold."

"Why, thank you."

Jon then glances at me and quickly looks away.

"It's me," I say, "Amelia. Don't you recognize me? I'm Amelia."

"I know who you are," he says and then refocuses on Joan. "How was your ride here? Where are you coming from?"

Joan tells him about her lodge and asks, "Do you ever have people who need a safe place to rehabilitate? Do you have a wife or a girlfriend who needs some guidance to change her life?"

"No, ma'am. I have no wife and no girlfriend," he responds with a smile. Joan returns the smile while smoothing her hair.

She asks, "What about you, Jon? Where will you go when you are released?"

"Ma'am, my future is not clear."

"Please call me Joan."

Jon abruptly turns toward me. "You should not be here. This is no place for a young girl from a loving family. I met your dad, remember? I know you have love in your life. You shouldn't be here. Go home. Why did you come all this way? There is no more Master Academy community. That's all gone. You're a lucky girl. You have love."

I dissolve into tears. Why is he mean to me? I was always good to him. I don't understand. I was important to him; I know I was.

Joan and Master continue speaking as if I'm not in the room.

Master ignores my crying. "This girl has a dad who takes good care of her and loves her," he tells Joan. "She should stay away from the likes of me. Joan, do you have love in your life?"

"Well, I love my home and I love my work."

"What about a husband? A pretty lady like you probably has one, right?"

Joan demurely smiles. "No, not a husband … yet."

I pull myself together, wipe my tears, take a long, deep breath and say to Master--or Jon or Whitey or whoever he is, "You owe me money, you know. All my artwork that you sold."

"You and many others, my dear. I am aware of my debts and transgressions."

"Laurie, everyone is entitled to make mistakes," Joan says sweetly. "It's recovering from them and then learning from them that makes us all better people."

"Yes," says Jon. "I agree."

Joan moves her head from side to side, if she had long hair she'd be tossing it. Master concentrates on her every word. I'm invisible to them.

Soon, the guard interrupts. "Five-minute warning. Visiting over in five minutes."

"Quick, Joni, give me your phone number. Maybe we'll be able to visit again," says Jon.

Joan complies, hastily scribbling her name, address, and phone number on a scrap of paper. She also finds out on which days Jon is permitted to receive calls. I watch everything. I have strong feelings and I know why I have them.

In the car ride back to the Lodge Joan asks me about Jon. "Did he have a wife? A steady girlfriend? Do you know when he will be released?"

"I don't know and I don't care. Didn't you tell me to put all this behind me? Well, now I can. I'm done with Master."

Joan doesn't respond. Although she's driving, she's deep in thought. I pay attention to the road so I can alert her if a red light is coming up. I'm definitely more well-adjusted than Joan.

"I once knew someone who was a lawyer in Milwaukee. Maybe she can help him. I'll call her tomorrow," muses Joan when she finally speaks. "There's something about Jon that makes me think I've known him forever."

IT WAS DISAPPOINTING TO SEE MASTER IN PRISON. AM I disappointed in him for being a law-breaker or in me for devoting myself to him for all that time? What makes a girl do that? Would Grandma have stopped me if she were alive? Does every teenage girl go bonkers if she doesn't have an older woman to guide her?

It's also disappointing to see Joan act like a teenager, but I can handle these disappointments. I guess I really am resilient. That's what Joan has been encouraging me to work toward and I'm there. I do occasionally wonder about Anna and Tom and all the other kids, but that's probably normal.

I have my last class with El Newman this week and then I'll pack up all my stuff from ACA and from the Lodge. I want to be home to start my normal life, and to get away from Joan. She might be nuts.

Just when I'm about to plan my getaway, Joan comes up with an idea that's appealing enough to keep me here longer. She would like to invite my mama friends from ACA and also El, to The Lodge, for a little farewell party. Also, the other girls' families and some community folks. Dad may want to come, too. Come to think of it, I haven't heard from him in a while. He must be overloaded with work.

After dinner Joan says she has something important to discuss with me. She probably wants to know more about Master, or Jon, as she calls him. She's been making calls on his behalf and writing to him, too. She has a poster in her office that quotes Freud. It says, *I cannot think of any need in childhood as strong as the need for a father's protection.* I am sure that she's been discussing that saying with Master. He told all of us in Master Academy that he was our protection. But now he thinks my own father is better protection than he is. He's right, of course, but he changed his mind rather swiftly.

I actually dread going into her office. Lately, the more I know of her, the more I think she might be not just weird but maybe dangerous or just plain out of her mind. Of course I had to tell Annette and Emily. "She's infatuated with a criminal. I know he's a criminal. I was once under his spell, too," I explain to them.

Annette asks me, "Is this bad for you? Does it bring back memories you don't want to have?"

"No," I answer. With all of Joan's ridiculousness, I must admit there is some good to her, or at least her work. "Honestly," I say, " I'm over Master. I'm over Master Academy. I'm my own person now. And I guess I'm over Joan, too."

It's true; I'm strong. All the more reason to leave. I tell Annette and Emily that I doubt their parents would approve of Joan's relationship with Jon. My father certainly would want me to leave as soon as possible, and I will. This little party and then home to New Jersey.

I'm on my way into her office now. As soon as I walk in, Joan says, "Please take a seat, Laurie. We have some final business to take care of."

"Oh, no. Does my dad owe you some money? When I last spoke to him he was taking some days off from work because he wasn't feeling too good. I know he'll pay you." All of a sudden, I'm chewing on my bottom lip.

"That too, but this has nothing to do with money. It's much more important. I need to talk to you about truth and lies and secrets. You know that I believe secrets cause problems."

"You believe that and so does your Dr. Freud, I know."

"Well, even though your life is on a good track now, I thought we should talk about why you got derailed, why you were sad, and why you ran away from home. I think it's because of your mother."

I brace myself. "You do know that my mother's dead, right? No wonder you hit it off with Master, I mean Jon. He communicates with my mother."

"That's what we need to discuss, Laurie. What if you learned that she is alive? Would that change your life?"

Why is she stuck on this? Maybe part of Joan's craziness is that she thinks dead people are really alive? That must be it. She has a hang-up about death. I'm sitting here with a delusional woman. I try to stay calm and talk sense into her.

"My mother died the day I was born. Everybody knows that. Stop talking nonsense," I patiently say as if speaking to a small child.

"Aren't you curious? You know how some adopted kids want to find their birth mother, this could be similar. The idea that your mom might still be living could be worth investigating."

"Please stop," I say, and my eyes go to the door. Why is Joan obsessed with my past. Maybe she really needs to investigate her past. I am secure. My grandmother loved me and never did anything to harm me. My father loves me and would never do anything to harm me. I'm certain of that. Would either of them know something that might harm me? If they did, would they tell me? Honestly, I hope not. I like my life now. I know with all my heart that my grandma and Dad have always protected me and taken good care of me. Curiosity killed the cat.

I look at Joan, she's hugging herself and rocking back and forth—and she is not sitting in a rocking chair. She's also mumbling something too low for me to hear. She's rocking and rocking and mumbling and mumbling.

"Enough!" I shout, interrupting her conversation with herself. "Stop. You're making me nervous. Why are you doing this? Because you want me to investigate my mother's death? You know that sounds crazy, right? I've heard of runaway wives. That could happen. But I never heard of a dead mother running away. I never heard of a mother who died in childbirth coming back to life. If that's what you're implying you are wrong. Dead wrong."

Finally, she opens her eyes and stops rocking. "You're right. You know yourself and you know what you need to know."

I'll never again trust this kook. Let's have the party and get out of town. It'll all go smoothly if I'm nice to her and I can do that knowing my escape is in sight. I'll alert Annette and Emily that Joan is getting wackier by the minute; they may want to leave earlier, too.

I smile at Joan and say, "Okay. You're talking my language. Now let's go over our plans for the event. It will be your annual gala and my farewell party."

CHAPTER TWENTY-ONE

Dot

AS SOON AS I ANSWER THE RINGING PHONE I HEAR A CLICK on the line, a pause, and then, "Oh, Blondie, it's been a rough day," Louie murmurs.

"You sound awful. Are you sick?"

"I wish it were that simple," he says, voice flat.

"Do you want me to come over?"

"No, Blondie, I'm not home. That's why I couldn't call to let you know."

"Let me know what? Where are you?"

"You know how I haven't been myself lately? You know how some days I couldn't get to work? Well, last night I couldn't take it anymore. All those memories of talking to Doc Joan. All those thoughts about how I ruined Laurie. I..."

He is scaring me. "Louie, what did you do? What did you do?"

"I didn't do anything. It was my body that did it. It was my head that got dizzy. It was my feet that flew me down the stairs."

I feel myself wilting with every word he says. "What are you talking about? Where are you, Louie?"

"I'm at Overlook Hospital, the one on top of the hill in Truesdale Center."

As always, I get my strength back when there's a task to do. "I'll be right there. I know where the Emergency Room is."

"I wish I could tell you I'm in the ER, but, no. They think I'm a danger to myself and they locked me up. It's true, Dot. I'm in the psych ward. They took away my shoelaces and my belt. They think I'm a nut case."

This is outrageous. I thought he was getting back to himself. I thought work would cure him. That Joan really did him in. I know he's a good person. I know he's normal and regular. He was a stable person until Joan got hold of him. I try to hide my blaze of anger and in my best nurturing voice ask, "What exactly happened, Louie? Tell me, please, from the beginning."

He tells me that he couldn't stop thinking about his conversation with Joan after we returned, and that every day since he has relived his abandonment of his wife. It got so bad that he didn't go into work—just ignored appointments and calls, and he stayed at home pacing around in circles.

"Finally, I decide to open some mail that's been on my desk for more than a week. One envelope turns out to be from Doc Joan. I thought it would be good news about Laurie coming home. You know, like a report card telling me all the progress about my girl. But that wasn't it. It was another bill. A big one. I always do the right thing, Blondie. I always take care of my family. But when I miss jobs I don't get paid."

"And that's why you tumbled down the stairs?" I'm not sure what to do. Is he being rational and thinking clearly? Maybe he does belong at Overlook in the psychiatry ward. What am I getting myself into?

"Honestly, Dot, I was going to the freezer. I figured some ice cream would calm me. And the next thing I knew I was downstairs, opening my eyes and crawling to the phone to get help. There were cuts on my arm, blood on my shirt. The cops came, the paramedics came, they took me to Overlook and when I told the nurses that I was angry at myself, and I hadn't slept in days, and I couldn't manage to work, they said I had to be watched over. And so here I am."

"It's not so unusual to do dumb things when we're upset." I try to normalize this, for his sake and for mine, too.

'Not like this, Dot. Not like this. I can't get over it. I ruined my kid."

My big strong guy is sensitive and scared. I try to convince him that Laurie is not ruined. "She's a lovely young woman. She's talented, she's considerate, and she's no longer interested in running away. Look at her through my eyes, not Joan's," I beg him. But he continues.

"I think Joan's right. Laurie was depressed in high school and I didn't even notice. What kind of a father doesn't notice his kid is depressed? And she had no mother. That's serious, Dot, very serious."

My blaze returns and I shout into the phone, "Louie, stop it right now!"

"Take it easy, Blondie," he says, "I never heard you raise your voice before."

"I won't take it easy, Louie, because you have it all wrong. You've been bullied. You listen to me, Louie. Put one foot in front of the other and get back to yourself. You did your best. Nothing was your fault and Laurie is okay now. That's all that matters."

"But I didn't tell her the truth about her mother."

"You don't know the truth. Think about that. Where is Suzanne now? You don't even know if she's alive, and if she is, you don't know if she's in a hospital or maybe living in another country or maybe married and living on a farm in Iowa with five kids."

"Dot. I did wrong."

"Secrets are not always wrong. Sometimes they're necessary. Come on, Louie, you are the guy who is always ready to act, ready to fix things. You're a strong man. I count on you. Get a grip, Louie, I need you."

He's quiet, absorbing my words. "You need me, Blondie? You do?" For the first time, he sounds a tiny bit hopeful.

"Of course, I do. You're the guy who keeps going, no matter what. No bully can shame you. Be proud of how you raised your daughter. Be proud of all you've accomplished. You are…"

"Sorry to interrupt. They're calling me. Try to do your magic, Dot, and get me out of here, okay? I need to go now and only one call each day is allowed. It's a little like jail and they're not doing anything for me, anyway."

I hope the hospital doctors understand Louie. Sometimes he acts tough in a way that could scare people if they don't see his sweet side, too. Sometimes his words are from the street and his manners rough. I hope he doesn't give the professionals at the hospital the wrong impression.

I HAVE CUSTOMERS WHO WORK ALL OVER THIS TOWN. JUST about everyone in Huntington has been in my diner and I know them all and I know what they do and where they do it. 'Meatloaf with Sauce on the Side' comes in every Wednesday and he works at Overlook Hospital. I get to the phone and track him down. I plead my case and he provides me with a name and extension number.

It takes several calls and many minutes on hold to cut through the layers of administrators and finally reach the pivotal person. In three days, the hospital management gets it right and a good doctor comes in to talk to Louie. Two more days and he is released with instructions to make an out-patient appointment with a counselor.

"Can you be my counselor?" he asks when I come to pick him up.

"No, but I will help you get back to yourself."

"But I don't want to be like those people who rely on a shrink before they make a move. I know what to do in life."

"Therapy can help you have an even better life. Obviously, Joan was not right for you."

"I could have told you that. That's why I didn't want therapy from her. I never signed up for it, but she did her damage anyway."

I must find a good shrink for Louie. I know many people who've had terrific experiences with the right therapist. I know people who credit therapy with giving them a good life, a good marriage, and more.

"Louie, please go into your house and retrieve your messages from the answering machine. Customers need to hear from you. Your business needs you. It's your duty to keep going no matter what. That's what a father does and that's what a business owner does."

I don't like to be tough, but he needs toughness now.

"I'll drop you off at home and I'll come back after I close tonight. You get your work going, Louie. Reschedule your appointments. I know you. Work is your therapy."

He begins working again and keeps up a good pace. Our life resumes. I stop worrying about him. Each week he puts in six full days and manages it all. At the end of my workdays I stop in to his house, bringing food from the diner. We put on mellow music, we eat, and we talk. Often, he talks to me as if I were a therapist. I'm not sure that's a good thing.

This evening there were several calls on his machine from Laurie, each saying, "Hi, Dad, call me. I'm ready to come home and I'd like you to attend the final ceremony here at The Lodge."

When Louie calls her I hear his part of the conversation: "Okay, honey. I'll be there. Dot's going to come with me. She soothes me and I need that these days. I promise we'll show up at your graduation."

It warms my heart to hear him speak about me like that. When he gets off the phone I join him on the couch. These last few weeks have been particularly good for him. I see my old Louie coming back. This is the right time for me to give him my commitment speech. I've been preparing it and rehearsing it for a while. Some people might not call it a commitment speech; they might say it's a proposal, a marriage proposal.

"Louie," I begin, "I like the way we help each other and ..."

He interrupts, "I beg to differ. You help me, but I haven't helped you in a long time. Not since new tiles for the diner, way back when."

He's making it easy for me. I continue, "In the course of a relationship there are times when one person needs more help and times when the other does. That's why it's good to know that a relationship is not temporary."

"I know that," he says. He looks at me quizzically. "You talking about us? Of course we're not temporary. I'm at the diner almost every day, and you stop in here almost every evening. Anybody who's paying attention knows we're not temporary."

"Louie," I say, as I wave my left hand in front of him, "a girl needs a signal to other men that she is taken."

He is quietly contemplating my flapping fingers. "What do you mean? ... A ring?" he asks. "You mean you want to ...what? Get married?"

My heart begins to pound. "I've thought of that, Louie. How about you?"

"I thought we could just stay like we are. Aren't you happy, Dot?"

I am truly happy that Louie is in my life. And Laurie, too. Of course I'm concerned about Laurie's mother. I suppose she could show up at any time. And then what?

Much of life has passed me by but now I'm in the thick of it with Louie and Laurie, and it's good. We could be a real family, do family things, live in a family home. I'd be proud wearing a ring from Louie. An engagement ring, a wedding ring, it's what my parents wished for me. I'm sorry they didn't live long enough to meet Louie.

I move closer to him, look up into his eyes, and say, "Yes. I'm happy. Louie, it's time for you to decide our future. I'm not saying another word."

It's difficult, but I stay quiet. Not another word.

He's silent for what seems like forever, then he puts his arm around me and quietly says, "Blondie, you're right. It's time for me to tell you how much I love you. I thought you knew."

And this evening Louie does seduce me, and I do spend the night in his disheveled bedroom. We awaken nestled together, smiling. I don't notice the dirty socks under the night table until morning when I sit up, place my feet on the floor, and hear the crunch of candy wrappers. That's when I look down and see everything, but by then he'd showed me his annulment decree and we'd already talked about a wedding.

"I'm scared. I admit it," Louie says, one night at his kitchen table, after dinner. "She might run away again."

Now that we're engaged, we discuss everything. I'm still his counselor, he hasn't looked for another, and his gloominess is hard for me to bear.

I know what I want to say to him, but I'm not sure if it's what a real counselor would say. I try my best. "Louie, anything can happen. Let's deal with the reality. She's coming home and she's better. Think about today, not yesterday."

"I can't help it, Dot. Yesterday is on my mind all the time now. How did I go for years without ever looking back, without ever worrying that I was harming my daughter?" His chin is on his chest and shame is on his face.

I reach across the table, over the plates, over the bowls, and grasp both of Louie's hands. "Stop worrying about Laurie. Lots of people keep secrets. Sometimes information can do more harm than good."

Louie squeezes my hands, and says, "Blondie, I'd be lost without you. Did you mean it when you said you need me?"

I nod, Louie relaxes, and we speak softly, planning our future and enjoying the comfort of truth.

CHAPTER TWENTY-TWO

Joan

THERE'S SOMETHING REASSURING AND SOOTHING ABOUT Jon. He's had bad breaks in life, but he's a positive thinker now. Prison rules allow me to call him once a day, except on weekends, and I do. Our conversations invariably start like this:

"Hi, Jon. How are you doing today?"

"I'm missing you, Joni, when are you coming to visit me?"

And then he tells me what he's thinking about and what he's learning in his daily mandatory counseling sessions. Today he said, "When I leave here I want to work hard. I want to experience contentment from dealing with people honestly. I used to think that taking from others was the sign of a winner, but I've changed, matured. I know now that taking depletes you; it's giving that fulfills you. I used to think that it was nice to be important, now I know it's important to be nice."

It warms my heart to hear Jon speak like that. "Jon, I'm trying to arrange a one-day release for you so you can come see what I'm doing here at the Lodge."

"If you can do that, I'd be most appreciative."

Our phone conversations are deep. I'm more comfortable talking to Jon about my innermost thoughts and dreams and memories than I was with the shrink provided by therapy school. I quit that shrink. I won't quit Jon.

That shrink, Dr. Nebb, was fascinated by my parents. He couldn't believe that they cared more about their swindles than about their daughter. He thought I was misremembering or downright lying. At one point I was so frustrated with him that I went to my memory box and showed him an old newspaper clipping that quoted my dad saying, 'One day our daughter will thank us for teaching her that the world honors people like us, people who know how to make a buck fast and easy.' That did it. Finally, Dr. Nebb was impressed that I grew up without any guidance and yet had managed to support myself since I was a teen. He didn't do much to help me, though. When I quit him he was disheartened; he wanted to hear more stories.

Yesterday, Jon asked me about my childhood. So, I described those years in New England, how it was cold in every way. Parents forbidding and grim, no friends, no assistance, no plans for a future. He asks why I never married. I tell him I had only one boyfriend and he lasted two days and then went off to a ranch in Texas.

"You mean that?" he asks.

"I do. I probably scared him away because I truly thought we were going to get married. I went shopping for a white dress to wear to City Hall. When I told him that, he told me he had to leave."

"I hope he treated you like a lady. He didn't take advantage of you, did he? Tell me about him, Joni."

"No. All we did was kiss. He warned me about guys like him, told me to stay away from them."

"Sounds like he cared about you. What was his name?"

"I don't know. I called him Tex. Why do you want to know?"

"Joni, I want to know everything about you," he answers. He's silent for a bit and then asks, "Where did you and Tex meet when you got together? Did you go to his house? Did he go to yours? Or did you meet someplace else?"

I explain that we met first in the street and then in a bar. He mumbles, "Thought so."

"What did you say? I didn't hear you."

"Nothing, nothing," Jon says.

I'll tell Jon whatever he wants to know, and I want to hear about his growing-up years. He says he has no secrets and when he took that writing class in prison he started thinking about his past and realized how much of an influence his parents and childhood had on what he thought he wanted out of life.

"Congratulations," I say, "you've just discovered Freudian theory." It's amazing to me that some people never realize that the adult they've become is a result of their childhood, their parents, and their early-life experiences. When the famous poet, William Wordsworth wrote, 'The child is the father of the man,' he wasn't kidding.

Jon says, "The idea for Master Academy came to me one night when I was supposed to begin my community service. They were handing out brooms to everyone in my unit. None of us wanted to sweep up Main Street but I looked at everybody's face. They were all just waiting for someone to tell them what to do and then tell them they did a good job. I could do that. I would also give them advice about the world. They wouldn't have to sweep. They could have good lives. I wanted to help. I could help because I was one of the few, out of all those boys, who knew anything.

"I read books and I watched documentaries and I asked a lot of questions. I was the only kid in the HNB—the official name for HNB is Home for Nice Boys, but we boys called it Horror for Neglected Bastards—who not only had a library card but read book after book. I considered the librarian a good friend. She asked my opinion about each book that I returned and then suggested others. She cared about me."

I stop him to say, "Oh, Jon, we're so much alike. I also loved the library when I was growing up. I practically lived there. We have so much in common."

He continues: "I wanted to tell the guys they were doing a good job sweeping, but I couldn't get the words to come out of my mouth because I didn't want them looking at me. They would notice my hair; I had removed my hat earlier in the day and my hair would give me away.

"My father warned me about my hair whenever he came to visit me at HNB. 'You have your mother's hair,' he would shout, 'and every so-called man in your mother's family was a weakling, a loser, a crybaby. Cover it up, hide it, shave it off, do something, but whatever you do, don't let anyone see your wispy strands.'"

Jon stops talking and after a minute or two he quietly says, "That writing class is paying off already. I just realized that nobody ever scrutinizes me, it's my own insecurity that gets me thinking I'm being dissected."

"I have no pictures of my mother's family, not even any of my mother. My father told me she ran off as soon as I was born. He never tried to look for her, just brought me to the Boys Home and visited once or twice a year. The day I turned eighteen they gave me a ten-dollar bill, a paper with my record of vaccinations, a map of New Jersey, and showed me the door. I never looked back, and my father never looked for me."

Jon tells me that he became successful without a role model, without advice from anyone, without an education. Television and books were his sources. I also had no advantages. We are a perfect match.

Jon wanted to be a hero but he went about it the wrong way. He tells me, "Now I know better. When I come out of here, I'll be a good person, an honest one. Maybe in some small way I can help you and truly be your hero."

As he speaks, I feel prouder and prouder of him, my prison crush. I think he likes me, too. I want to show him off to everyone who'll be at the Lodge celebration. I will prove I'm not an old maid.

"Joni, I hope you don't have reservations about getting to know me because I'm locked up," he says one day.

"Not because of prison," I say, "but I am concerned about your academy. Cults are known for nasty stuff."

"I'll tell you the truth, Joni. I never hurt anyone, never touched anyone. I really wanted the best for those kids; I wanted them to learn to work hard and to succeed. There were some things I did I'm not proud of, but it was only words. My insecurities needed those kids to help me, to say things to me, but it was only words, I promise you. Here, in this prison, they've given me help and it's made a difference. I'm a different person now. Believe me, Joni, believe me."

I tell Jon that I do believe him. That's the truth. I explain that I'm trying to get him a twelve-hour furlough so I can pick him up, he can spend the day here for the Lodge festivities, and then I'll bring him back. I don't mention that I have to sign a pledge guaranteeing supervision. That seems demeaning. Nor do I tell him that I am in touch with someone who knows the ropes. The ropes about getting early parole. That will be my next project.

I ask if he feels ready for that one-day release. "Jon, how does that sound to you?"

"Sounds like you're *my* hero, Joni."

I also haven't mentioned to him that I'm almost finished with the deprogramming business. As soon as these three girls are gone, I'll be ready to live my dream, and he can live it with me.

The money's piling up and I've already chosen the contractor. I won't get caught. I won't be locked up. All this cash and I didn't hurt anyone. I didn't break into a house; I didn't shoplift.

I used my brain and my advanced psychological training to say the right words to men who were lonely. I gave desperate men hope for their future. I did good deeds. I earned this money because I was clever and helpful. I deserve all the money that I've stockpiled.

It's possible that in my enthusiasm to help the isolated desolate men maybe I went a little too far. The ads I placed in *Romance Magazine* offered men someone to write to, someone who would listen to them, understand them.

Some weeks I had ten, eleven, even twelve pen pals at a time. I truly helped all those men; they were not alone anymore. When the men asked to meet me, I said *no*. I said *no* to protect them. I was thinking of their well-being. They were happy and hopeful when they thought they were corresponding with the young and beautiful woman, the gal with long strawberry-blonde hair in the photo I sent, and I didn't want to disappoint them.

My standard line was, "I'm so sorry. I've just come down with a serious illness. It's contagious and I don't want you to suffer like I'm suffering. The doctors insist I stay in bed and have no visitors."

Week after week, they wondered why I didn't recover. "Oh, soon, I'll be better," I said. "I'm just saving up money to get the really strong medicine."

It wasn't wrong to keep the money that was coming in the mail every day. Their generosity made them feel good about themselves. What was wrong about that?

When Jon is released I'll invite him to live with me and by then The Lodge will be transformed into an upscale family resort. We can run it together. He will never leave me.

CHAPTER TWENTY-THREE

Louie

UPSTAIRS IN MY HOME OFFICE, WHEN I SIT AT THE DESK I can turn off the lights but I cannot turn off my thoughts. I cannot stop thinking about years ago. This is all Joan's fault. She therapied me when I didn't ask for it and didn't want it. And now, after all these years, when I have a beautiful woman waiting to marry me and a beautiful daughter wanting to live with me, I have thoughts about Suzanne. And not just any old thoughts. No, these are tough thoughts.

My mind is overwhelmed with cruel questions. How was I able to block her out of my mind all these years? And how come I can't now? And why did I do what I did, anyway? Was it the docs at the hospital who made it too easy for me to listen to my mother. I must take responsibility … I did listen. I abandoned the mother of my daughter, my young wife who was sick and who never did anything wrong. Why?

I can't relax. I don't sleep at night. I have a twitch in my right eye. Just when I thought everything was going to be good in my life—Laurie's back, Dot will be my wife—I've become a nervous wreck. All Joan's fault.

Dot's been extra-busy at the diner. One of the waiters is out with a bad shoulder, one of the line cooks is out with a dental emergency. "Louie, I may not see you until the end of the week or the weekend," she said last Monday, when she finally had a moment to return my calls. She is efficient and unflappable. She does it all and never complains.

"I have a lot of work to do, too, this will give me time to catch up," I say. "I'll miss you, but just think, soon we'll be married and come home to each other every day."

I'm relieved that Dot is busy, and that Laurie is not yet home. It gives me more time to do this privately. I know what I need to do, and I'm doing it. Dot's super-organized style stays in my mind and I carefully plan task after task. The proof that I've got my mind back is that I've been accomplishing this and keeping up with all my jobs, too. I didn't miss one day of work and I've managed to make these important phone calls every day. I've written more letters in the past month than ever in my life. I've filled out more forms than ever, too.

Dot might have accomplished this quicker or more efficiently, but I don't want to start our marriage with her cleaning up a mess that I've made. I'll be proud to tell her that we finally have an answer.

I did it. I contacted the folks at Winter Falls Chamber of Commerce and the folks at Winter Falls Municipal Building. I spoke to the owner of the storage place and to the manager of the new chain drug store that replaced the

small pharmacy. I connected with the psychiatry department at the big medical center, the one that replaced the
old community hospital. The head of that department
took the time to hear my story and put me in touch with
a doctor from twenty years ago. He's the one who knew
where to look. It took phone call after phone call and lots
of paperwork, but finally it's done. I even tracked down an
old neighbor of ours. And while I was talking to the folks
in the Record Room I got them to send me the change of
name form for Laurie Sue Franno's birth certificate.

I also asked them about Suzanne's family. At that
address there now is a group home for men who need special care. That real estate was part of a trust left for Joel's
protection, and was a donation to Winter Falls County
Health Department. The parents both died a few years ago.

I'm gratified to inspect the piles of papers spread
across my desk. They're evidence of my hard work and
my determination to get to the bottom of things, to find
out what happened to my blameless wife. Why did it
take me all these years to face the fact that she's blameless and I'm guilty?

I'm proud that I can look at this paperwork and study
these forms and letters with the interest I usually reserve for
exotic floor tiles. It took guts to do this. With every call I
made I heard my mother's voice telling me 'don't bring sadness into your life,' and 'stop thinking about bad things.' It
was tempting to listen to those instructions, but I prevailed.

The final piece of the Suzanne puzzle fell into place
yesterday when the registered letter arrived. Amazingly, my
eye twitch vanished and I had a decent enough sleep last
night. It's official. Suzanne Franno eventually recovered,

left the hospital, retrieved all her items from the storage facility, and ultimately went to work as a pharmacy tech.

Now I need Dot's opinion. Not a therapist's opinion, just Dot, my best therapist. We need to know if anything is gained by telling Laurie the truth. Especially now that she'll have Dot, she'll have that mother influence in her life.

I wouldn't want Laurie to spend years trying to search for her mother, if that were even possible and if she wanted to, and then to find out that her mother is not interested in knowing her. The mother might have another family and doesn't want an intruder, or the mother, God forbid, could be mental again.

Next week we go to pick up Laurie and settle her back in Truesdale. We're arriving the night before her graduation, if that's what they call it, and then promptly leaving after the ceremony. This is not my idea. I didn't want to travel all the way to Chicago just for a couple of hours. I did that once, not on purpose. I don't want to do it now as a planned trip. We could say congratulations when Laurie comes home. We could say congratulations on the phone. But Dot thinks it's important we both go. She thinks it's good for Laurie to be proud of finishing the program and it might make up for her not qualifying for her high school graduation here in town. Dot thinks of everything.

CHAPTER TWENTY-FOUR

Joan

TODAY THE MAIN ROOM OF THE LODGE IS A GALA PARTY space, celebrating the completion of a successful year. Tables decked with bright yellow tablecloths hold mints and chocolate bars, pretzels and red licorice sticks. Chocolate-covered strawberries sit next to fruit tarts and mini cupcakes. There's a serving platter overflowing with raisins and nuts—cashews, peanuts, and walnuts—and a round, crystal glass bowl bursting with an explosion of colorful jellybeans.

Emily provides background music as guests arrive; Laurie was adamant that there be live music. Dot and Louie are on the way from their motel, Laurie's ACA gal pals are coming together in one car, Emily and Annette's families are already present, and the town mayor is here, too.

The mayor asks us to begin promptly, even though not all guests have arrived, and I do so. I'm proud of my Lodge and I want to stay in the mayor's good graces. When I start my new venture I'll need some zoning variances.

The speeches begin. The mayor gives his regular platitude talk, I say a few welcoming remarks, two of the town's big shots who just happened to drop in—they were not invited—introduce themselves, smile and pretend they're my friends while ogling the tables of sweets. It's Laurie's turn to get the mic. It's evident I know how to be a deprogrammer because Laurie is no longer an angry, confused, skinny girl. She is articulate, poised, and pretty, too, now that the hideous blonde hair is completely gone.

Laurie begins: "Thank you everyone for coming to the Lodge's annual spring gala which happens to also be my graduation. I call it my graduation because I'm on my way to the next stage of my life. I've been through a lot and now I know there's more to life than meets the eye. I'd like to tell you about all that has met my eyes."

Laurie talks about growing up in New Jersey and she talks about choices she made—some good, some not so good.

"Then there was Master," Laurie says, as she points to Jon.

Jon looks to his right and then to his left.

"Don't pretend to forget that you used to be called Master," says Laurie. "You had many young people, people like me who were looking for something, a family, a place to belong, obeying you. Remember my mantra? You made me recite it all the time. Now, finally, I know that doing that is bizarre, very bizarre. But I did it. Why? Because I thought you could give me what I needed, and you did, for a while, and I thank you for that. You actually helped me move on to more mature ways of getting a life."

Oh, my. What is Laurie doing? I stand and motion for her to stop speaking. I wave my arm. I snap my fingers.

She ignores my signals, so I fake a big smile and hope she doesn't continue with these outlandish statements.

Here she goes again. I wave again. I smile a broader smile. She continues speaking. My face is stretched to its limit. I sit in defeat.

"Joan," she points at me, "I hope you and Jon have a good time together. You taught me that Freud said happiness and fulfillment in life come from having meaningful work and having meaningful love. I hope you've found fulfillment from your work. Your work succeeded in getting me to forget about Master, and ironically it also led you to him. Coincidences are interesting, aren't they? Now you can try to be successful at love with him. You do know who he is, right?"

I really can't take this. In a loud voice I say, "Laurie, please, let's celebrate you and your accomplishments. Your portrait of your dad is extraordinary. Your talent is … oh, look, here comes your dad now."

Louie and Dot enter The Lodge, arm-in-arm, and both are surprised to see Laurie standing in the center of the room, all eyes upon her. They hesitantly take their seats at one of the brightly covered tables near the front.

Laurie continues, "My dad tries hard to be a good dad. And he succeeds; he's a very good dad. He's had to be a mother and a father to me. And he made it look easy; I never realized, until I grew up, that it couldn't have always been a piece of cake. He must have struggled, but he never let me know about his struggles. My dad is one tough dude.

"I messed up big time when I went off to parts unknown, yet he forgave me. He's made this trip from his home in New Jersey to me, here, in Chicago, several times, even though he has had to miss work and even though he didn't always feel so good. He was worried about me and he consistently showed me his support."

The room is quiet. Laurie has the ability to command attention. Not everyone has arrived, yet she speaks as if she's addressing a nation.

"So, Dad, I'm a little different than I was when last I lived home. Even though Joan bothered me with her Freud stuff and her psychology stuff, and her countless counseling sessions, she did help me figure out what I need. It was hard for me to understand myself at first, but now I'm getting good at looking back and thinking about things, and I'm brave enough to feel my feelings...at least sometimes.

"By the way, when it comes to knowing my needs, I now know that I need more than just a car." Laurie pauses, scans the audience until the laughter subsides, and then continues. "It's true; I confess, that's what I thought until recently. But now I can look into myself and I can admit that more importantly I need the closeness of a family.

"Dad, when Grandma left I needed another mama-figure in my life, but I couldn't face it. Now I understand that even though I'm an adult I still need a mama even if it's just a 'now and then' mama."

Louis abruptly stands and says, "Allow me to cut in here, Laurie. I apologize to you. In front of this entire group of people I tell you I am sorry. I am sorry that..."

Dot pulls on his shirt. He looks down and says, "Dot, stop it, please. Stop pulling on me. I want to tell Laurie the truth. It's time to stop keeping this secret."

I cannot let this go on. I stand and declare, "Louie, certain conversations should be private. Perhaps you can wait until you are home to talk to Laurie about personal matters." He must stop.

"No, Joan, no," Louie replies, "Stop trying to boss me around. I want this to be public." Dot has a horrified look on her face as Louie continues.

"Laurie, I am sorry that you've been deprived of a motherly influence. I want you and the rest of the world to know that Dot is going to move in with us. She has agreed to allow me to marry her. She can be your 'now and then' mama."

Laurie squeals with delight, claps, and says, "Now, I'll have all the mothering I could ever need."

I truly cannot let this continue. Louie told me his story. He told me the truth about his wife. This marriage cannot occur. He shouldn't promise Laurie something that cannot happen. I jump up, "Louie, there are legal issues here."

Laurie challenges me with a stern face. "What legal issues, Joan. What are you talking about?"

"I'm talking about the fact that your father is not free to marry." This is my chance to tell Laurie the truth. She's entitled to know the truth. Do I say it now, in front of everyone?

"What is she talking about, Dad?" asks Laurie as she looks at Louie and Dot, who are sitting shoulder-to-shoulder and clutching each other.

"Don't ask him," I say. "Ask me. I speak the truth. I don't keep secrets. Laurie, there's something…"

Jon stands and with his face just inches from mine, he grabs both my arms and says to me, "Joan, leave good enough alone. They will be a family. That's a good thing."

"Jon, you don't know. There's more here than meets the eye, like Laurie said. Louie cannot marry Dot."

Jon insists, "Joan, give it a rest. They're good people."

I don't know why, but Jon has a big influence on me. I stop talking. I sit.

Louie has everyone's attention now. From his seat he speaks: "I've had enough of your bossiness. Joan. Enough of your bullying. Of course, I can marry. Legally and any other way, I am free to marry. And if this fella Jon is who I think he is, I want my money back, Doc. Your job was to get Laurie into a new environment. But this guy looks a lot like Mister Master, a criminal from back in New Jersey. He shouldn't be here, not with Laurie here, anyway."

Laurie still has the mic. "Oh, Dad, it's okay. He's harmless now and I don't care about him or his ideas anymore."

"But, but...why is he here?" Louie sputters. "Why is your doc harboring a criminal?"

"Dad, take it easy. I'll explain it all to you on the way home. It's okay Dad, they're a good match, a very good match, they deserve each other. And, like most things in life, the idea of it is worse than the reality of it."

It's time for me to put an end to this so I purposefully stride up to the podium and loudly announce: " Laurie has worked hard and knows what she needs. I, too, know what I need, and for the record, I am not harboring a criminal."

The audience members are turning from Laurie to me to Louie and they seem bewildered, but nevertheless they're enjoying this unexpected show.

Louie stands and says, "Laurie is coming home where she belongs, and we are leaving. Are you ready, Laurie?"

"Yes, but I want to wait for my ACA ladies. They'll be here any minute, and I'd like to say goodbye to them. I know it's time for the airport; just a few more minutes of waiting, okay?"

Laurie faces the audience and continues, "While I'm waiting I want everyone to see the success of Joan's program. Look at me now. I'm smiling. I'm not searching anymore."

Awkward, but true. She was the girl who was malnourished, gaunt and grim. A few of the folks in the audience applaud.

I'm proud that Laurie has publicly acknowledged my program. I ask Emily to play again and I invite the audience to taste all our sweets. Folks wander around, listen to the pleasant music, and enjoy the snacks. Annette will speak next, after a short break.

Laurie puts the mic down and walks over to me.

"By the way, Joan, I know a lot now, more than you think I do."

Does she know about her mother? Did her dad tell her? My heart is beating wildly. "Come," I say, "let's steal away for a few minutes." We walk to a side table which has two chairs next to it. It's meant for an unexpected guest or two—the director of the town's Water Board sometimes shows up at events, and if refreshments are served he tends to bring along his secretary.

We sit and Laurie begins. "Joan, here's the main thing I learned during these months: I know that I should say it hurts when it hurts. I understand that secret sadness is not a good thing. Proud of me?"

I don't know what to say. That's not a great accomplishment for most people, but coming from Louie's daughter who began her time here in total denial of an inner life I suppose it does mean something.

Laurie continues, "Joan, you want my father to spill his guts to me, and I finally figured out why you're so concerned about secrets. It's the feelings stuff again. My dad keeps his feelings secret. He never speaks about what it was like being widowed at a young age, and with a newborn baby. He never talks about what he felt then or what he's feeling these days.

"You were thinking that if he expressed his emotions then I would learn how to express mine. Right? Am I right? If he talked about loneliness, instead of keeping his loneliness a secret, then I would realize I was lonely, too, is that what you thought?"

I nod in agreement and tell her that she is thinking the way a mature, psychologically healthy person thinks.

She continues, "Joan, all the times you wanted me to think about stuff from years ago I thought it was stupid, but I don't think it's stupid anymore. My ACA friend Suzie talked to me about looking into my heart and she taught me to be brave enough to delve. Suzie and I have had a ton of intense conversations.

"Now that I look back, I realize that it would have helped me when I was younger, and even these days, too, to look back. I could have figured out why I was staying in my room and feeling miserable so often. I had no clue what I needed. After my grandmother left I was sad not to have a mother, but I couldn't face it."

I'm proud of Laurie and proud of myself, too. I got her to think. I got her to break down that wall that cut off her past and cut off her emotions.

I stand—a signal to Laurie that we should rejoin the group. But she's not done. This is typical Laurie, commandeering a situation. She had months to reach these revelations and talk to me about her insights. The party is

going on around us, I hear the music as well as snippets
of conversation, I see the guests enjoying luscious sweets,
and I, the hostess, am trapped away from the action, away
from my guests.

"Joan, I didn't realize that you were right until my conversations with Suzie. Now I'm not scared to think about my
past. Not only was I deprived of a mother, I also was deprived
of talking about what it feels like to not have a mother."

"Tell me, Laurie," I gently ask, " what does it feel
like?" I sit.

Laurie looks at the floor. "Not having a mother feels
like I'm a freak. Or, at least it did when I was growing up.
I was the only girl in school without a mother. Not having
a mother felt like I had no protection. I don't mean big
things like wars or hurricanes; I mean everyday things like
nasty kids and letdowns and history term papers. Every
day it was just me against anything or anyone that came
my way. Feelings of sadness and loneliness were always
popping up in my life.

"When I had my grandmother I was okay. She was a
buffer between me and the world. But when my grandfather
was offered that prestigious job, opening a new *House and
Yard* in Florida and being in charge of the whole thing, they
just picked up and left. We didn't talk about it. She didn't
prepare me. Maybe she thought I was tough like she. She
was the type to make up her mind and do something without feeling anything about it. My grandfather said she was
strong; he called her 'tough as nails.' When he would say
that, grandma would say, "I'm proud of my heart of steel."

"Suzie explained that if my dad had talked about his
feelings I would have learned how to talk about mine. She

said emotions are manageable when they're out in the open, but not when hidden."

So, it took Suzie to get this girl on the right track. Suzie's not even a therapist.

Laurie continues, "Thank you. I'm not mad at you anymore for harping on dad's secrets. I understand it was for my own good."

I'm stunned. I want to defend myself. It wasn't all Suzie. And those aren't the biggest secrets. There's a doozy still covered up. But I have no time to respond because Dot walks over and whispers something to Laurie.

Laurie apologizes to me, says, "I gotta run. It's time." She rushes to scoop up her painting and her luggage, and she and Louie and Dot swiftly link arms and walk out the door. I watch from the window—they don't look back as they hurry toward their rental car in the outer parking area.

They don't notice Suzie and Irma and Linda walking toward The Lodge entrance. Suzie, however, spots a side view of Laurie. She sees her snug between a man and a woman. She stops walking just as I go out to greet her and the other two ACA women. "Come on," I hear Linda say, as she prods Suzie. "We're late enough as it is."

"I'm sorry, I'm not ready to go in yet. I'll meet you there in a few minutes. I need to stay out here and look for something," Suzie says, as she lowers her head and rummages through her handbag.

I welcome Irma and Linda. After escorting them inside I go out to Suzie who is standing in the parking lot. She's stopped fiddling with her bag. She's looking at Laurie and Louie and Dot, scrutinizing the three of them as they scurry to the car. Suzie remains riveted until their car is but a speck in the distance and then she walks toward me and says something which I don't quite understand. She says, 'All's well that ends well.' Beaming a beautiful, big smile, and holding her head high, Suzie proudly strides into the celebration.

THE END

Laurie

DOT ASKED ME TO COME WORK AT THE DINER SOON AFTER she and Dad were married. I was getting known as a portrait painter but had plenty of extra time and she didn't want me to mope around. She wouldn't take *no* for an answer and before I knew it, I was an experienced diner worker and then manager. I also fixed up the place and the bright new look attracted new customers.

Every morning a group of guys who worked over at the bank would come in for breakfast. They livened up the diner with their spirited talk, flirty remarks, and enthusiastic eating. (Young men consume more food in one meal than Dot and I together eat in a day or maybe two.) Abraham was the handsomest one, still is, and it didn't take long for him to ask me out. On our first date I knew he was 'the one.' When I met his mother she told me he came home from work one day and announced, "There's a new girl working at the diner. I'm going to marry her." His mother advised that he get to know me, take me on a date, and at least find out my name. "Don't doubt me," he insisted. When our children grow up we'll tell them about love at first sight.

Abraham knows all about my life, my high school fiasco, my Master years, my Joan year. I pretty much had forgotten about Joan until the time we got a collect phone call from a women's prison. It was someone saying her name was Joan and she asked to talk to Louie Franklin. However, Abe and I don't accept junk calls or collect calls, and certainly not from prisoners.

Soon after Abe and I were married, Dot and Dad unexpectedly showed up at our house one evening. She and I had worked together during that day and she didn't mention there was anything on her mind that couldn't wait until the following morning.

I got nervous. Why was she here? She had a pile of papers with her and explained, "We have some legal maneuverings to attend to. Let's do this now, sign all these pages, please, where you see the x, and tomorrow morning the lawyer and notary are stopping in to see us at eleven."

And just like that I had a real mom. Dot adopted me.

After Zach was born, Dot had more papers for me to sign. She said, "Retiring from the diner will be easy for me because you can do everything I can do, and you do it all with added charm and grace. The customers adore you, the employees appreciate you, the vendors like your banter, and the bottom line rises each year. You deserve this, Laurie." I am now a fifty percent owner of Dan's Diner.

It was unexpected when one morning, after the breakfast crowd was gone, Dot turned to me and said, "I've been planning a plan. The best time for me to have started college was years ago, and the second best time is now." She's a chemistry major at Lehigh, yet manages to stop into the diner now and then to catch up with her favorite long-time customers.

Dad works as much as always and takes pride in all his projects. But most of all he's proudest of his wife, the college student; his daughter, the business owner; and his grandson, the cutest, smartest, boy in the world.

Dot was wise when she suggested they move. They've started over as newlyweds in a brand-new home and Dad is more easy-going than ever. When they come over for their Sunday visits, Dot plays with Zach and Dad relaxes in our comfy living room chair, looking up at the *Dad Louie* portrait on the wall. That portrait makes him smile. He stares at it a lot.

On slow days, if I have extra help in the diner, I take time off to work in my home studio painting portraits. One of the projects I'm working on now is a portrait of Dot. I hope Dad will hang it in their bedroom. And moms hire me to paint their babies' portraits and are relieved when I tell them the baby doesn't need to sit and pose.

Whenever I look at the portraits of Zach and of Abe that I made for our hallway, and the other portraits I've painted, too, I'm reminded of El and all that I learned from her. I also learned from Suzie. She gave me significant psychological advice and inspired me to examine my life. She actually taught me a new way of being. I can still hear her saying, "Laurie, dear, the goal is to be present for life; this is not a dress rehearsal." She also told me, "It's never too late to create a family." Did she know I was going to meet Abe and have Zach? Did she know Dot was going to adopt me?

Fortunately, I still had the photo that Linda sent me years ago. It was a picture of Irma and Suzie sitting at our table at the ACA. While Irma looks a little mean in that print, Suzie looks beautiful. Her black curly hair and blue eyes are clear and vibrant, so I used that photo to create a Suzie portrait.

Suzie is a wise woman and I would have liked to stay in touch with her. I hope Abe, and Zach, too, might meet her someday. When we said our goodbyes she told me she was overloaded with commitments and would be an unreliable telephone pal. She did say, though, that when she approaches retirement age she'll have fewer obligations. "Maybe when my life is less frenetic and you're about 30 years old we'll get together for a special lunch, just you and me. I'll send you a note when the time is right."

I'm comforted by all the portraits in our home, particularly the two I decided to hang on the living room wall facing the doorway. *Dad Louie* and *Suzie* are framed side by side.

DISCUSSING THE PSYCHOLOGICAL ISSUES IN *A GOOD LIE*

- Some psychiatric practices used in the middle of the last century are considered barbaric today. Which of today's practices might be considered barbaric years from now?

- How is postpartum depression (PPD) treated today? How does PPD differ from baby blues?

- Is Suzie being a good enough wife if she never tells Harry her secret?

- What symptoms of depression did Louie miss during Laurie's adolescence?

- Dot believes that work is Louie's therapy. What is therapeutic about work?

- Suzie writes in her memoir that love is not enough to hold a marriage together. Is that true? What else do you need?

- Do you agree with Suzie that the best revenge is a life well lived?

- Did you ever find driving in a car an easy way to speak about sensitive issues? Why?

- What was the appeal of the Master Academy cult?

- Explain 'The child is the father of the man.'

More Ideas to Discuss

Sometimes in life we don't know what we don't know—said by Louie.

Writing your memoir helps you make sense out of your life—said by Suzie.

A health exam should be an annual physical and an annual mental—said by Laurie.

The way to a peaceful life is to join the resistance. Don't argue; agree. When the emotion is eliminated, common sense prevails—said by Suzie.

You fall in love and stay in love because of the feelings that other person engenders in you—said by Suzie.

As long as a child has someone to believe in him, someone who cares about him, he can grow up okay. Every child deserves to have someone whose face lights up when they see him—said by Carol.

Be present for life; this is not a dress rehearsal—said by Suzie.

You will turn into your friends, so choose your friends wisely—said by Joan and Suzie.

Like most things, the idea of it is worse than the reality—said by Laurie.

ABOUT THE AUTHOR

Roberta Temes is a psychotherapist who has practiced in New York City and in New Jersey for decades. She is the award-winning author of many well-received professional books, magazine articles and essays. *A Good Lie* is her first work of fiction.

Dr. Temes lives with her husband in New Jersey and in Florida. She can be reached at www.DrRoberta.com and may be available to Zoom into your book group.

Made in United States
North Haven, CT
11 March 2022

17015054R00186